Saltic the Fifth

Lauren Logan

For my besties, who are sick of my shit

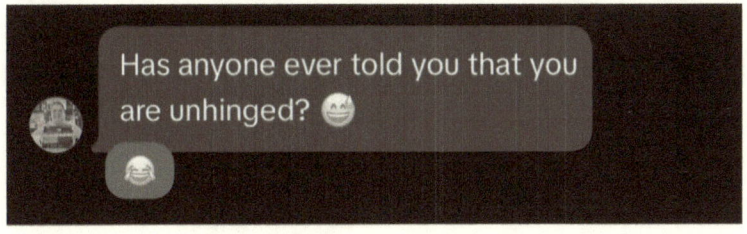

www.authorlaurenlogan.com
Copyright © 2026 Lauren Maxwell Logan
This is a work of fiction. All references to events, persons, and locale are used fictitiously, except where documented in historical record. Names, characters, and places are products of the author's imagination, and any resemblance to actual events, locales, or persons, living or dead, is coincidental.
Published by Lauren Logan. All rights reserved, including the right of reproduction in whole or in part in any form, except in instances of quotation used in critical articles or book reviews. Where such permission is sufficient, the author grants the right to strip any DRM which may be applied to this work.

Front Cover Art: Sean.Ex.Savior

Instagram @seanexsavior

Front Cover Design: Allen Wahlström

Instagram @Bafacoach.W

www.asenzathletic.myportfolio.com

Editor: Beth Sullivan

BSullivanEdPro@gmail.com

Writing Assistant: Kathy Hunter

Content Warnings

Content warnings for Saltic the Fifth are listed on www.authorlaurenlogan.com

Saltic the Fifth is strictly for mature readers of 18+

Please protect your mental health.

Chapter 1

Marry Me?

Two deals, two possibilities for profit, yet they both ended with me fucked. I'm not allowing this day to become worse, so, by the poolside with alcohol I will remain until the daylight is dusk. Kortul toasted to the light blue sky and sighed with satisfaction at his decision. Two bright system stars shone high in the sky, and he pulled his shades over the two largest of his four eyes as he lowered his drink. He wrapped his lips around his flattened straw to suck down the sweet liquid. *Maybe I can drink this awful day away. I should be drunk for the next meeting, or all my future meetings. Thank fuck I don't have another meeting for a month and a half.*

The rooftop pool, covered patio, and pool house on his high-rise building were vacant as usual since it was midday during a typical work week. He knew he had several hours before anyone would make their way to the pool house and disrupt his peace. *The next high-rise apartment building I reconstruct, I want a larger pool.*

A flash of intense, scorching light had Kortul rolling

from his sunning chair and onto the searing hot pool deck. "I know my meetings went bad, but this is out of hand. Have they resorted to shooting heat rays at me now?" He peered over the edge of the now tipped over white sunning chair to see what had been shot at him. It was a foreign escape pod and not some bomb or projectile. *Is there something inside? Or someone? I hope they know Corbatton laws. This planet was extensively exploited for resources in its early history by multiple species from nearby systems and our people are strict about who can be here.*

Filled with an odd thrill, his thoughts swirled as he approached the pod. He took a moment to adjust his swim trunks and tied them just in case he needed to run. He was ill-equipped for a fight, and hoped whoever he found inside was one of his people. If they weren't, they would be due for a visit from the authorities. If any of the planetary surveillance sensors caught what just happened, a planetary border authority transport would be on the way.

Kortul was cautious as he approached the pod to peek around the side and into the window. A beautiful woman with black hair and bright fuchsia skin was inside, and he wondered if she was from anywhere in his galaxy. None of the many planets in his galactic neighborhood had beings with coloration quite like hers. *What the fuck am I supposed to do now? I can't just leave her here. I'm sure Mabit and Tyce will kick my ass for this, but I don't think any of us have a choice.*

He came around to open the top of the pod and it released billowing steam. The woman's mouth was stuffed with fabric, and her hands and feet were tied together with layers of rope. Her sheer underclothes were soaking wet as sweat poured from her skin. He pressed his hand against her forehead, and she appeared unconscious due to overheating.

He only had a few choices, and none of them were acceptable. "It doesn't look like this was her choice, and I won't let her pay such a steep price for a mistake." He called out to his virtual assistant, "Corver, message Tyce and tell him to come to my apartment right now. It's an emergency." *I know I'm jeopardizing my freedom. I don't care.* As he lifted the mystery woman into his arms a quick tone signaled Corver sent the message. He peered down at the unconscious woman, and he noticed the antenna in her hair. He lifted her to see her back, and through her wet underclothes he could make out her glossy black wings flush against her skin. "You're a little moth. Too bad you landed on Corbatton. You'll be stuck with me for a while if you want to remain here. It's a shame I can't first explain what needs to happen."

He watched as her eyes remain still under her eyelids. He took a few steps from the pod. "Corver, transport me to my living room."

In a split second, he stood in his living room holding the little moth woman. He was gentle as he lay her on his long gray plush couch before he answered the door, knowing Tyce would be there. The door slid open, and his friend glared at him. Tyce was a healthy mix of skeptical and confused. Kortul demanded, "I need you to trust me and not ask questions. Do you understand?"

Tyce snarled but rolled his solid black eyes and agreed, "Fine. What the fuck do you want now?"

Kortul grinned like he had stolen a precious gemstone and locked his door at the keypad before showing Tyce the bound woman on his couch. Tyce spun on his heels and started running for the door, but Kortul stopped him and narrowed his four eyes at his closest friend. "You agreed not to ask questions."

Tyce was furious, and his usually solid white face became a heated light blue as he countered, "What the fuck is this? You said an emergency, not a crime!"

"She appeared on the patio in an escape pod. I can only assume she is in danger and needs help considering she is tied and was gagged. You know our laws, and you know what happens when people land here who are not members of an established family or have clearance to visit. What if the authorities send her back to Vumenko and she's harmed? I need you to marry us right now so she's not hauled off when the authorities arrive in about five minutes." Tyce glared as though he wanted to throw Kortul from his high-rise window as he raked his fingers through his brown hair. *I know he has thought about it more than once.* "I will do no such thing. This is low, even for you."

Kortul shot a conniving smile at his best friend. "You do realize you and I will also be accompanying her when the authorities arrive."

Tyce seemed murderous yet thrust his hand out with a scowl. "Give me the fucking knife!"

"I knew you would see the light." Kortul handed Tyce his family's ceremonial marriage knife from the display table beside them and offered his hand to be the first to receive the slice. He and Tyce approached the woman, and Tyce adjusted her bonds to access her palm before he gently pressed the knife into her flesh, cutting her across her skin. Clear blood emerged, and Kortul pressed his palm to hers before he presented both their palms to Tyce. Tyce retrieved his interactive communicator from his pocket and submitted their mixed blood samples. "I need you to change the date. I know what I'm asking."

Tyce scowled at him with fire behind his eyes. "You have asked for a lifetime of favors in the course of a few minutes. If you ask for one more thing, I believe you will finally be the one who owes me!"

The buzz of police transports outside the giant window of the apartment drew their attention, and Kortul reached down to untie the woman as the authorities began broadcasting. "Our sensors show a being transported to this premises. You are required to present any unauthorized entries to our protected planet to local authorities or incur the consequences of breaking Corbatton law. You have two minutes before we will perform a search of your premises. Any resistance will be seen as an act of hostility, and you will be detained."

Tyce screeched at Kortul, "How the fuck are we supposed to explain the woman tied up?" Kortul shrugged as though he wasn't concerned as he finished untying her. "We just need to hope she wakes up and is cooperative before then."

Tyce stood nearby glaring at Kortul, and this time anger overrode his bewilderment. *Great, here we go. He's about to explode. He might throw me through the window this time.* "You always drag me into these fuck ass disastrous messes! I am not answering your call anymore." Kortul knew Tyce was lying. They had been friends for the majority of their life. Kortul had done plenty for Tyce over the years. He knew damn well Tyce wasn't going anywhere.

The woman opened her big green eyes, and didn't seem as distressed as Kortul thought she ought to be. She raised her hand and stared at the cut, lightly touching the fresh wound on her hand before looking over at Kortul and seeming thankful. *That is somewhat unexpected. I need to know who she is and how she ended up here like it's my entire purpose in life.*

Happy to be alive, Tolina inspected her bloody hand which made her suspicious a ritual involving her occurred. There were authorities outside, these men had untied her, but the furthest one seemed distressed to a point of panic. The closest man to her had black hair, fire orange head, a solid black neck, and a tan torso. Each of his limbs were black and white striped and his hands and feet were solid black. She returned to the cut on her hand and looked at his hand. *Oh, there is a cut on that orange faced man's hand too. He better not have...* She pulled her hand close to her nose and smelled her palm, detecting much more than just her own blood present. *Searing fucking honey, he did not. I know enough about common cultural practices to be aware of what this means.* She pointed to the man standing over her and his cut hand with a scowl. He grinned at her, but as authorities began to bang on his door, his carefree demeanor melted. His pleading, solid black eyes begged her to play along. He took her unharmed hand and rubbed his thumb along her knuckles in a calming and reassuring gesture.

When men with sleek guns, masks, and protective gear overrode the door lock and forced it open, they rushed into the apartment. As the authorities surrounded them, Kortul smirked at her without taking his eyes away and kissed the back of her hand. Tolina looked around to find all the guns were pointed at her and not at him. *I'm playing along and saving my fucking skin. That sounds like a great plan. How did I let this happen?* The back of her head ached where she had been hit with a blunt object. *Had it even been two days on Emendo before someone kidnapped me and shipped me off to another planet? Two fucking days of freedom was all I had?*

None of the guns pointed at her head upset her. She had been through much worse scenarios. What bothered her to her core was the wound on her hand, and this man who was resolving whatever issue she caused. *What the fuck did he do between us to fix whatever is going on? Why am I even asking myself that? I know what he did! All I wanted was freedom, and here I am fucking trapped again! If I'm bonded to this man after what I went through back home, I'm going on a killing spree at my first opportunity.*

Once the orange faced man handed over a tablet to the authorities, they lowered their weapons and began filing from the apartment. Tolina watched as one of them sent some sort of digital citation to the tablet. *This fucking translator better start working quickly because I need to know what is happening.*

Kortul wasn't sure how he would explain himself, and he knew even if she had an implanted translator, it might be weeks or months before their translators could decipher their languages. He was glad she didn't panic or cause a problem when the authorities arrived. *That could have become a disaster for everyone, but why was she not panicking? She should've been terribly upset there were firearms pointed at her face.* Her unnatural calm was a blaring red flag added to a list of other red flags. *Unfortunately, she's perfect for me. I fear I may be obsessed with her.*

The moment the door shut behind the last man in combat attire, the woman stood with a sour frown, pointed to her palm, then pointed to his. Kortul grinned at her sweetly and shrugged. "Sorry mysterious moth lady, you're stuck with me for a while at least." Kortul pointed at himself, "Kortul," before pointing to his friend, "Tyce."

She rolled her eyes and pointed to herself. "Toli-na."

When her gaze met Tyce's, Tyce stormed out of Kortul's apartment. The door slid shut behind him, leaving the two of them alone. She noticed a physical color pattern with their people, Tyce had a solid white head, brown hair, brown neck, and his arms were striped deep brown and white with brown hands. *I wonder if all their people have markings like these.* She couldn't see any of the authorities as they were covered head to toe in combat gear, but now she was curious to see the rest of the people of this species.

She noticed his ears were pointed like hers before Kortul broke her observations by waving to follow him into one of his spare bedrooms. He didn't make it far when she came up behind him and swept his feet from underneath him, sending him crashing onto the hard floor with a grunt. She flipped him over and pinned him to poke him in the center of his forehead twice before pointing to her palm then grabbing his hand and pointing to his.

"What the fuck did you do?" Tolina needed answers and she needed them now. Her brow furrowed in anger as she pointed to her hand again.

She is even more gorgeous when she's furious. I regret nothing. I'll do anything to keep her. Kortul wasn't sure how else to explain it to her, so he took the hands he had sliced and joined them together. He linked each one of his fingers with hers while he stared at her, hoping she could gather some sort of intuitive explanation. The longer she stared at their joined hands, the more she started to shake her head no. He just shrugged and smiled at her trying to be reassuring before he lied, imitated the guns pointing at her and blasting her away before he tapped their hands.

"You're telling me I'm fucking stuck with you, or I die? Oh, sweet nuts, are you a damn spider?!" Kortul's webbing elongated from where his fingertips touched her knuckles, and when he pulled his hand away, he brought his fingertips together and spun his hand around, breaking the connections. He lay still, staring at her with his big black eyes before she slowly climbed off him.

I am stuck again, and it's with a spider. A four eyed spider. He rose from the ground, and she wasn't sure what to do as she stood studying him, and he did the same to her. *Him being a spider explains the markings. It's a shame I hate him so much. I think he might be the best looking man I have ever laid eyes on. His friend was cute too. Maybe I can make this living arrangement work, and I can date while I stay here.* Fury bubbled in her as she remembered she didn't know the laws here, and she might not be able to date. She breathed through the murderous anger. *In the nose, out the mouth. Don't kill the gorgeous man with the orange face. Unless he deserves it. I need to be careful here. I can't just be killing people.* She guessed it was her turn to reveal a bit of who she was, so she took a few steps back before she unfurled her black wings from her shoulders down to her calves. They spread behind her, and Kortul was enthralled.

"Well, Tolina, you're not a moth at all. You're a butterfly. Where did you come from?"

Chapter 2

Little Guest

Pointing to the bedroom door, Kortul led her to a room she believed was larger than her entire apartment back on Hyret, her home planet. She had been bonded to a member of the most prominent elder family in their society, but she had never even seen a bedroom this spacious. There was a plush white seated living area with a central table and a hologram floating above it, and it was arranged on a large furry white rug. On the other side of the room was a massive wall of windows similar to the open kitchen and main living space. As Tolina took in the beautiful space, she noticed the large round bed with white sheets and fluffy white comforter behind her. There were two long white dressers on either side against the wall. *This is outrageous.* She wondered if this was his room, and he was just showing her. He could not expect her to stay in here with him. *I don't care how beautiful this asshole, and his apartment are, I refuse to stay in a situation in which I have no choice. I will be leaving him as soon as I have the means.*

He led her into a spacious bathroom with a large natural crystal tub and shower along the wall of windows, and the area led into a deep closet, which was bare, save a few bath robes, folded towels, and sleep attire. *This is not his room.* She noticed the particle replicator in the corner and sighed with relief. Tolina would be able to make clothes for herself, and she wouldn't have to bother anyone to do it.

When she was finished surveying the room, she met his eyes, and he smirked before he waved for her to follow him. He led her from the bedroom and down the hall to double doors at the end, and when he opened them, she was unprepared for what was on the other side. *The man is so wealthy I feel uncomfortable. I don't want to touch anything. I need to get out of this apartment before I break everything in here.* She was the clumsiest and most accident-prone Vo-Pess she knew, and while she hated admitting it, she almost failed training. They had let her slide just because of her wing type, which was called a Short Wing. When it came to speed and maneuverability, her wing type was the best, but she, however, was at the bottom of the best list, and she was usually too proud to admit it. Being at the bottom of the list meant she ended up an assassin assigned the lowliest and scummiest of all the targets. They were the type of people no one wanted to be around. *I really think I will miss cutting up those disgusting people. It truly was the greatest joy of my life.* She often reminisced about some of her favorite kills. One time in particular, she made two of her victims choke on their own fingers while they were tied together. This was after they begged her to stop shoving their severed digits inside their orifices. *What a rewarding workday. I love shoving their digits in their holes, especially when they have the same number of victims as they have fingers. Big gnarly bloody toes fit so well in the asshole of a screaming, begging man.*

She turned around and swooped her hip to the side to avoid bumping into a glass table. *Why does everything in this home need to be made of glass?!* Beyond the table she avoided hip checking, there was an enormous circular bed in the center of the room with curtains dipping down from the ceiling and surrounding it. Glass display cases lined one wall, and she was drawn to the contents of his collection. Each piece was something usually found in a museum of artifacts, from ancient clay pottery to primitive electronics to fossils and finally, at the end, she reached precious gemstones.

She stepped back from the display and ran into something hard as a rock. She whirled around to see Kortul standing before her, still shirtless and smirking. *Will you put some fucking clothes on? I know those are swim shorts. Wait, this dumbass can't understand what I'm saying. I might as well just say it aloud.*

"Hey, dumbass, can you put a fucking shirt on?" He gave her a devious stare as he bit his bottom lip, and he smiled before he waved for her to follow him into the bathroom. "I met you just a few minutes ago, and I already hate you so much." When she walked in his bathroom, he made a gesture in the air with his hand and what happened next caused her to stop and shut her eyes for a moment, trying to process what occurred. *This fuck has a whole waterfall for a shower and bath. Who is this man?* He cleared his throat, and she opened her eyes, just to glare at him. He gave her a beautiful grin and led her into a two-story closet, with a spiral staircase and a balcony circling the room above her. She promptly turned around and walked out, uninterested, and thoroughly ready to be away from this exuberantly rich man. *If he shows me one more fancy thing, I will punch him.*

Kortul followed her from his room, and she went back to the first room they visited. When she reached the doorway, she turned around and gestured to the keypad, making it clear she wanted to shut the door. "Are you asking me how to shut the door so that you can shut the door on me?" He laughed as he showed her how to shut it, and she pushed the button. The door slid shut right in his face, and he could see his stupid smile in the reflection of the polished metal. *I think that might be the most gorgeous woman I've ever met. No, she is without a doubt the most gorgeous.*

He turned around to Brock, his Eckolie companion, standing behind him. Brock was a curious two-and-a-half-foot tall man with a lumpy bald head, mossy colored skin, and wide saggy lips. Kortul, like all the Wendi people, believed the Eckolie to be exceptionally adorable as well as generously helpful. Every Wendi had at least one living in their home. Some Wendi had entire families living with them, which was considered an incredible blessing and something Wendi were expected to boast about.

Brock spoke in his childlike, slow voice, "Is someone new?"

Kortul answered his sweet little companion, "Yes, we have a new housemate, and she will be staying with us from now on. She doesn't know it yet, but she won't be leaving."

Brock slowly opened and closed his droopy eyelids over his enormous eyes. "Kortul did kidnap?"

A nervous laugh escaped Kortul as he tried to explain, "No, no kidnap. She is not Wendi or Eckolie, so I had to marry her. She just doesn't quite understand yet." Brock seemed unsatisfied by that answer, and carefully took one step after the other, backing away toward the kitchen. Kortul watched him as he made his way around the corner, and it sounded like he had begun cooking a meal, which Kortul presumed would be their dinner tonight.

The Wendi were unconditional in their care and love for their Eckolie companions, and Kortul was no different. He had immense respect for the little man who had lived with him for over ten years. He also believed Brock to be hopelessly adorable and could not understand anyone who didn't also think the same way. Brock's room was by far the largest, and that was typical for most companions.

Tolina must be hungry. Kortul knew people evolved from moths had a diet of sugars, so he was presuming the same about the little ray of starlight he had as a wife. *She might be gamma radiation starlight, but that's just a technicality.* Her murderous gaze sent delicious chills down his spine, and he gave up waiting for her to open the door, so he joined Brock in the kitchen. Brock was sautéing some white bird meat with vegetables and a light oil along with several of their favorite spices. The aroma of the savory root vegetables filled the space and Kortul couldn't wait for dinner. He approached the replicator in his kitchen and searched the menu for all the different types of sugary substances and syrups he could find before ordering everything.

Tolina opened her bedroom door and checked the hallway to be sure he had left her alone before shutting it again. "This translator needs to hurry and learn this language. Maybe he will take me in public, and it can start learning." She spotted the holographic projection across the room and thought it might be some kind of multimedia source. She approached and tapped on the glass, hoping the controls would be in symbol form. She saw a symbol resembling a sound wave, so she pressed it and could hear a voice speaking. She increased the volume just enough that the translator would pick up the words before she went to the bathroom to shower.

"I smell like I haven't had a bath in a year. That transport technology becomes so warm I must have sweat a bucket." *I don't think I've ever been this thirsty for water before.* She stuck her head under the sink and gulped down several mouthfuls of the cleanest water she had ever tasted. *Hyret water tasted like industrial chemicals. This water tastes too good to be true.* She took a few more drinks before she made the same gesture in the air as Kortul had to turn on the shower. It worked, and soon hot water poured down like rain over the shower and reservoir for the bath. Feeling a spark of glee, she stripped off her sugary sweat-soaked clothes, and they slapped the floor. She climbed in the sprawling shower and a force field formed to hold in the heat and steam.

She used the soaps, shampoo, and conditioner she found in the alcove of the shower, but she was unable to place the floral scents, wondering if the flowers were unique to this world. After the most luxurious shower she had ever taken, she reached for her towel and realized she never grabbed one. Dripping water on the floor on the way to the closet, she found a towel and dried herself before she approached the replicator in the corner. Once she had ordered two doll sized sweatshirts, she gave up and went to retrieve her clothes from the floor. They were crunchy with the dry and crystallized sugar from her sweat flaking away. "Gross." *I can't put these back on.* She looked down at the towel wrapped around her and scowled. She would need to ask Kortul for help. *I would rather waterboard myself in the shower for an hour* than ask that pompous rich boy for help. He was too handsome to be real, and she assumed it cost him a fortune. His pretty face made her hate him even more. *No one is born looking that good. I bet he has calf and chin implants. I want to punch him hard enough to find out.*

She finally gave in, and approached the door to her room, and mentally prepared to walk down the hallway. She tucked her towel around her bust and wrapped her arm around her middle to hold the towel in place. She opened the door and crept down the hallway where she could smell and hear dinner being prepared in the kitchen.

Tolina came around the corner to find a short, saggy skinned greenish man cooking while Kortul arranged over fifty jars of syrup, nectar, and honey on his long glass dining table on the other side of the kitchen island. Kortul retrieved the last few jars from the replicator before he noticed her standing awkwardly in a towel by the hallway. "Oh, you have no clothes. I guess you wouldn't know how to read the replicator, would you?"

Brock faced Kortul, and scowled with deep wrinkles and his sweet voice was overflowing with disdain, "Left the new woman no clothing?"

Kortul hated when Brock scolded him. "It was a mistake. I'll help her replicate clothes right now."

Tolina was struck by the odd interaction happening in front of her. *Is that really a tiny old frog man cooking him dinner and talking to him? Did he just scold him? Did I consume a hallucinogen? I'm asleep. That has to be it.* Tolina pinched her own side. *No, no. I am not dreaming. Damn, this is real. Well, at least the frog man seems to not like Kortul as well.*

Kortul, still not wearing a shirt, could not escape Brock's

scrutinizing glare quickly enough. He gestured for Tolina to follow him to her closet where he began plugging away at the machine. He handed her articles of clothing which looked like they were a perfect size for her. Once she had hung up a small new wardrobe of clothing, he seemed satisfied and left for her to dress. *Is he allergic to shirts or what?*

Chapter 3

Tricksters

Wanting to be comfortable, Tolina came from her room wearing black leggings and a grey tank top. The door whooshed open as she rubbed the place on her neck where her nano-tech armor tab once lived. The skin was softer from all the years it stayed in the same place. Losing her nano-tech armor to the people who sent her here was something she would need to spend some time grieving. Her armor had been designed to link with her nervous system, just like all the Vo-Pess spies and assassins. She felt silly admitting to herself that she would need to grieve over a piece of technology, but it had been integrated into her nervous system as well as being a point of protection her entire adult life.

She knew the door would make a sound when it closed, but she didn't want to alert Kortul she had left her room. *His eyes are creepy.* When she looked over toward the kitchen, Kortul was staring at her from down the hallway. *Damn! I wish the doors were quieter. Maybe I can mess with the tech and slow it down at night. Why does this man still not* have a shirt on? *Well, he did put actual pants on, so I guess I can't complain.*

"Quit staring at me with those creepy eyes of yours." Tolina passed by him and his four eyes followed her all the way to the table where she approached the collection of sugary options for her to eat. Sitting down next to his little old man companion, Kortul didn't take his eyes away from her as he began eating his plate of steaming vegetables and white meat. The old man peeled his lips back at her, which she realized was probably a smile, and she did her best to smile back at the view of yellowed teeth and lumpy gums.

She shifted her attention to her choice of dinner options and opened a few of the jars to smell the contents before she settled on one, which had a delicate rosy scent with a citrus undertone. She unrolled and dipped her long tubule tongue in what she discovered was a honey and syrup blend, which was delightful. Tolina had never tasted a sugary meal like this, and she was now desperate to try the rest without being too obvious. *Maybe he will leave them out. I can sneak out here tonight when everyone is asleep, and then I can open and try them all. I've never even seen this much food before.*

Trying to be nonchalant, she looked around the room, and his eyes were still laser focused on her. Although they were solid black, she could tell where he was looking. She wound her tongue back into her mouth as she set the empty jar on the table. The little old man hopped from his chair and collected the jar before disposing of it in the particle recycler opening on the side of the replicator.

"Thank you, Brock. Are you going to bed early tonight? I plan to take our new guest on a walk through the art district," Kortul explained.

Brock stared at him from next to the replicator. "Unwilling wife."

Pausing to sigh, Kortul agreed, "You're right. I'm working on fixing it. I need to expose her to our language, so her translator will work. Once it does, I will explain the situation, and she can decide what she wants to do."

Brock seemed satisfied for the moment but narrowed his big eyes at Kortul. "I go to bed early, but I not happy."

Brock shuffled off to his room which was on the side of the kitchen that met the wall of windows. When it opened, and Brock went inside, she saw lush greenery as well as a waterfall and pool filled with lily pads. A willow tree dipped its leaves in the water. *Is his room an amphibian habitat?* A bit of steam escaped before the door shut, and she must've looked shocked because when she turned around Kortul had a shining, gleeful smile on his face. *I really want to kick in those pretty teeth. I don't know why I hate him so much. What am I talking about? Yes, I do. he's fucking insufferable. He has cute, happy cheeks, and why does that make me wanna punch him in the face so badly? Even his frog roommate is irritated with him. I wish I knew what the fuck they were saying. Whatever. I plan to just sit here and try different jars.*

She sneered at him, but that didn't deter him whatsoever; in fact, he was more enthusiastic than he was before, which pissed her off further. "I have brutally tortured and killed people who I hated less than I hate you right now." Kortul appeared delighted with her, and she imagined cutting his ears off. He rose up and took his plate to clean it, and he watched her as he made his way around the corner toward his room. When he came back wearing a warm jacket, she scowled. She didn't understand why he was coming back. It looked like the system stars were setting outside. He showed her a stylish, long plush coat and waved for her to follow him.

He held the coat up for her to slip her arms in, and she complied. Kortul selected some option on the wall and a compartment opened with multiple walking shoe options shown on a display screen. "Oh, great fun. I guess we're off for a walk. I hope his stupid ass is taking me somewhere busy so I can at least learn the language. I will miss being able to openly call you a 'dumbass' when it starts working. Now that I said it aloud, I don't know if I can stop. It feels too good. I might have to keep doing it anyway. Dumbass." He reached over and guided her to step onto a sensor pad, which he had spread onto the floor.

The sensors worked and produced a pair of perfectly fitted walking shoes. She liked the style, and she felt like she was walking on a cloud. *Maybe this walk won't turn out so bad, but if this fucker tries to hold my hand, I will break his finger.*

He led her into the center of his living area, which she found odd, before he spoke words she couldn't understand, "Corver, transport us to the lobby." In moments they stood in an enormous room with a luxurious garden lounge and bar on one side, and on the other was a full-service gym. The gym included a lap pool, and she could see the frog and spider people both swimming. Next to the gym was a large food market where she could see more of the frog people pushing little baskets which were sized down for them. Each market display had a small staircase along the side to give the short frog people easy access to the items on the higher shelves.

Besides the floor, everything she could see around her was made of glass high-resolution hologram surfaces, which were fully interactive. People would appear at random on the pad as they arrived in the lobby, and she was sad to think her own society might have had such advancements if their ruling elders had not been so obsessed with retribution and repopulation.

She thought about her sweet former husband, an unfortunate member of the elder Van-Well family. Trel had saved her from brutal abuse at home after the horrendous abuse she had received during her training. It was common for Vo-Pess men, especially within the elder family to abuse their claimed wives for many years before they were ready for breeding.

Not only did her sweet husband never lay a hand on her, but he also didn't desire any sort of breeding from her. They did *try* to produce a batch of eggs, but quickly learned she did not have the anatomy he preferred. Trel would always be profusely apologetic to her when he was not able to perform his breeding duties, which was never, and it broke her heart that a society would prevent a natural flowing coupling as two people of the same gender because the coupling couldn't produce direct offspring. How infinitely asinine when it was so simple to impregnate a willing surrogate. She could have given him several batches of eggs if he had been able to find completion with another willing male partner. Her heart seemed to twist in on itself with the sweet memories of Trel. It was hard to take a breath because she knew she would never see him again. *Did I make the wrong choice? Should I have stayed?*

Kortul stole her attention when he lightly gripped her elbow to guide her through the building doors, which were more like giant sections of the glass wall. They were rolled back on either side, leaving a wide opening. The weather outside looked clear, and she was on the verge of sweating in her jacket as they went toward what she realized was a force field.

When they crossed over the threshold, she was shocked at how frozen the air was. Her breath, along with everyone else's, came out in frosty clouds. "The two system stars here must warm the surface significantly during the day if it becomes this cold every night. I bet the planet is far away from the system stars. Maybe at some point this asshole will show me a map of the solar system and galaxy." Her words were more under her breath and to herself, but Kortul made it clear his intent was to listen although there was no way he could understand her yet.

He assumed her translator needed at least a few weeks' worth of average communication to pass through the sensors in order to decipher the language. Most translator tech could learn quicker when exposed to large crowds. He intended to take her on multiple busy outings to speed up the process.

The sidewalks were filled with people, and she sighed with relief. *I guess translator technology is the same here, and he knows how it works. Damn, he's staring at me again.* "You gawking at me won't make the translator work quicker. I'm sure that's why we're out here taking a walk through the city. Right?" She looked up at Kortul and pointed to a few conversing people before she tapped her ear, and he grinned at her.

"Yes, we are here so your translator can learn our language."

She had no idea what he was saying so she just moved along, and he began guiding her toward an archway with abstract colorful swirls and lights strategically placed among a mix of vibrant and deep hues. *Maybe he brought me to some sort of art market.* As they passed through the creative archway, stood booth after booth of independent artisans, bakers, confectioneries, painters, and jewelry makers. *Fine, I take it back, this is damn delightful. I still want to punch him in the mouth, but maybe a little less now.*

Kortul approached a booth with a young man who had a kind, light purple face and he bought two rainbow sweets on glowing sticks shaped like a double helix. He sampled his first, and she followed, wrapping her tubule tongue around the sweet before pulling it back into her mouth. Kortul did his best not to seem like he was staring at her eating, but she could tell where his eyes were pointed. There appeared to be an iris with a convex lens shape in the center of his two large pitch-black eyes, giving her a glimmer of where his gaze was pointed.

All his eyes blinked at the same time, and she noticed the young man in front of them with six eyes did the same. Those of his people with extra eyes always had them positioned along their brow before their temples. She noticed his people also had variations of tiny spikes along the top of their forehead before their hair started. She suspected that the patterns might be unique to each person.

What she guessed was a family, with over twenty children who looked identical to their parents standing behind them. Kortul noticed where she was looking and began chuckling, causing her to turn and look at him. She did her best to hold back shock and disbelief, but he saw it written all over her and shrugged. "We can afford to have as many children as we want, and some couples I think might go a little overboard."

He tried to be discreet as he pointed to the group and made it clear a large family was not something he was looking for as he waved his hand and grimaced. Something in her found great relief at that, although she wasn't staying with this man because she was certain she was not having anyone's babies. She had been through too much violence in her life to think about something like that. The thought of a child made her skin crawl after her own childhood, and she shut down those thoughts as she did her best to ignore the rowdy group of chattering children.

When they were far enough away, she relaxed and continued to taste her sweet on a glowing stick. "How could anyone finish something like this?" Just as the words left her lips, next to her, Kortul crunched down on his sweet and turned his light pink mouth and white teeth a bright blue. He licked his lips, and they turned a muddy brown from the blue mixing with the fire orange of his skin, and she giggled at him. He frowned before pulling a thin clear communication device from his pocket and holding it up to his face to check his mouth.

He whirled around to check behind him if the young man was still at the table, and he discovered that the young man and his sweets were gone. He stared at the empty table for several seconds before he gently took back the sweet from Tolina and tossed them both in a particle recycler. "It's going to take me an hour to scrub this blue dye from my teeth. I never know when a sweet vendor is really a trickster dealer. They con me every time." He grimaced, knowing there was a temporary location tag in his gut after that last swallow of his sweet. He would need to let his staff at the front desk of his building know that there would be local tricksters trying to set up traps or art tagging aimed at him in his building.

Without hunger or a lack of housing, the crime in his world had taken an odd turn, and it had become an epidemic of practical jokers with light displays of anarchy. Their queen delighted in the stories of tricksters and their lawlessness, and in lieu of punishment, they were often offered artistic positions in the Queen's Palace.

Violent crimes, like rape, were uncommon, but it still happened, and the consequences were appropriately extreme. There had not been a murder on the planet in several hundred years, which was due to the tireless work of the Corbatton queen.

She took her set of prying and soldering tools and began working at the flush edge of the keypad next to the door. During her efforts to pull off the keypad, the door slid open, making its usual whooshing sound. *Well, so much for that.* She kicked away her tools and peered around the quiet hallway. *Maybe he didn't hear the door this time.* She tiptoed into the kitchen and over to the table where she found her little collection of sugary treats. Pulling the chair out, she sat down and began devouring jar after jar. She had been feed on rations for as long as she could remember, so she gorged herself for the first time in her life.

After eating four jars, she looked around the room and felt silly sitting by herself at the huge glass table. *What if somebody walks in here?* She grabbed a few jars and sat on the floor behind the island to continue gorging herself on two at a time before returning to the table for more. Eight jars down and she was just opening the ninth and tenth, when she heard something. She froze, listening in the darkness of the apartment. *Could it have been someone upstairs? Did he have someone living above him?* She didn't see anything, or hear anything further, so she delved back into the little jars of delectable nectars and syrups.

She felt the air shift and froze. She was not alone in this room. She stood quickly, and surveyed the room, but found it empty, which confused her and sent her mind into a tailspin. *I have heard of spirits remaining behind and scaring the living. If this fucking apartment has a ghost, we're moving. Everyone. Even Kortul.*

She felt eyes on her, and her skin prickled as she felt the gaze roam her body. Before she could look around, she was spinning too quickly to see anything except a blur. Now dizzy, she couldn't tell what was happening until she came to a stop facing Kortul, who held her up by her shoulders. She wiggled and discovered she was encased in spiderweb from her shoulders to her thighs. Fury blossomed in her quicker than it had ever before, and she screamed in frustration.

Kortul looked down at Tolina as she leaned her head back and yelled, and he couldn't help but grin, she was so cute when she was mad. He fought the urge to reach down and kiss her, but he was afraid she'd bite his lips off, so he refrained. Her light fuchsia skin was beginning to flush a deeper tone, and he set her down to begin tearing away his webbing before she combusted. When he freed her, he was kneeling at her feet balling up the remains of his webbing, and she shoved him to the ground.

He rolled backward into the chairs of his table. Landing between two chairs, Kortul shot to his feet and rushed toward Tolina. She sucked in a sharp breath and jumped to the side to try to evade him. He caught her body as she leaned to the side, and he changed his trajectory to match hers for momentum before he spun them both to the ground. By the time they reached the floor, Kortul had her on her back and he was looming over her with a grin of triumph.

Tolina had enough of this. She didn't care *at all* that this rich ass-face could match her in sparing. That was a lie. She did care. This made him more annoying than she knew how to express. Tolina swiftly punched him in the side of his perfect abdominal muscles and watched his pretty smile fade into a frown as he slumped onto the floor next to her. He groaned and grabbed his gut where she punched him as he curled into a ball, and she didn't wait to see if she had done harm before walking off. She went right back to her room, grabbed the tools next to the door, tossed them into a drawer, and crawled in her comfortable bed.

Listening as Tolina's door shut, Kortul lay on his kitchen floor reminiscing about having her all bundled up in his webbing as he recovered from her gut punch. He was sure she had bruised his organs as he checked the tender spot.

Brock appeared above him with a sour expression, his long lips curled into a deep grimace. "Why on floor? I worried you become very stupid." He glowered at Kortul and didn't look away.

I fear he might be right. Kortul's brow creased as he sat up to respond, "I heard a sound in here, and it was Tolina crouched and eating behind the counter. I may have played around and caught her in my webbing, but don't worry, she got me back by punching me in the stomach." Brock was silent, and Kortul held his breath. *Oh, great. Here we go. I'm about to receive a lecture.*

Brock's upset expression, morphed into anger as he found his words. "What if she comes from hunger. Four eyes and no thoughts."

Well, that stung, but he's not wrong. What if she did come from somewhere that doesn't have readily available food for everyone? I know there are plenty of places in our galaxy where food is not a right. He peered over at his replicator, and it occurred to him how wealthy he really was. The same went for everyone else on his planet. Everyone having unlimited free access to shelter, clothing, transportation, education, and food, and it made his planet a leader in technology furthering their progress in the galaxy. His people learned early on that if you don't need to worry about the necessities of life, the resulting collective boredom facilitates extreme progress and a multitude of creative fields. His planet had a vast surplus of resources. They were able to permanently feed six border planets, giving them the ability to develop stable economies.

He was exuberantly wealthy, but the least wealthy people on his planet were entitled to the exact same things he was. The reality that she could have come from somewhere focused on anything other than their people's well-being settled in and he couldn't shake the brewing guilt. *I feel terrible for sneaking up on her. How the fuck can I make up for this?* Brock disappeared back into his room, and Kortul was left staring at his replicator. *This calls for something this machine can't give me.*

He went to his room, grabbed his tablet from his nightstand, and began searching for high rated off-world syrup, honey, and nectars. Vumenko was where the Vitolas, or people who evolved from moths were from, so that's where he started. The top connoisseurs of sweets in the galaxy all had confectionaries on Vumenko, and he knew their selections would be the best in the galaxy for the new woman in his life. His gorgeous, unwilling, and adorably grumpy wife. If the small collection of sweets he provided her made her sneak into the kitchen for more, maybe he could provide her with an exotic selection, and she would hate him a little less. *Maybe?*

He searched on his tablet and quickly found the company he heard was the best. Once he had his cart filled with exotic nectars, syrups, and honeys to the degree that even he cringed at the price, he added some delivery protections and made the purchase. The delivery notification claimed his package would be at his door in the morning.

Checking the time, he realized the morning was only a few hours away. He didn't need much sleep. Kortul grabbed his long, black coat before he slipped on his house shoes. He made his way into the kitchen to recycle Tolina's leftover jars on the floor before he made himself some tea at the replicator. When it was finished, he walked to the center of his kitchen. "Corver, transport me to the patio." Before he could lift his steaming cup to his lips, he was standing on the patio of his building, admiring the glowing city. He felt a tremor through the building and wondered how bad the earthquake was deep below.

His building, like all the others in the Corbatton Capital City, had been built over a massive marsh with a deep aquifer. To avoid sinking down into the murky waters beneath the shallow crust, every structure, including the roads, had enormous mechanical piers drilled down into the depths of their planet. The only solid thing on the surface were the crystal islands spread throughout their great oceans.

The crystalline metallic core of the planet was volatile and sent earthquakes through the piers of their buildings. The deep piers were designed to sway and tilt underneath the buildings and reduced the movement above, so the explosive power of the earthquake only felt as vibrations. All their metal was a crystalline metallic alloy which made their structures able to withstand the common cyclones as well.

As he gazed beyond the fading glow of cityscape's nighttime lights, he could see the Corbatton double system stars light shining through the mountain sized crystals. The crystals jutted from the small islands spread over the sea. His ancient people carved and polished the crystals to harness their distant double stars' light and spread it over their world, providing them with a rainbow of color. The most vibrant color being the reds which shone bright pink on the clouds. *The clouds are the same color as Tolina.* The colors cast in various directions changed based on the time of year, and since it was cyclone season, they appeared as light beams through the humidity. At the horizon, he could see hints of one of the first seasonal cyclones forming. Teeny blips of lightning were striking the surface of the ocean as well as reaching up into the atmosphere above the clouds in sprites. Without pollution on his world, he could see storms a day or more before they struck.

He sipped his orange vanilla black tea as he watched the sunrise and went back inside as he began to chill. He deposited his empty teacup in the replicator and went to check the front door for Tolina's package. The door attendant was just walking up with the package, which was enormous, and Kortul met him halfway down the hall. "Thank you. Have a nice day."

The door attendant nodded and replied, "You, too, sir."

Kortul came inside and opened the box in the kitchen before deciding to slide it down the hall by her door. He hated the box just sitting there and pulled a cart from the kitchen to organize the jars on it. When he was finished, he didn't have time to return to the kitchen and wait for Tolina because she was standing behind him. He had not heard her door open. Her cold glare made him squirm, and he decided as soon as she went back in her room he was transporting back to the patio.

Tolina stared at the collection of sugary treats on the cart in front of Kortul and knew it was for her to keep in her room. *I don't care how nice and thoughtful this is. I still fucking hate him.*

Chapter 5

Crooked Finger

Back on the patio, Kortul frowned at how chilly it still was outside from the cyclone which would soon arrive. He heard echoes of giggles from the street, and he peered over the side of his building to see what the laughter was about. A long way down on the street, he saw people pointing at the windows. Tricksters painted a mural on his building in the night, and judging by the giggles, he was concerned about what was on the mural. "Corver, transport me to the lobby."

The computer initiated the transport system, and he appeared in the lobby in an instant. Wrapping his jacket around him and concealing his lounge clothes underneath, he emerged from his building and looked at the mural painted on the windows. He had been marked for a tagging with the sweet from the art district, so he knew something was coming, but he was utterly shocked at the comic the trickster had painted. It started off with him drawn next to Tolina in the art district, then it moved to the two of them in an intimate embrace in his apartment, and the final depiction was the two of them entangled in his web with his cock buried inside of her pussy. It was pornographic, and he was a strong blend of delighted and horrified.

A small crowd gathered and began a wave of increasing giggles as each one looked over and recognized Kortul as the man in the comic. The street erupted into laughter, and Kortul was left screaming inside and demanded, "Corver, transport me to my apartment."

The computer complied and whisked him off to his apartment living room where he found Tolina staring at him from the hallway. *Should I show her the comic? Should I act like I don't know? I'm doing it. She needs to see it. It's too perfect.*

Kortul always had the choice of any woman he wanted, but the only woman he wanted now was Tolina. He ran his tongue over his filed down fangs and wished he hadn't allowed his father's ex-boyfriend Mabit to talk him into the procedure when he was a teenager. No one who had the gene for fangs ever kept them, so he knew it was ridiculous, but he wanted his full fangs back so he could sink his teeth into that curvy ass of hers. *I haven't spoken to Mabit in a few days. I need to introduce him once her translator works.*

"Does your translator work yet?" Kortul asked as he approached her.

She stared at him with a blank expression as he passed by her to grab her coat. *Well, that's a no.* He slid it over her shoulders and guided her to the center of his kitchen. "Corver, transport us to the lobby."

Tolina understood the word transport and was relieved her translator was learning words. *It won't be long now, and I can tell this smug asshole I want a divorce.* He grinned at her, and she frowned back. Before they exited the building, he stopped her and mimicked licking the sweets they had from the art district. He made an odd face and twisted his mouth around before he pointed to the windows.

"What are you trying to say to me?" Tolina was beyond confused as they rounded the corner until she saw what he was trying to communicate. There was a three-part comic of them meeting with the sweets, embracing in the apartment, and the end was a pornographic image of them having sex in a spider web.

She kicked Kortul in the shin before stalking off and he grunted before chasing after her down the windy, cold street. *Why the fuck is it so cold? Why the honey trap is there porn of us on the window of this man's building?* She felt a gust of air rush by her as Kortul caught up. She wished he hadn't. She walked quickly, trying to avoid him, but he caught up again, and guided her to turn a corner. When they did, the wind was much less gusty, and she relaxed her tense shoulders. The cold wasn't the worst thing; it was the wind. *I hate strong wind.*

Beside her, Kortul pointed to a shopping center, and she was reluctant as she nodded, complying only because any type of crowds would help her translator learn his language. It was already detecting words, so it wouldn't be long before it understood his full language. *Hopefully the holo-media in my room has helped it learn quicker.*

They passed by a boutique shop, and then five more until Kortul stopped at a store with twisted pastries and bought one for himself and a sweet drink for her. He handed her the drink and as she took a sip. She wondered if his people had an affinity, or a need for sugar, because the drink she was consuming was almost syrup with its sugar content. She eyed him suspiciously before they moved on and passed by several dress stores. Her eyes must have told on her because he stopped and pointed to one of the stores. She shook her head no before she bolted away, and he had to walk at a brisk pace to catch up.

Tolina sensed him catching up and walked quicker to try to escape him, but as she passed by a large gathering of chatting people, she noticed she could understand what they were saying. *My translator works!* She twirled around, and Kortul almost slammed into her. He had to step around her to keep his balance. "I hate you, and I want rid of you. How do we do it legally? Hire someone now. Is it called a divorce? I want a divorce." Tolina spoke loudly enough an entire group of people turned around and stared at Kortul, whose smile fell, and brow creased as he noticed the people now listening to their conversation.

He sighed as he tried to explain, "If you will just give me a chance to..."

Tolina cut him off by grabbing his arm to pull him away from the far too many eyes pointed at them for comfort before she continued in a lethal whisper, "If it won't kill me, or send me off planet, I don't ever want to see you again. You repulse me, and I want to punch you in the face every time you smile."

I think I could love her. Delighted, Kortul couldn't help his grin as he shrugged and admitted, "I have bad news for you."

Tolina narrowed her eyes at him, and he could feel the angry heat of her gaze on his skin. "What the honey fuck does that mean?"

Did she just say, honey fuck? I'd love to fuck that honey of hers. "It means if you were to legally end our relationship now, you would be returned to wherever you came for violating our ecological planetary protection laws. You're welcome." Kortul held his hand out to show her the scar forming, and she gently took his hand, and before he could react, she dislocated his middle finger. He held his crooked finger up to his face. *How the fuck did she do that so fast? And where does she think she's going?* His finger now throbbed, but all he could think about was tracking her down before someone called the authorities and they had to explain their marital tiff.

If anyone fought in public, the government would force them to attend therapy. The last thing he wanted was to sit in front of a therapist and have to explain the situation in a way that would prevent them both from ending up in trouble.

His fear unfolded right in front of his eyes as a member of the planetary guard walked straight up to Tolina before he could reach her. When he neared, he could hear the guard speaking, "Are you in distress? You have been reported for a public disruption regarding a disagreement. You must explain yourself or report to the court for instruction. What is your official statement?" Kortul stood frozen just out of eyeshot from her, and he could already see his life crashing and burning.

Tolina scowled at the man and acted like the guard had offended her. "Can't you tell kink play when you see it?"

Kortul's mouth fell open at the same time as the guards. The guard cleared his throat and took a step back before sighing and briskly walking away as he avoided eye contact. He made sure to bump into Kortul's shoulder and gave him a sour snarl before he disappeared in the crowd of the shopping center.

Kortul lifted his bent finger. "Is this kink play too?"

"How stupid are you, exactly?" Tolina reached over to set his finger, and he had to hold in a yelp of pain as the action was less than gentle.

"Stupid enough to want to save your helpless ass when you landed on my building in the middle of the day."

Tolina stood up a little straighter and replied, "Fine. What do I need to do to be rid of you, and stay here?"

"We need to remain married for a year, but if we split legally within the first five years, we would need to prove we tried to make it work. The only loophole is if you marry someone else before then." Kortul refused to lie to her about that, even if it meant the potential of losing her to someone else before she gave him a fair chance. *I'm not my father. I will not hurt her.*

Tolina felt like she would be sick, and she grasped her shirt at her chest. Her suppressed turbulent feelings were doing flips. "I've been through worse. I can deal with this," she was speaking to herself before she looked up and addressed Kortul, "I only accept these terms because I must. I will fake things with you, but I expect you to allow me to date other people. I need a job as well, and not something stupid. I was an assassin before, and I may have defected, but I loved my job. Something in security would work."

"You? An assassin? How could I have ever guessed?" Kortul asked with thick sarcasm, and she looked around to see if anyone was watching before she reached over and stepped on his toe, making him grimace.

I've never met such a vicious woman. I love it. She's perfect. "Careful, that's kink play now." Kortul knew what was coming and side stepped her as she tried to punch him in the stomach. When she missed, it infuriated her, and she stormed away making him run to keep up. She was almost at a jog on the way back to his building and stood glaring at him with her arms crossed in his lobby when he finally caught up.

"Corver, transport us home."

The transporters deposited them in his living room, and Tolina threw her jacket in the coat alcove by the front door and went straight for her room. Kortul stared down the hallway and sighed before he looked up and closed his eyes. "Corver, give Tolina full access."

"Does this include access to your galactic ships?" Corver asked.

He agreed, "Yes, I consent to full access. Give her full access to the ocean top factory, and the crystal island too. She has authority over anything I own as my wife, and she receives everything upon my death." The computer answered him with a confirmation tone just as Brock emerged from his room. Steam seeped from the edges of the door as he passed through.

"I have good news. Tolina's translator now works, and she is fully aware of the situation." Brock slowly blinked and didn't say a word as he scrutinized Kortul. "Should we ask her? Would that satisfy you?"

Brock ignored him and returned to his room. Brock knew Kortul hated when he was upset. He was not letting up until Tolina was happy, and Kortul knew that. Kortul wanted Tolina happy too. *How the fuck am I supposed to make the angriest woman I've ever met content? I want to keep her, and that means I need to find what brings her joy.* He looked down at his throbbing finger and wondered if he really was the dumbest man in the galaxy. *I guess I will find out.*

Chapter 6

A Father's Love

Kortul stood by as Brock cooked them dinner. Brock kept shooing him away to leave the cooking alone. Kortul was a terrible cook and only ever assisted. Wendi were expected to cook alongside their Eckolie, but Kortul burned food often and it irritated Brock far too much to allow Kortul to help anymore. Brock had been Kortul's companion since he was fifteen after he had passed him on the sidewalk one day. Wendi usually waited until they were twenty and on their own for an Eckolie companion, but if there was a strong connection earlier than that, a bond could form at any time.

Kortul was at the end of the island chopping carrots and listening to soft string music when Tolina came from her room. "Am I expected to eat with you?"

Brock grinned at her, and Kortul twisted his mouth in a bashful half smile as he responded, "I was hoping you would." Tolina cracked a hint of a genuine smile for the first time, but Kortul knew better than to think it was aimed at him. He looked behind him, and Brock had a wide yellow grin.

"I'll stay for Brock, not you." She went around the island and sat at the table to wait for them to finish cooking. Tolina didn't know the customs here and wanted to learn for dating purposes. Just because she hated Kortul, didn't mean she didn't find him ridiculously attractive, and she didn't mind watching him chop vegetables. She was fine with whatever species he was, just not him specifically. The little frog man was growing on her though. She was starting to understand why Kortul adored him. No matter how it looked on the outside, it was clear Brock was the one in charge here, and that gave Tolina great relief.

"Brock, do all of Kortul's people have companions like you?" Tolina decided she could just ignore Kortul if he would be eating with her and Brock.

"Yes, Eckolie and Wendi people are bonded species. We have lived symbiotically for millions of years."

Tolina looked over at Kortul wondering if he was noticing her ignoring him, but she saw he was enthralled in the holo-screen. Kortul frowned as he stared at the news stream on mute, and Tolina interjected, "What's wrong, Kortul? What are you making that rotten face about?"

Kortul chewed his lip and turned to look at her before he admitted, "One of the people I'm in a long-term contract with was just accused of violating the Common Galactic Trade Agreement, or CGTA laws. Ancient Corbatton ecology was once threatened by several off-planet mining companies, so we established strict laws to protect the planet from outside harm. This caused a movement for widespread ecological and societal protection. The CGTA was established by an ancient Corbatton queen, and it includes over sixty systems and almost a hundred protected planets. The only planets in our small galaxy not subject to the law are the border planets, but the common systems all supplement and support them with the surplus so they can live decent lives. According to the report, exploitation practices were discovered at Vespuc Cobbles mines. He has been hiring underage off-world miners and confiscating travel documents to keep them there with no pay. They released over three hundred teenagers who had been told they would be receiving pay, but who had hardly even been fed." He shifted his solemn gaze to Tolina and asked, "You want a job fit for your skills, am I right? Do you want to be my personal protection for meetings?"

"You want me to work as your bodyguard?" Tolina closed her eyes trying to decide whether she wanted to protect him or not, and for some reason the idea of someone harming Kortul seemed inconceivable. *The only person dislocating his fingers or cutting off his ears will be me.* "Fine. I'll do it. When is your next meeting?"

"Not for several weeks. We have plenty of time to prepare you." Kortul sighed as he knew it was time to introduce her to his late father's ex-boyfriend Mabit, who lived in the apartment under him. Mabit had first been his father's bodyguard and then his bodyguard after his father died. At one hundred, Mabit was far overdue for retirement, and Kortul wondered if Tolina might be a permanent replacement if he could talk her into it. Mabit was also far more than just a bodyguard. He had loved Kortul like his own son since Kortul's father had brought Kortul home. Mabit had been more of a father than his actual father had ever been, and he wasn't sure how this introduction would go. He hoped Mabit would like Tolina, but he had never introduced his overprotective father figure to anyone but a few friends before.

Brock finished cooking the white bird meat and vegetables, and he and Kortul made a plate before they joined Tolina at the table. She waited until they sat down and began eating before she opened a few of the jars and devoured the contents. Her mind wandered as she thought about what preparations and gear she would need, and who would be preparing her for her new job as she slurped up a few more jars of nectar.

Kortul finished his meal and as Brock cleared the table. Kortul waited for Tolina to meet his eyes. "Would you like to meet the bodyguard you will be replacing? He's like a father to me. His name is Mabit, and he lives a few floors down."

"Sure." Tolina stood up and deposited her used jars into the side of the replicator before she followed Kortul to the center of the kitchen. "Corver, transport us outside Mabit's door."

The computer complied, and they were standing in front of a tall door. He used to keypad to ring the door, and a voice answered from the keypad, "Kortul? Why didn't you just walk in?"

"Are you not looking at your camera?" Silence followed until the front door opened, and a kind, brown faced man with short black hair stood before Kortul and Tolina.

"Who is this?" Mabit grinned and seemed thrilled to meet Tolina, which made her feel strange and giddy inside. She wasn't used to people enjoying her company or wanting her around. She would take it, though, because something about him felt safe, and she needed a friend. He ushered them inside and she felt comfortable enough to spill some of the truth.

"I'm Tolina, Kortul's new, unwilling, *fake wife*."

Mabit blinked and narrowed his eyes at Kortul. "Please, continue Tolina. I would love to hear how this happened."

"I left my home planet looking for a new life, and I was drugged and abducted from the street on the planet I was visiting. I was there to see if it was a fit to start over. All I remember was blips of being at a lab, bound, and shoved inside a modified escape pod. My captors must have been experimenting with transport tech and sent me to the patio of this building. That's when Kortul found me," she held her hand up to show him her marital scar, "and I understand we are stuck together for a while so I can stay here." Mabit's and Kortul's mouths dropped open in unison.

With his eyebrows raised in surprise, Kortul spoke first, "I didn't know that." He wished he had kept his mouth shut because Mabit frowned at him and gave him a dismissive wave.

"Tolina, I would love to know more about you. Would you like a drink? We should all sit under the moons on the patio." Mabit seemed to float across the floor to his kitchen and Tolina followed with Kortul behind them. Tolina could tell by how Mabit walked he had extensive physical skills. His balance and grace were impeccable.

Once drinks were poured, Kortul asked, "Corver, add a force field over the top of the building and make it comfortable for swimming. Warm the pool, too." They all stepped closer together in the kitchen. "Corver, take us to the patio." In a split second they were standing on the patio and Tolina relaxed in the warm air.

"Does the force field act as a sound barrier?" Tolina asked as she admired the night sky.

Kortul sipped his drink before he answered, "It does. I installed privacy tech all over the building when I rebuilt it."

Tolina hated the Vo-Pess and couldn't wait to spill everything. *Maybe not everything. How am I supposed to say I failed at being a spy, so they gave me the dirty kills no one wanted?* "I come from a world kept hidden for thousands of years. Our planet Hyret was a secret from the rest of our galaxy until the first spy defected, and then it was a cascade. I was an assassin for my people's leaders, but they were exploitive and abusive at best. I was bonded, or married, to a family member of our leaders, and I was *very* lucky. He was kind and treated me well. He just wasn't interested in me like a couple ought to be interested in one another. He was in love with a man he worked with, and all I ever wanted was to see him happy. When our operatives began to defect one after another, our society fell apart. We both knew it was time for me to leave and start a new life somewhere else. He and the man he loved planned to leave and have the life he always deserved while I went to a planet called Emendo in my galaxy. It was only my first day on Emendo when I was captured by an enemy to my people and sent here in what I assume is a transport technology experiment."

"She has asked for work, so I offered her your old position as my bodyguard, and I was hoping you could spend some time working with her and make sure she is a good fit." Kortul was facing Mabit who aimed a curious stare at Kortul before he downed his drink.

Mabit changed the subject abruptly and Kortul should have seen it coming. "You two are aware you'll face the queen if you're caught. You better start acting married or the planetary guard will open an investigation. Do you have any idea how invasive that investigation is?" Kortul had nothing to say as he was clueless to the investigation process, and Mabit knew that, so he continued, "I didn't think so. Tolina, I am sure you are an honest person, however, Kortul, you cannot walk into my apartment with a bodyguard replacement you just met and forced into a fake marriage, just so she can stay on the planet." Kortul stood speechless. He and Mabit both knew he was thinking with his dick again. He swore sometimes it had its own brain and made its own decisions. He felt it move from its slit and curl in his pants and he scowled. *Now is not the time.* He couldn't help thinking of Tolina nude and spread for him, moaning, and rocking her hips as he licked up her cum. "Kortul!" Mabit snapped, "Are you listening?"

Kortul grinned at Mabit. *What did he say?* "No. I wasn't listening. I was too busy thinking about how Tolina might taste." *Did I just say that aloud?* Tolina swiftly smacked his arm and scowled at him. Kortul had stars twinkling in his eyes for her even though his arm was stinging.

Mabit snarled at Kortul and turned to Tolina to apologize, "I'm sorry he is such an ass. I did try with him, but some obstacles you never conquer. I was with Kortul's father for many years while I was his bodyguard. I've known Kortul since he was an infant, and he's the exact same now as he always has been, only a lot larger."

Kortul scoffed in offense holding his hand on his chest. "I am not the same as I was as a child. That is a vast stretch. My jokes as a child were not nearly as inappropriate."

A scrunched nose was all Mabit could muster for a response, and Tolina guzzled her remaining drink and smashed it in Kortul's chest before demanding, "Listen Kortul, if I must be stuck with your dumb ass, I'll need a lot more alcohol."

Mabit threw his head back and roared with laughter, "HA! I love her!"

Tolina couldn't help a giggle herself as Kortul mocked him with a frown and a sarcastic, "I love her," as he went to refill her drink at the replicator.

In Kortul's short absence for a refill, Mabit leaned in, studying Tolina. Mabit intrigued her as he asked, "I can see more than most. Things which exist above and below, and sometimes in between. You hide your pain well, but I can still see it. May I ask how long it went on?"

Tolina had never had someone rip her in half like a soggy sheet of paper before. He had revealed her soul as if it were effortless for him. *If this man helped raise Kortul, there must be some good in him.* "My training, it was brutal. They made us do awful things to one another. There was a sadistic man who led the training academy, and he must have had some kind of torture kink. He would sit and watch every physical arms class and loved it when one of us was wounded. After the training was over, my first mission went wrong." Tolina felt Kortul behind her, so she reached out for her drink, and he was silent as he handed it over. "I located and moved to eliminate my target. He was on the run for murdering his wife, and I caught him when he returned to his home, which was also the scene of the crime. When I went in for the kill, I didn't know he had an ax in his reach. He was a keeper of the spawning forest, and he brought the mallet side of his ax onto my right leg several times before I could end him. I had to crawl for miles with a shattered leg before I had a signal to call for help. Our planet is in a nebulous region and much of our communication was ground lines. My right leg bones are a lightweight alloy now."

The patio was silent as a calm, warm breeze passed over

Tolina's skin while she breathed through the trauma of that day. She had been so young and so new at her job, and she had no idea the crime scene crew would leave the murder weapon behind. The memory of having to drag her body in agony along the forest floor with every bump and move making the journey more excruciating always tied her insides in knots.

Before she realized what was happening, Mabit had his arms around her, and she was hugging him back. He smelled like vanilla, and he felt like a stone, but his demeanor oozed care and affection, and she felt safer than she had ever before. She was so comfortable in his arms her antennae drooped down her hair and went limp.

Chapter 7

Cyclones and Cigars

Tolina prepared for Mabit to rush her as she crouched on the mat, but Mabit surprised her by side stepping at the last second and slamming into her from the side, sending them both rolling. Tolina was able to slip from his grasp, but he was always one step behind her and ready to pounce once she was free. They continued this routine for over two hours while Kortul lounged on the mat and watched while he pretended to work on his tablet. He was recording them, and Mabit shot him a glare, suspecting Kortul of doing exactly that.

It was still a slight surprise to him Mabit had accepted Tolina so quickly, but then again, Kortul was practically in love with Tolina, and he had known her less than a week. The more she overtly hated him, the more he wanted her. He was hopeless with dating and only seemed to like the chase, and then when it was over, his interest would wane. Tolina hating him was like mixing drugs and candy, and he knew he would lick the dirt from the soles of her shoes if she asked him. *I want to lick a lot more than that.* He imagined how she looked when she orgasmed, and he had to fight a groan.

He wanted everything from her. He wanted to taste her, and then he wanted her to peg him and pull his hair while she did it. *I hope she's a mean fuck too.* Kortul nearly came in his pants and had to press his cock back down between his legs when the imagery of her furious and pounding his ass with a strap on blessed his mind. *How the fuck am I supposed to let her date other people?* He already wanted to kill them all. *I know I can convince her to go on a date with me. All I need to do is tell her we need to make sure we have evidence in case we are questioned. I'll take her to the island. No one can resist a man with an island, right?* He laughed to himself because on Corbatton things like that didn't matter. In reality, his island may have had his name on it, but it had been open to the public for generations, long before the name Saltic was on every other electronic on the planet. It was one of the places the Wendi people had originated from, and he loved it there. It was his responsibility to preserve it, and that was the part of which he was most proud. The island had flourished when he inherited it. Even the resort who leased from him had been more successful since he had taken ownership after his father died.

Tolina and Mabit finished their practice, and Mabit came over and kicked at Kortul's foot. "Have you been keeping up with your workouts?"

Kortul frowned. He was in the best shape he had ever been in. He usually worked out in the mornings right after he woke up. "You can't tell? I'm offended." Mabit shook his head as he toweled off his sweat and walked away.

Tolina approached, guzzling a glass of water. "Now that Mabit approved me, what is the first job?"

Kortul stared at her and knew he was wrong for his first motives, but he decided being drastic in his security from now on wouldn't be a terrible thing. "I'll need you anytime I leave for business, and we need to be seen together soon to show we made some kind of attempt to make this work." Kortul wasn't sure how she would take that last bit, so he waited for her to think about it.

"You mean for when I date other people. I am not staying married to you, no matter how great your dad is." Kortul ignored over half of what she said as he grinned at her. *She's already calling Mabit my dad. I don't even call him that. She's not wrong. He is much more of a dad than my father ever was.*

Kortul rose from the ground, and Tolina stepped closer. "Corver, transport us home." In moments, they were standing in his living room. Tolina was walking off to shower when he noticed the light rain outside, meaning within a few hours the building would be tilted over in the wind. The emergency alert system would be initiated, and a magnetic force would be enacted on all the items in the building to keep them in place during the commotion. The cyclones on his planet could easily reach three to five hundred miles an hour or more, and the small amount of wetland the city was built on always flooded, so their streets had mechanical lifts to allow the seawater to drain below.

The building's emergency siren began, and he scrunched his nose with the screeching sound as Brock came from the living room with his window cleaning supplies. The floor cleaning robot rolled by as Brock looked over at Kortul and slowly blinked. "Bad one coming. Worse one in years, expecting sideways buildings."

Kortul sighed, he was glad they had the static and

magnetic fields in the building to hold all the items and people in place while the storm ravaged the area. No one in the city ever had more than a cracked window after a storm was over, but the part he really hated was all the sea life trapped in his pool. It would take two days for the rescue teams to retrieve all the fish, which were mostly protected wildlife.

It was too late when Kortul realized Tolina would be clueless about the weather, and moments later she came flying from her room in a towel with wet hair. "What the fuck is happening?"

"Don't worry. We have a cyclone approaching. The building will sway a lot, and we could be sideways for a few hours."

"Sideways?"

Kortul shot her a nervous half smile as he explained, "Since Corbatton is primarily open oceans, we have storms with wind speeds well over three hundred to five hundred miles an hour. The building is designed to lean all the way over and rest on the next building to withstand the wind gusts. We do have static and magnetic force fields in place, so it will feel very uneasy, but I assure you we are safe. You should get dressed."

Tolina blinked at him. She was not a fan of windy storms, and she knew it was part of her people's nature. Butterflies don't last long in windstorms. Her heart was picking up speed, and she hated when this happened. This is part of why she failed spy school and ended up a bottom dweller assassin. Maybe that's not entirely true, she failed a lot of classes too, but maybe part of it was because she had anxiety and a list of other faults she couldn't control. She knew she wasn't stupid. She was just terrible at school.

A strong warm hand was holding hers, and she looked up to find Kortul concerned and far too close for her comfort. He made her feel awkward and bubbly inside, and she hated it. It felt like her insides were squirming around, and now she was overheating. "Do you need to sit down? The wind is picking up and we will start leaning soon. I can grab your clothes."

Tolina was doing everything she could not show how upset she was, but she was losing the battle in a landslide of heavy thoughts. Too much had happened in the last week for her to be facing a major fear. She felt Kortul guide her to his long, curved couch in his living area before he helped her sit down.

"Brock, can you please bring Tolina some water?" Kortul could hear Brock in the kitchen before he brought the water to Tolina and handed it to her while Kortul went in her room for her clothes. She drank the glass and handed it back to Brock. Brock gave Kortul a concerned look when he passed him to sit back down next to Tolina. Brock went to his room while Kortul's hand died from Tolina's iron grip, and he wasn't even sure when she had grabbed it.

"Tolina, if you squeeze my hand any harder, you might break it." She gasped and recoiled her hand before she took a shaking breath and dared to look at the storm outside the window. "Here are your clothes." He handed them over and turned around for her to change. She went silent when she was finished, and he sat back against the sofa.

Outside straight-line winds and sheets of rain pounded the glass. They had a few more minutes before the building would begin to lean, but it looked like the storm was already at its worst to someone who had never experienced the Corbatton storms. "The building is still upright, and you look like you might pass out, do you want a sedative or maybe a drink?"

Tolina turned to him and grabbed his forearm in a bruising hold. "Please, I need a drink, or maybe something more." Being vulnerable was not something which came easy, but her insides were screaming at her to run and hide, so she was wide open and there wasn't anything she could do about it. *This is so embarrassing. Why the honey fuck did I land somewhere with cyclones?! The one thing I cannot control is a storm. I hate storms.*

The building began its slow lean to the side, and Kortul could see Tolina's lime eyes widen with the tilt of the building. He patted her leg and crawled over the back of the couch instead of walking around it and he headed straight for his replicator where he ordered a drink and a leaf cigar with calming properties. By the time he made it back over to her, the building had tilted so far, her hair was now lifting from the back of the couch and dangling behind her head.

"You'll need to sit forward in order to drink this."

Tolina twisted around and when she did, he saw her distress and slid the cigar behind his ear to crawl over the couch and help her sit forward to sip the drink. Instead of sipping it, she guzzled down the stout liquor and pointed to the cigar behind his ear. "What is that? Will it help me?"

"It's a calming leaf cigar. My father used it all the time for anxiety."

"Well, hurry up." Tolina gasped and grabbed at the couch as the wind shifted and the building groaned in response.

Patting the cushion beside him, Kortul scoffed, "Fuck, I forgot the lighter. Corver, ignite the end of this cigar." The computer complied and a little flame burst to life at the end of his cigar. He puffed on it a few times before he handed it over to her.

She sucked on it like she was trying to take a full breath from the cigar, and Kortul chuckled knowing she would cough until snot came from her nose. She did exactly that moments later, and he pat her on the back. "Corver, I need an emergency bottle of water."

When a bottle of water appeared in his hand, he opened it and helped Tolina take a drink. When she lay back against the couch, she melted into it and looked over at Kortul with thanks as she reached for the leaf cigar again to take a much smaller inhale. As they finished smoking, she was finally at ease.

"That worked well. I feel much better. Thank you."

Tolina had not spoken to him with such a soft tone before, so he took his opportunity. "I want to take you to one of the crystal islands, and you could go flying there. I was thinking we would go for a couple of days, and that would be a sufficient start for proving we gave this relationship our best effort."

Tolina could see right through him and narrowed her eyes she replied, "Fine. Only because we *must*." The storm was too distracting for her to keep up her attitude, and she closed her eyes trying to block it out. Kortul handed her the leaf cigar again and she remembered taking that last drag, but that was all.

Blinking, Tolina looked round her room and sat up to check outside, finding it clear and dark. She was still in the same clothes from earlier, but now she was in bed and hours had passed. Aiming for the restroom, she climbed out of bed, but when she passed by the sink in the bathroom, she noticed her toothbrush and toothpaste were sitting out. She smacked her mouth a few times and snarled her lip. *Did he brush my fucking teeth? Is that weird, or should I say thank you? I feel like that's weird. Why am I thinking about this right now? Is it early in the morning or late?*

Tolina went back to bed after relieving herself and awoke to a soft knock on the wall next to her door. "What?" She scowled at the bright natural light.

The door slid open and Kortul was in swim trunks ready to leave. "When you're dressed and ready, we can board my transport for the island. Wear swimwear."

Kortul let the door shut, and Tolina stared at it wondering if she should just go back to sleep. "Does he ever wear a shirt?"

Chapter 8

Wife

Tolina stood in a black bikini behind her door, staring at the shiny metal. *How did I end up in this situation? I just wanted to be free and now I'm trapped all over again, but this time by a fucking four eyed spider. Freedom seems so far away I don't know how I can keep this up and not snap. I don't trust Kortul, and I miss Trel.* She wasn't ready to accept she may have made a mistake in leaving her home world. That fear rattled her down to her soul. She knew if she didn't find purpose for her life here she would end up doing despicable things, and the awful urges left over from her former career would return. She yearned to hear the gurgling screams of a deserving victim as badly as she wanted loving affection, but she had to brush away all those ideas. She would need to act like a good little wife until she could escape. Tolina closed her eyes and prepared herself for a nauseating vacation.

When she built up the nerve to face the living room, she came around the corner where Tyce and Kortul were talking. They both became quiet when she approached.

Tyce frowned at Kortul before he looked over to Tolina with kindness and addressed her softly, "Are you faring well here with him? Has he been treating you well?" His sincerity and Kortul appearing to roll his solid black eyes made her far more trusting of this white-faced man. She couldn't honestly tell if Kortul had rolled his eyes, but with the face he was making, he might as well have.

She sighed and admitted the truth, "He has given me no reason to kill him in the middle of the night."

Kortul seemed a bit shocked at her answer and scoffed as he replied, "I caught you in the kitchen eating honey in the middle of the night, and I made you an entire cart of honey for your room, but I'm only on the other side of murder?"

"Did you tell him I dislocated your finger?" Tolina crossed her arms over her half naked body. She was second guessing listening to Kortul's instructions on attire and felt uncomfortable with such a revealing outfit in the apartment. A beach or pool was fine, but it was chilly, and she felt odd. Her bathing suit cover was much more sheer than she anticipated, and she had picked a very revealing bikini on purpose, but now she regretted it. *I've never been modest before. What's wrong with me?* Beside her, Kortul completely ignored what she asked, yet stared at her like he wanted to take a bite. She almost shivered and was tempted to stomp on her own toe to make the internal squirming stop.

Tyce cleared his throat as he gawked at their awkwardness together. "I will be leaving now. You two have fun."

Kortul knew Tyce was still furious. He had two choices, either let Tolina go, or convince her to give him a chance. He could never let her go. She was far too perfect for him, and this little hating game of hers was the most thrilling experience of his life. This was the kind of woman who could keep him interested and guessing at every turn. *The more she hates me, the more I love her. No wonder I have never found love before. It was never toxic enough for me.* He sighed at how knowing this woman might murder him in the night made his cock so hard it ached.

They were transporting down to his ship, and it occurred to him he might need to explain that since she arrived on the planet under traumatic circumstances by transport. "We are taking my ship, and the ship will transport to the island hanger. I know you have been ground transporting, but a ship is much closer to how you arrived and I don't want to make you uncomfortable."

Tolina was a little surprised that he considered her feelings, but as long as they weren't transporting into any cyclones, she would be fine. "It does not bother me." If it had been anybody else, she would have said thank you, but she wanted to dislocate his finger again for the way he was looking at her. She hated she could not tell precisely where he was looking, but it was easy enough to figure out, and it was always clear his thoughts were despicable.

"Corver, transport us to my ship." In the matter of a moment, they were standing on the bridge of a ship which made every other ship she had ever seen before seem primitive in comparison. The entire interior of the bridge was a hologram showing the hangar outside the ship. As she and Kortul approached the center of the bridge, two holographic chairs emerged from the floor like liquid. Tolina watched as Kortul sat down on what should have been collected points of light, but somehow, was now solid. Her face revealed her thoughts, and she could see Kortul's smug meter rising by the second. "Our holograms can be programmed to become solid. Did you not have this technology? It's similar to particle replication and combines holo-tech creating a particle organizing system."

Tolina pretended to ignore him and sat down, sinking into the chair. A forcefield tingled as it rolled over her like a chill, and the ship's controls appeared as a solid hologram in front of Kortul. He scrolled through a list of destinations before he tapped on an option labeled, 'My island.' Tolina groaned to herself. *This is HIS island we are visiting? How did I not catch that before now? This man is impossible.*

Within moments they were in another ship's hangar, and Kortul rose from his seat with his hand out for hers. Reluctant to pull her arms away from her exposed, chilled skin, she relented when Kortul made it clear he was not moving until she took his hand. Why was she so concerned with her own skin? She had never cared before. When her hand slid into his, she wanted to yank it back. His touch always made her feel like her insides were fluttering, and she hated it. *I don't know why the fuck that happens, but it makes me want to cut my damn skin off!*

Kortul held her hand, and she rose from her chair before he asked the computer, "Corver, transport us to the front desk." The computer complied and they were standing at the desk before Tolina could finish taking in a breath. A beautiful woman with six eyes, light cream skin, and warm chestnut hair looked up and scowled at them as they approached the counter. The room was constructed from crystal blocks and Tolina was struck by the bright, colorful beauty of the spacious lobby. The crystal and lights created an ethereal space and she noticed only a few people were walking around.

Kortul smirked at the woman and leaned on the glass counter, "I want the seaside room on the top level instead of ground level this time." The woman with a deep brown neck and deep brown and white stripped arms with a tan resort button-down short sleeved shirt tugged on the hem of her shirt to straighten it.

"You could have at least called," she scathed, but Kortul returned a smile.

He leaned in and stared at her before he answered, "Nire, I don't recall being in any kind of relationship with you which would require a call."

Now fuming, Nire seethed, "Fuck you, Saltic, and your new toy."

"My name is Tolina. That's no way to speak to the owner of the island and his wife," Tolina interjected, and she watched Nire's face fall. Kortul looked over at Tolina, and she hated the satisfaction on his face. She took his hand and bent his finger in an unnatural position causing him to shake with internal laughter as he batted at her hand.

When Nire turned away, Kortul swiftly grabbed Tolina's wrist and held it in his iron grip until they walked down the hall. He pulled her to him and whispered against the shell of her ear, "My wife? Have you changed your mind?"

That wriggling feeling was crawling down her spine again, and Tolina clenched her muscles, trying not to tremble. She knew she was supposed to be keeping up appearances and pretending to be his wife, so she remained still. He was more than pleased. "Corver, transport us to our room." The computer had them in a top floor room in seconds. Kortul wrapped his arms around her, which she was sick of, so she elbowed him in the gut, and he fell to his knees.

"I thought we were doing so well," Kortul groaned as he grabbed his stomach where she elbowed him. He already had a healing bruise there from her, and he was sure she made it worse.

Ignoring him, Tolina walked off to look from the wall of windows out onto the beach and ocean below. She remembered him saying something about her being able to fly here, so she opened the door to the patio and tossed away her swimsuit cover before she peeled her wings from her skin. Holding her bathing suit down, she waited until her wings were fully spread before she readjusted and tightened her suit. The breeze and the purple-blue color of the sky made her feel delightful.

This world is beautiful, and I need to find a way to remain here without having to stay with Kortul. He makes me feel squirmy, and I fucking hate it.

Inside, Kortul sat up when she unfurled her wings from her back and legs, and they spread out behind her. *She's the most beautiful being I've ever seen. She can think I will allow her to date other people all she wants, but this woman is mine.* He walked out behind her to admire her wings, and he fought the urge to run his finger along the raised veins. She fluttered them to prepare to take off, but she sensed him take a step closer. "Your wings are beautiful. May I touch them?"

Tolina froze and swallowed trying to wet her drying throat. Her wings were sensitive. Lost in pleasure sensitive. Touching her wings was an intimate act, and her desperation for him *not* to touch them seemed to be enticing him more. He stepped around her wing to look at her and tipped his head, waiting for her answer.

I don't want him to, but I know if I say no, it will make him want to touch them more. She nodded in agreement, and he narrowed his eyes at her reluctance before he moved behind her. She felt his warmth at her back, and she regretted giving him permission. When he touched her, her heart squeezed as she realized he knew wing anatomy. He ran his finger along the place where her wings connected to her back and then trailed it along the upper edge. She could have moaned with the way he stroked his finger along her right wing, but when he began touching her left wing, she couldn't take the overwhelming pleasure anymore and had to clench her muscles to prevent a colossal shiver.

When she felt his finger trail down the center of her spine, she burst. She flapped her wings and launched from the patio, desperate for space. In the air and far enough away from Kortul, Tolina released her building shiver, and it lasted so long she almost fell from the sky. Furious and flapping so hard she felt her wings stretching with the force, she circled the mountain sized carved crystals jutting from the ocean.

Now that she was alone, she was in heaven as she soared through the salty air. The warm breeze enveloped her skin like an embrace. Bright streams of light cast from the crystal tip onto the sea, and she basked in the colorful light as she skimmed the crashing waves.

She landed on the tip of one of the mountainous crystals, and joy overflowed from her as she watched a school of flying fish soar by her as they hunted and ate swarms of insects. She wondered what other curious creatures this planet had as she peered down into the clear waters, realizing she could see to the sea floor because of the clarity of the water. She jumped from the top of the crystal and soared over the ocean to admire the sea life. Enormous fish and whales, as well as massive octopus lived in the waters below, and she wondered if they had sharks too. She was beginning to love this planet, which made her stomach curl. She had to find a way to stay here and escape Kortul, but her control was weak. Finding him attractive did not mean she wanted to be with him. She rolled her eyes, remembering the pornographic comic painted on the side of his building.

When she prepared to land, she saw him standing on the patio in only a pair of loose linen pants, hanging far too low on his hips. Kortul had a bruise in the center of his stomach, and she knew the bruising was from her. Her mood changed quickly, and she cringed when she landed.

Chapter 9

Girls Girl

After a long, quiet meal on the patio with Kortul staring at her like he wanted her for dessert, she was now waiting for him to fall asleep so she could confront Nire. As much as she hated Kortul, she would not tolerate someone being disrespectful of him. She could be a brat all she wanted and complain about him, but the reality was she landed on the wrong planet and he was doing her a life debt of a favor. What she would not allow was anyone thinking it was acceptable to offend Kortul, especially considering she was his new bodyguard.

Beside her, Kortul's breathing evened out, and she slipped from the bed and quietly went to the balcony where she had left the glass doors open. Wearing loose linen sleep pants and a loose crop, Tolina didn't want to fly down and flash the people having a night swim on the beach, so she looked around the side of the balcony and noticed a mechanical fire escape lift on the side. The poles it moved along were the perfect size for her to wrap her hands around and slide down. She could climb them later when she returned to her room.

Holding the poles, she slid down and the moment her feet touched the sandy ground she felt a rush of excitement. She walked through a small, manicured garden of bright pink island flowers with long yellow pistons before she found a paved pathway to walk on. She passed through a small seated area before reaching the patio of a restaurant. After making her way around the patio, she found a door with a map indicating she was traveling toward the front desk.

Tolina arrived at the front desk and was quite disappointed to see Nire was not there. In her place was a man with a kind tan face; however, he seemed nervous and unsure. *Perfect.* She approached the counter with a smile. "My friend Nire was working earlier, and I thought she was supposed to be here. I was coming by to see her. Is she off work now? Did I have her schedule wrong?" She leaned in close and continued, "If I forgot to meet her after work again, she will roast me."

He nodded and whispered, "She's at the resort restaurant drinking at the bar. Her shift ended over an hour ago. You better hurry. She had a hard day and she's not staying much longer." Tolina gave him a bright shining smile before she pranced off in the same direction she had come in and right back to the restaurant she passed by.

Spotting Nire tucked at the end of the bar, Tolina came up and sat right next to her. Nire twisted on her stool to face Tolina and frowned. "What do *you* want?"

Tolina leaned against the bar and stared at her, refraining from showing any emotion. "I want to know what your problem is, and why you think you can speak to Kortul the way you did?"

"Kortul Saltic was in my bed last month fucking me. That's why."

Tolina stared at her with an apologetic gaze and was delicate as she spoke, "That explains nothing. Did he declare a relationship with you? Where is your self respect?" She knew he had not been in a relationship with Nire, and it was confirmed with Nire's tears growing in her eyes. "Out with it. You're safe." Tolina watched Nire slump at the bar as she her hard exterior cracked.

"Kortul and I had been having sex off and on when he visited the resort, but I haven't seen him in a while, and now he shows up with you." Tears rolled down her cheeks and she drank the rest of her beverage before she tried to slip away.

Tolina reached for her arm, and Nire whipped around. With Tolina's antennae raised, and with contact to Nire's skin, her senses were strong. Tolina detected Nire was not telling her everything. Something terrible had happened to her. "Nire you're hurting, and I know it's not about Kortul. I assure you. You're safe. I might be able to help."

After looking around the room, Nire wiped her two biggest eyes, the only ones with tears, and nodded before she pointed outside to the restaurant patio. Tolina followed her and they sat down at a table in the corner away from everyone.

Nire didn't hold back as she gushed, "When Kortul didn't return for a while I became upset, and I did something I regret. It was a week ago. I was just off my shift, and in here for a drink before I went to walk on the beach." She paused and took a breath before she continued, "I walked too far down, and wasn't on the resort land anymore, which isn't protected by the automated security. It's a part of a public park on the island and with a group, it would have been safe. We know better than to venture there alone because of wild animals at night, but what happened didn't involve that kind of animal." Nire took another pause before she went on, this time slower, "There was a man. He had bright blue face, white hair, and he was very handsome. He was leaning against a crystal rock wall, and I walked near him before I realized he had been drinking. I tried to escape but, he caught me."

Before Tolina's eyes, Nire shut down and began staring at the table between them. Tolina needed confirmation, so she reached out and held Nire's hand as she asked gently, "Nire, did he force himself on you?"

She looked up at Tolina and nodded in confirmation. "He's still here at the resort."

Tolina was firm but kind as she spoke. "You are taking me up front. We are friends who are breaking a few rules and looking up a guy we saw. Do you understand?" Nire stood with new confidence and waved for Tolina to follow her. Tolina began thinking about all the ways she would make this man hurt as they approached the counter.

The man Tolina spoke to earlier seemed delighted to see them together, and Nire introduced her to him, "Evek, this is my friend Tolina. Can we use the console alone for a bit?" Nire winked at him, and he smiled as he walked away. She turned around and began clicking at the touchscreen before she scrolled through pictures of guests at the resort. After a few minutes of scrolling, she paused when she saw a man with a blue face. "That's him." Nire whispered, "Sanfen Wertik, room 7002."

I know they have sharp knives in the kitchen. "Nire, I need two knives to peel and cut up some fruit. I need them to be very sharp."

Her eyes widened at Tolina's request, and she became quiet. "Who are you?"

"I'm not someone you make enemies with," Tolina replied flatly, sending a visible chill through Nire before she gave Tolina a brilliant smile.

As they went toward the restaurant, Nire pointed for Tolina to move back to the patio where they had been sitting and Tolina made her way to the table. Moments later Nire sat down. "We are so lucky. I just set aside his room service order from the rack before it could be delivered. This way you can steal a uniform from the locker room, and you'll be able to deliver it to his room." Nire handed Tolina her purse and then patted her pockets. "I emptied the contents of my purse into my pockets, and you can just take the purse. The knives are inside. Destroy everything in a particle recycler afterward."

She would be able to find the target's balcony from the food delivery. Tolina was impressed with Nire's assistance. Tolina could tell Nire was desperate to know what Tolina would do, but she would need to find out the next day after the authorities arrived. She only needed to ask one last thing, "Can you loop the surveillance system on level 7?"

Shaking her head, Nire replied, "No, we have no access to it. You will need to deliver the food and then use the patio entrance. There is no surveillance inside the rooms or on the balcony though. Only the area on the other side of the balcony is recorded, so be quick when you arrive and hide your face."

That was not good enough for Tolina, "Where is the security camera on the porch?"

Nire thought about it and lit up when she realized she knew the answer, "It's on the wall, and it's a grey strip. You could cut the feed if you stabbed the smaller knife into the edge where it's soft. They just have a rubber coating on it. I saw one of the maintenance people working on it once."

Smiling, Tolina reached over and took Nire's hand. "You're too good to be moping around about Kortul. Don't let any man drag you down." Tolina rose from her seat and stalked off with the purse and the tray food in her hands. She moved down the hallway at a steady pace until she saw a door stuck open with lockers and a staff changing room inside. She slowly leaned over to look at it and slid inside without anyone noticing her.

Knowing there would be no surveillance cameras in a changing room, she quickly changed into a resort restaurant uniform and stuffed her clothes into the purse. Eying a back door, she went through it and found a staff only staircase without power. The sign said it was under maintenance. *Perfect*. She sprinted to the seventh story, skipping several stairs as she went. When she made it to the top, she stuck her head from the door she pried open and checked both ways before she ventured out and found room 7002. She set the order down and moved to the end of the hall where she found a lift to take her back downstairs. In the lift, she waited for him to take the order. When he came out and grabbed it, she rode the lift to the bottom level and went to a restroom where she took off the uniform and stuffed it in a particle recycler. She dressed in her former loose clothing before she checked the replicator.

Once she knew the uniform was deconstructed on a

molecular level and added to the replicator resources, she moved from the bathroom with the purse to walk around the building and locate the man's balcony. Once she saw it, she noticed a drone hovering the area and it appeared to be the point of security for the beach side of the resort. Destroying it would be necessary as she unfurled her wings, and they opened under the cover of some trees. She retrieved the knives from the purse and flapped her wings to stretch them as she made her flight plan to eliminate the surveillance drone. She would come back for the purse to recycle it and the knives before returning to her room.

Running toward the edge of the property, she flapped her wings and shot into the sky. Positioning herself far above the drone, she used the pull of gravity and the power of her wings to slam into the device with the spines of her knives. She broke it into a thousand pieces before she aimed and landed on the roof of Sanfen's patio. Once she had the video feed cut along the balcony of the porch, she dropped down onto the patio. She angled for the open doors as her wings receded, and with her feet on the floor she charged into the room for the man eating on the couch.

"What the fuck?" was all he had time to say before Tolina had him pinned on the ground with a knife to his throat.

The terror in his eyes gave Tolina such delight she couldn't hold back a grin. "Do you like the taste of your own blood? I hope so. You'll be tasting a lot of yourself tonight." He tried to scream but as his lips parted for the sound to escape, he passed out. Tolina had been holding pressure on his neck with the side of her blade, and when he lost consciousness, he slumped over with a gaping mouth.

Tolina rose up and looked around for something to tie

him with, and she saw the laces in his shoes first, so she pulled them free as he twitched. Once she had him stripped and tied face up on the living room table, she frowned at his crotch. His penis was inside of his body. "Well honey fuck me raw. How do I open that damn slit?"

He woke up, and saw Tolina hovering his crotch, and she knew a scream was coming, so she punched him in the mouth to silence him. He gargled around the impact as he lost consciousness again, and Tolina quickly began her work. She knew he would be loud if she didn't gag him first, so she took his shirt and stuffed it in his mouth before using his belt to strap it down. He woke again and whimpered around the gag.

"I need you to show me your dick. How do I charm it from your slit so I can cut it off and make you eat it. This is very important to me. If I don't make you eat at least one part of yourself, I did not have enough fun, and then I'll think about this forever. I really don't want that. Do you know what? I think we can start with a toe, and the pain can force it out."

Sanfen shook the table as he fought the shoelaces holding him down. Tolina grabbed his little toe, causing him to scream around the gag. She was so delighted by his scream she could have giggled, but she had toes to cut off, so she reached down and wedged her knife between his toe bones before pushing it through. His own movements finished the severing job, and he gargled as he cried.

Tolina had enough waiting for his dick to emerge, so she left the toe on the table, and she wedged the knife in his slit to begin working it apart, causing Sanfen to buck so hard the table groaned. Annoyed, Tolina slapped him as hard as she could on the lower belly and his dick burst free. "Yes!" She grabbed his white, fleshy penis, causing him to thrash and a sorrowful high pitched scream poured from around the gag. Tolina scoffed, "I don't know why you're so upset about me cutting it off. I would be far more upset about what I'm planning to do with it, and your toe." He sobbed around the gag as she reached down and sawed off his penis. She took her time and made sure she hacked at it a bit before she fully separated it. Blood spurt out, but she hopped around to miss it.

He started to blackout, and she was having none of that. Tolina slapped him a few times, causing his eyes to widen, and she loosened the belt to pull the gag from his mouth. He cried to her, "Please have mercy. Whatever I did, I'm sorry!"

Tolina smiled with his severed dick in her hand and then pursed her lips. "Whatever you did? You mean who you raped?" His guilt was evident in his terrified eyes.

"You deserve this." Tolina smiled as she grabbed his jaw to force it open before she shoved his penis into his mouth and wedged it into his throat, preventing him from breathing. She took his belt and slid it back over his mouth and tightened it down.

Tolina stepped back and watched him fight for breath as she noticed his toe. "Oh, I forgot your toe! Silly me." She went over and grabbed his severed toe before reaching up and shoving it into his nostril. His look of pure horror was joyous, and she burst into laughter. She hovered over him as he suffocated on his own dick, and she began to wonder if she could ever really live without some fun torture and a murder.

Chapter 10

Colossal Creatures

Tolina made it back to her room and was standing in the bathroom staring at her pleased image in the mirror when she noticed blue blood droplets drying on her crop top. She looked over at the replicator knowing it beeped when it finished and Kortul might wake up.

She sighed and stuffed her soiled clothes into the machine anyway and selected the same outfit. Needing to wash away any evidence on her skin, she started the shower and quickly scrubbed herself while the replicator made new clothes. Tolina started drying and noticed Kortul staring at her from the open bathroom door.

At the moment, she didn't care about him seeing her nude. What she cared about was that he was awake, and she had to speak to him. She wrapped her towel around her dripping body. "What?"

"It's after midnight. Why are you showering and having the replicator make you new clothing?" Kortul seemed confused as he stared at her.

She sighed. She was not explaining anything, and she knew there was one solid way to distract this man. Tolina dropped her towel and bent over showing Kortul her entire ass and pussy, just to take her clothes from the replicator tray as she lied, "I had a bad dream and sweated. I needed a shower and dry clothes."

Kortul was too interested in staring at her to pay attention to her words, and she dressed knowing he wouldn't ask any more questions. "I'm tired, and I want to go back to bed."

He followed close behind her as they went back to the large bed they were supposed to sleep in together. Watching him climb in the bed, she would not admit this to him, but she missed having someone sleeping with her. Although she and Trel tried and failed at sex a few times, she and her former husband always slept together, and he sometimes even held her at night. She especially enjoyed his affection after she made a brutal kill, but tonight she would just be happy she wasn't sleeping alone.

When she crawled into the bed and looked back at him, Kortul seemed curious as he watched her find a comfortable place. "What are you looking at?" she asked as her head sunk down into the soft pillow.

"Something feels off," Kortul admitted, but he didn't take his eyes from her.

She brushed him off. "You're sensing a couple fighting in the next room or something. I'm trained in using empathic abilities, and you would be surprised what even a normal being can detect."

Giving up, Kortul closed his eyes, and his breathing evened out. Tolina fell asleep shortly after. When she woke, she climbed from the bed to stretch before she went into the next room. Kortul was standing in front of the holo-screen and he had a news segment playing on silent.

"I was right about my bad feeling last night. Someone was brutally murdered on the seventh floor here at the resort. The resort owner just called and told me to turn on the news, I didn't wake you during the call, did I?" Tolina was the worst at concealing her feelings but she did everything she could to squash the delight swirling through her as she pretended concern.

Tolina moved to stand next to him to watch. He increased the volume, but the segment ended, and he huffed and turned it off. "They said his name was Sanfen Wertik, and he was wanted for rape and murder of two women off world, but he had just undergone facial reconstruction, so our security system didn't pick him out. The investigation reported no leads, and whoever did it took out the resort security drone. It sounds like someone hired a Vumenko Rallion for a hit, but that's not possible."

Tolina stared at him, and he seemed satisfied with his own conclusion, so she changed the subject. "Do we have plans? I want to go to the beach today. I've never been to one." She watched as he looked over at her and he seemed to be having trouble processing what she said.

He appeared pained. "You've never visited a beach?"

"No. I didn't have days off. I've seen a beach before, but I've never been near an ocean beach until yesterday." Tolina wished she had just kept her mouth shut as she watched pity grow in his expression. "I don't appreciate pity," she whispered under her breath.

He frowned at her. "I don't pity you. I was thinking you deserved better, and we can spend a few more days here at the beach if you want. We have some time before I need to confirm the lithium shipment on B'Otipe. It's an ugly dead world with salt and lithium mines from a dried ocean, and I don't like traveling there. I don't understand how their people managed to pollute so much they overheated and dried their home world, but they did, and they were lucky they had another water world in their system, or they would have gone extinct as a species. The people evolved from sharks, and while most of the people are kind and learned their lesson many generations ago, the worst of their people stayed behind on their old world to strip it."

"Why don't you find new sources?" Tolina asked, and she wished she hadn't, Kortul looked disgusted as he sat down on the couch behind him.

"I would, but my late father decided to sign the contracts with the company I inherited, and not with him specifically. Since contracts are with my company Saltic, and I own the company, I am stuck in bad contracts with shady businesspeople for the next forty years. I've already survived the first five, and if I can make it through next forty, I'll sell the company and retire since I'm not having children."

Tolina already regretted her next question. "Why are you not having children?"

Kortul paused and tried to push away the many memories of his father's abuse. It was always a cascade of feelings because his father didn't abuse him outright. He was covert and manipulated everyone in their life to abuse him instead of doing it directly. If he ever tried to defend himself, his father would take away something he loved, or worse. His heart cracked thinking about when he was six and his father threw away his collection of sea life fossils, which were gifts from Mabit. It was all because his father accused him of breaking an expensive statue. His father had broken it while drunk. The blame for everything fell on Kortul, and he would never have children because setting his eyes on a child who looked like him would be unbearable. He might as well be at least partially honest. It would come out eventually. "My father was controlling, selfish, and cruel to me as a child. I don't think I could do it."

Tolina felt her hate for him fading, and she wondered if she had been too harsh. She should have known a carefree ass like Kortul could be using humor to cover his pain. "Let's go to the beach." She was not accustomed to heavy personal discussions, and she didn't know him well enough to be asking further questions. That could wait until later.

He agreed quietly, and they dressed in swimsuits before he made towels at the replicator. "Corver, transport us to the beach." In a split second, they were both shading their faces with their hands in the bright light as their eyes adjusted.

Kortul spread the towels out while Tolina wiggled her feet in the sand. She sat down on the towel and ran her fingers through the sand, lifting it and allowing it to sift through her fingers. Kortul held his hand out. "Do you want to try the water? Do you know how to swim?"

She allowed him to help her up, and they walked to the edge of the water, but Kortul became still as he whispered, "Shit."

"What?" Tolina looked around but all she saw was a handsome Wendi man with a grey face approaching.

Kortul sighed as the man walked up, demanding, "Why haven't you answered any of my messages? Who is this?"

Distressed, Kortul took Tolina's hand. "This is my wife, Tolina. We married recently."

The man stared at Kortul and blinked a few times,

scoffed, and walked away. Kortul looked over at Tolina who was giving him a threatening side eye. "Who was that?"

Kortul took a long breath before he answered, "I had a prolific dating life before I met you."

Tolina dropped his hand like it had poop on it, and she remembered what Nire had told her the night before. "You're a sleazy asshole, and I can't believe I almost didn't hate you for a moment." *He is impossible. Now I fully understand why Tyce was so angry when I first woke up on this planet.* She stormed off in the sand, which was not giving her the satisfaction of storming away like normal solid ground, and she growled under her breath as she fought to make it to the water's edge. She ran into the warm water and began swimming away from the beach. She was almost as good at swimming as she was at flying because of her training. Her stomach curled remembering the cold pool she once practiced in. She could hold her breath for four minutes, so she decided to have a little fun with Kortul. He had fun at other people's expense, so it was only fair.

Tolina took a few long breaths before she held a deep breath and dove down into the mild salty water. She opened her eyes, and they stung a bit, but she could see well. The sea life was picturesque, and she swam down to the sea floor, scattering the fish. She didn't care. She was aiming to look at the interesting crabs. They came in a plethora of shapes and sizes, and she laughed to herself about this planet and how things like crabs, spiders, and frogs were dominant creatures here. *The crabs and spiders make sense, but the frogs are a whole other topic.* One of the crabs had massive pinchers, which gave her a fantastic idea. She looked behind her seeing Kortul swimming in her direction. *Perfect. I hope it pinches his nipple off.*

Tolina reached down and grabbed the shell of the crab to avoid being pinched herself, and when Kortul reached her, she thrust the huge wriggling crab at him. Kortul screamed and fought the crab as Tolina smiled and swam away. She peered back and watched as he pried a pincher from his arm and kicked at the crab before he broke away. She laughed the entire way back to the surface.

Swimming back to the beach, Tolina felt Kortul wrap his hand around her ankle. *Oh, shit.* She sucked in a breath as he yanked her under the water, and they spun around making her dizzy before he popped up with her. "That crab fucking pinched me!" Tolina lost her cool as she laughed and choked on saltwater all while Kortul stared at her with fury in his eyes.

"Good! You're an asshole for the way you've treated people. I'm glad I know the truth about you. Now I will know better than to fall for your bullshit. Let me go."

Kortul smiled at her, which was *not* what she wanted, before he whispered, "Deep breath."

Tolina watched him take in air and she did the same, wondering what he was planning. He took them under the surface and when he began swimming, they moved faster than she could have swum herself, and she wondered if he had webbed toes or if he was cheating with technology. He took her by a reef with long red tubule worms and a rainbow of colorful anemones swaying in the current before showing her a wide flat area with nothing on it except a few barnacle looking creatures attached to the sea floor.

Barnacles don't usually attach to the seafloor, do they? She looked up at Kortul and he gave her a devious smile before he stomped against the surface. *Oh, no. What the fuck did you just do? Fucking honey balls is the ground moving?* The vibrating ground grew into intense shaking under their feet and Tolina frowned at Kortul before tightly grabbing onto him. She was glad she did because they were shot up and away from the surface they had been standing on. They whirled through the water and when Kortul stopped their spinning, Tolina looked back and saw a colossal crab teetering toward a crevasse in the sea floor. It was the color of sand, but it was larger than an entire floor of the resort. She had never seen anything so incredible before.

Kortul was careful with her as he swam them up for air. When they broke the surface, Tolina was too delighted to be pissed off, and screeched, "That was the most fantastic thing I have ever seen!"

Chapter 11

Waves

Simple distractions didn't work on Tolina, so by the time they reached the beach, she was forming questions. They collected their towels from the dry sand and they were heading back to the room when Tolina asked, "Do you want to explain to me why you were Mr. Sex-guy before I arrived, and all of a sudden you not only want to be married, but to somebody who doesn't want you back, at all. What the fuck is wrong with you?"

Korţul just smiled at her and bit his lip before walking by her, ignoring her question. *I thought I hated him before, but now I hate him even more. He is such a smug, honey fucking assface!* "Are you ignoring my question?" Tolina had enough of his silence by the time they arrived at their room, and demanded, "If you're choosing to ignore me, you can take us back because I am finished with this."

Korţul grabbed her towel from her and tossed it away before he pulled her into his arms and hugged her to him as she squirmed. He looked down at her and answered, "It's simple. I care about you, and I want to be with you. I think you're perfect for me, and I didn't like them."

"Let me go! What the fuck does that mean? Why were you fucking people you don't even like? Wait. Don't answer that last question." Tolina wiggled from his grip and stood in front of him with her hands on her hips.

She's adorable when she's mad, and I want to fuck that little mad mouth until it's full of my cum. "It means I chose you over them. If you keep pressing this, I'll show you exactly how much more I care about you than them, but something tells me you're not ready for that."

Her nipples felt like they would burn off, and Tolina hated how much her body wanted Kortul. It betrayed her with every heated gaze he shot at her. Every touch was like lightning, and his words were like spinning fire spreading inside of her, but she wasn't falling for it. *It's just lust.* "I'm sure you said all of these things to them too."

Kortul couldn't help but laugh. He had never so much as told another person he *wanted them.* "Not once, ever."

Tolina could feel her face fall. *What does that mean? No one just flips a switch like that. There is no such thing as love at first sight. Maybe lust at first sight exists, and if that's what this is, that means this is not real. It's just chemistry.* "What happens when I give in to you? What happens when I give you what you want, and then you don't want me any longer? I've already been married to a man who didn't *want me like that.* I can't endure that again." Tolina was on the verge of tears, and she knew it would be so easy to use her wings and fly away, but what would that achieve?

She walked to the balcony and faced a chair toward the ocean before she sat down. Kortul started to come outside, but she snapped, "Leave me alone," and for once he listened. She loved her former husband, but he didn't love her back in the way she wanted or deserved. *At least with him I had a sweet and caring best friend.* Her heart ached for him. She hoped he was happy.

"A toe in his NOSE? Tolina, I know you're needing a quiet moment, but you need to hear this! The man who was murdered on the seventh floor had his own severed toe in his nose! Whoever this killer is, they are diabolical, and I must admit, I love it. I never thought I would be happy about a murder on my own island, but this one has turned out to be spectacular."

Tolina was not religious, but in that moment, she prayed. *Please help me wind spirits, I will kill this man if he doesn't shut up.* The memories of her victim screaming were a soothing music, and she sighed as she sat back in the chair. A few moments passed by before she could hear Kortul making some commotion in the kitchen. He came out and handed her a tall drink.

She glared at him, but drank it before handing it back empty, and he raised his brows before returning to the kitchen to refill her drink, or so she hoped. When he returned with another full fruity alcoholic drink, she drank half of it down then held the cup in her lap while she glared at the tropical ocean view.

"Tolina, look at me."

She briefly closed her eyes and sighed before she turned to face him. "What do you want?"

He quietly peered at her before he explained, "I've never been married. I haven't had any kind of relationship before because I never wanted one. When I say I want you to stay my wife, it's not a game. I didn't marry you to only save you. If I had, I would have made that clear. I don't give a fuck how it sounds. I married you because *I want you as my wife*."

As sincere as he seemed, she was far from stupid to believe a few pleasant words. "You will need to prove it by allowing me to date other people. If I decide *after* dating that I want to try things with you, we can try then. I will not make a decision about *us* until I have experienced dating, and I need to be sure I know who you are."

Kortul seemed discouraged, but agreed, and whispered, "Fine." He thought for a few moments and stood to go back inside. This was a new experience for him. He had never had anyone reject him. With his drink still full, he set it down and started to go for a walk, but when he went to change, he stopped in the doorway and turned back to the patio. He approached Tolina and insisted, "If you are dating other people, you can date me too. That's only fair."

"Fine," she breathed before she finished her drink quietly. He changed his mind and went back to grab his drink. He joined her on the balcony, and this time he remained quiet. They sat together in silence for an hour before Kortul quietly suggested, "Why don't we have dinner at the restaurant downstairs?"

She nodded in agreement. Tolina had been daydreaming about how she wedged her knife in that man's dick slit as she tried to pry it open. He thrashed and screamed in her mind, and she felt much better. It had been a delightful moment, and she realized if she wanted to be happy here, she would need to find another piece of scum to murder.

Something wonderful occurred to her. *I bet Kortul will introduce me to plenty of awful people. Oh! I can make a list!*

This may turn out well after all. I may be lacking at keeping a straight face, but I am damn good at killing and covering my tracks.

"Come on," Kortul suggested as he stood from his chair and reached his hand out to help Tolina up. She ignored his hand and went around the chair the opposite direction to avoid him. She went straight to their room to access the replicator to find herself something to wear for dinner.

When she had her outfit picked out, a comfortable white linen loose crop and shorts set with gold strappy sandals. She came out, and Kortul went in to dress. He came out wearing comfortable pants cut like slacks and no shirt. "What is your problem with shirts?" Tolina was beyond annoyed already. "We are eating dinner not sitting at the beach."

"It's hot, and when I put it on it stuck to me. So, I took it off. It's my island I can do whatever the hell I want." All four of his eyes were narrowed on her, and she wanted to thump the spikes along his hairline.

Tolina blinked at him a few times. "So, it is. Whatever. Let's go, I'm hungry for once."

Kortul asked, "Corver, transport us to the resort restaurant."

The restaurant was bustling, and Tolina was shocked at all the people. Many of the people were without shirts, and she rolled her eyes. "What is happening?"

Kortul smirked at her as he guided her around the crowd to a private table on the patio. "It's a business convention. The resort is booked with conventions for the next two weeks, and they won't have another slow week like you saw for a year. There is only maybe two weeks a year when the resort is slow, and it's only because of room maintenance and over half the occupancy can't be filled. It's the only time

I visit for more than a day." Tolina was never one to be star struck, but the profits this man must bring in from leasing this island alone seemed unreal. "What's wrong? Are there too many people for you? We can go to the beach and have dinner there if you would like."

"No. It's not that. I am just wondering why an absurdly rich man like you wants anything to do with me. I know my personal worth, and this is not about that. You could have anyone. Why are you so stuck on me when you don't even know me?" Tolina wasn't all that surprised when he just smirked and began plugging in their order on the table holo-screen.

"Everyone on my planet is absurdly rich, Tolina. I am simply one man who generates a substantial portion of it." *Where did this woman come from that she doesn't understand how a people's economy works?* "I have a fancy shower at home, and I have a ship with transport tech, but those are things available to anyone if they wanted to book a flight or have a fancy shower. I may be the owner of several successful businesses generating high profits, but I am heavily taxed and rightfully so. Our economy has remained strong for thousands of years, and during that time, we've prospered with technology and medical advancements. We achieved all of this by understanding the value of each person in our society and spreading wealth where it belongs the most."

Tolina just blinked at him. Her own society intended to be similar, but a vastly different factor playing out for the Vo-Pess. The people at the top of Tolina's former society hoarded all the wealth and didn't redistribute it. They called it a people's government, but it was a lie. *You can call a ruling entity whatever you want, but if you look around and your people are miserable and suffering, you've become a hypocrite.*

"Everything about my former society was centered around harsh control of the population. Everyone worked until they died, no self expression, no chance to advance, and if you became disabled or couldn't work anymore, you were cast off and given the bare minimum to survive. I killed the scum the government wanted gone. If you were a person of honor, you were drowned in the lake by the city. If you stepped from the line far enough beyond murder, like betraying the Vo-Pess secrets or defecting, they would hook you up to a neural cycle, which was a neural linking program. It sought out your worst nightmares and fed them back to you as torture. My former life was different from everything here. Leisure was unheard of." Tolina sat back in her chair as a man came by and set covered plates in front of them before placing filled water glasses by the plates.

Kortul wasn't sure how to respond as he pulled the cover from his dinner, which was a steaming fresh fish caught earlier in the day. "I'm sorry you had to live that way. Oh. I just thought about something important. How old are you?" Kortul realized he hadn't even asked her yet.

"I'm thirty-five." Tolina saw Kortul shift in his seat as he gave her a sly grin.

"You're older than me." Kortul took a bite from his fish as he watched Tolina remove the cover from her plate. "I'm twenty-five."

Big fucking surprise. Tolina couldn't help a deep sigh as she lifted the bowl of nectar and was delighted by the floral scents and flavors. She lost herself in the sweet liquid until she finished it and set it down.

When she looked up, a handsome man was approaching,

and he was staring in her direction. Her heart jumped around in her chest, and she tried to move herself away from Kortul without being obvious.

Next to her, Kortul noticed and grabbed the arm of her chair to prevent her from moving any further, causing her to shoot him a glare promising profound pain.

Chapter 12

Dating

A stunning man with a light green face approached them. His black curly hair sparkled under the lights. He wore a black suit with an unbuttoned white shirt underneath showing his black neck and light brown chest. He had six eyes, and they were all focused on her, or so it appeared. He was confident and walked with confident purpose causing Tolina to swoon over him long before he arrived at the table.

"Kortul, please introduce me to your guest," he purred as he reached down for Tolina's hand.

Kortul scowled and stood up, towering over Tolina in her chair. "This is Tolina, my wife."

"It's a technicality. I am not remaining his wife. I am single, *and dating*." Tolina was as discreet as possible as she stomped on Kortul's foot, and he grunted under his breath before sitting down in a rush. As Kortul reached down to grab his foot, Tolina stood up and she gave the man her hand.

The handsome man had a seductive aura and Tolina

sensed it fully when he kissed the back of her hand. "I am Lanute Graphel, and if you are as single as you say, I would love to invite you for a stroll through the gardens tomorrow. Have you seen the flying fish up close when they come in for their mid-day rest among the willow trees?"

Kortul leaned in and blew air on the bare sliver of her back under her crop, and she waved her hand at his face to stop. "I would love to, that seems wonderful." Behind her, Kortul grabbed her wrist and brought her hand to his lips and sucked on her fingers. Tolina gasped and she yanked her hand back to wipe it off on her napkin. *I will fucking kill him.*

Lanute grinned at her with a hint of a smirk. "I'll meet you here at the restaurant right at midday tomorrow?"

"That sounds perfect." Tolina bit her lip as he walked away.

As soon as Lanute disappeared, Kortul spun her around. "You crushed my toe. It's still throbbing."

"You'll survive." Tolina looked down at his foot and noticed he had webbed toes. "Do all your people have webbed toes?"

"We all have webbed toes and many of us have webbed fingers." He took a bite of his food as Tolina became lost in thought.

She scrunched her nose. "I know so little about your people and this planet. I haven't even asked you what city we live in."

Kortul swallowed his bite and answered, "I think Brock explained part of this, but we are called the Wendi. Brock's people are called the Eckolie, and the planet is called Corbatton. We live in Corbatton Capital City."

"What is this crystal island called?"

"Saltic Island," Kortul answered as he took another bite.

Tolina closed her eyes and tried not to be annoyed. *This fucking island has the same name as him.* "How does it look written?"

Kortul pointed to the napkins which had the island name on them, 'Saltic Island.' Tolina's mouth dropped open. She had seen the word 'Saltic' advertised everywhere since she had been here. "What do you own exactly?"

Kortul grimaced. "You mean what did I inherit from my greedy, cruel father? That's a long story, but to answer you, I own a nano-chip manufacturing company, and we make almost all the programable nano-tech micro-chips on the market. It's been in the family for generations. Long ago my people became sick of the dirty business practices with other planets, and soon we had a movement to make ourselves the most successful planet, and my ancient people ensured the money would always be shared instead of hoarded. The plan worked so well it eventually brought peace to our galaxy and incredible advancements to Corbatton. Sometime during the movement, one of my Saltic ancestors built a tech company, and it has grown and evolved ever since. When my father was alive, he worked every illegal loophole, and he was lucky he was never caught. He did increase company profits higher than ever, but correcting things means I've had to reallocate it back to the places it was squeezed from. It's been over two years of slowed growth, but I've reversed most of his exploitive damage. It was worth it to have things back how they were when my grandfather was alive. Some things cannot be undone though. The CGTA laws have worked well to keep people like my father from gaining too much control, but my father still found a way to fuck *me* over."

The undone things he referred to meant the bad

contracts he mentioned before. Tolina had been itching to ask, but didn't want to pry about what happened to his father if it would be painful, but he appeared not to miss him. "Do you mind if I ask what happened to him?"

Kortul finished his meal and set the cover back on top before he leaned back and looked at her. "I don't know. Mabit came back from one of my father's business meetings with his dead body, and Mabit said my father had been poisoned." He paused and chose his next words with care. "A few days before, I had come home early from a visit here when he was away. When he came home, he didn't know I was there. He was drunk and dropped his tablet next to him when he fell asleep on the couch. He woke up and believed I was reading about his illegal deal, but I was just trying to adjust the volume on the music blaring from the device. He grabbed it from me, and he beat me until I was half dead. He made me swear not to repeat anything I read. It was the first time he had ever been violent to that degree toward me, and Mabit caught him before he killed me. I have never seen fury like that. Mabit's anger made my father seem tame in comparison to how furious he was. They went to my father's meeting the next day, and that was the last time I saw my father alive. It was five years ago."

Tolina had a whole new respect for Mabit, but she felt bad for Kortul. Maybe his father's abuse was the root of many of the problems he's had. She thought about her own abuse during her training. Being abused and tortured by instructors and fellow students to learn how to be an assassin wasn't something she wanted to talk about, but she knew Kortul wasn't cheering up so easily this time. "I wasn't abused in any way as a child, but when it was time to attend the military academy, I was warned by my former husband about what I would go through, and I didn't believe him. The actual training was so much worse than he said. I have seen my own internal organs from an accident during practice with live weapons. They repaired my cut open abdomen on the mat."

Kortul was horrified and pulled her into his lap and squeezed her to him. She could hear his heart racing. "Fuck. Tolina, what the fuck. You said that so casually, like it was a common occurrence." He kept his grip on her tight and she squirmed trying to free herself.

"I am fine. That was years ago, and that sort of thing *was* a common occurrence." He wouldn't budge. She had been able to slip from his hold before, but not now. "Kortul, let me go."

"Who the fuck *exactly* did all of this to you?" Kortul sounded lethal, and she stopped moving as he rested his head on top of hers, waiting for her to respond.

Tolina sighed and looked away as she answered, "My former instructors and fellow classmates. It was part of my training as a Short Wing. Some of the people who hurt me are dead now, but most of them are back on my home planet. It wasn't their fault."

"Tolina, look at me. Please tell me you had some kind of pain relief while these barbaric injuries were repaired."

Meeting his eyes, Tolina couldn't help but twist her lips to the side and burst into laughter. "What? Never. The only time I was given any pain relief was after my leg surgery, but I was out of the academy and at the main military hospital in the capital."

"I need to be honest. I am having a tough time accepting this." Kortul felt like his heart would rip from his chest and slap him in the face if he didn't expel some of the negative energy brewing inside of him.

"I can tell. You've been crushing me since you pulled me in your lap." Tolina admitted as she tried to take in a full breath but couldn't.

Kortul shot up from his chair and set her down. "I am so sorry."

Tolina stared at Kortul and blinked while consumed with confusion as she tried to understand the roller coaster of emotions from their day. *One minute I fucking hate him, and the next minute he is wonderful. Right now, he looks like his head will explode any second, so we need to take a walk before that happens.*

She swore to herself not to tell him about the time she was shot in the side and her mission partner had to dig out the bullet. Tolina held back a gag remembering her teammate's fingers digging into her side to push her organs out of the way to reach the bullet. "We should take a walk on the beach."

Kortul nodded and linked her arm before bolting off toward the waves. They were drudging through the thick dry sand before they reached the packed wet sand. She was being half dragged along until he stopped and knelt to grab a star fish stuck in the dry sand. Lifting it up to see better under the stars, he flipped it over and brought it closer to his eyes and whispered, "I think it's still alive."

He rolled his pants up and waded up to his knees before gently tossing it out in the deeper water. He met Tolina back on the shore, but he didn't seem any more settled than he was when they left the restaurant. "Why are you so upset?"

He stared at her with a heated intensity. "I told you I want you. I care about you. What do you think that meant?

Do you really think I would be fine with hearing about how you were brutally tortured? I want to find everyone who hurt you and murder them all."

She was quiet, but direct as she explained, "You don't understand the type of life I lived before. This went on for twenty years, so I'm calloused to it. I came from a harsh society where everything was aimed to protect the Vo-Pess and procreation. Only the Vo-Pess people mattered. Nothing else. Personal pain was my sacrifice to my people just as taxes are yours."

Kortul shook his head at her. "That is not even in the same realm of reasoning. Where are your scars? Did they mend your skin with medical tech to erase your scars?" He narrowed his eyes and bent down to face her. "Do not lie to me."

She was not answering. He knew they repaired her and used a dermal bonder with a glue and amino acids to prevent her scars from showing, but under a bright light they could be seen. *I hope he doesn't know that.* Kortul stared at her waiting for an answer, but when it didn't come. He swooped her into his arms. "Corver, emergency transport to our room."

In a fraction of a second, they were standing in the living area of their room, and he stalked toward the bed to set her down. "Kortul, I know what you're doing. You don't want to do that."

He leaned over her face and pointed at her nose. "Do. Not. Move."

Tolina froze. He had not spoken to her that way before. It was demanding and powerful. She didn't move as he returned with an ultra-luminous flashlight from the replicator. *Honey fuck, he's about to be very upset.* The specific glue residue from the scar regeneration serum would light up. It was a similar tech developed on many worlds, and she was quickly realizing, in other galaxies too. "Kortul, stop."

Ignoring her, Kortul turned on the light and lifted her shirt to underneath her breasts. "Tolina, how am I supposed to accept this." She looked down and saw her exposed flesh and all the healed lacerations running over it. She sighed and sat up to stand. *Fuck it. Maybe he'll drop this if I willfully show him the rest.*

In front of Kortul, she stripped her clothes off, and he dropped the light after shining it onto her. She was riddled with scars. He stood in front of her too stunned to speak as she dressed.

"Do you want a drink?" Kortul offered, his voice soft and kind.

Tolina nodded, "That would be great."

He brought a bottle into the bedroom and poured them each a glass before he sat on the bed, and she sat beside him. They drank in silence and when they were finished, Kortul took their glasses to the kitchen. When he returned, he crawled onto the bed and grabbed her as he lay down and pulled the plush white covers over both of them.

"Kortul, this doesn't change anything." Tolina was not giving in as she felt him pull her close. He wrapped around her with one arm crossed the center of her chest and his other arm was around her middle.

Kortul tightened his arms around her and whispered into her hair, "I don't care. I'm holding you tonight."

Chapter 13

Lanute Graphel

The next day, Kortul stood on the balcony as she dressed in the bedroom for her date. He could hear Tolina approach the open glass door, and he tensed knowing what was coming next. "I'm leaving now."

He remained in place as he replied, "Be careful. Just ask Corver to transport you downstairs. I don't want you taking the common lift down the hall since the murderer might still be in the resort."

She stared at the back of his head before she went to stand in the living room. "Corver, transport me to the restaurant."

She disappeared, and Kortul checked behind him to make sure she was gone before he clenched his fists. "Corver, emergency transport me the chameleon armor owned by Kortul Voutin Saltic the Fourth."

A tone sounded above which meant Corver was unable to complete the action.

Kortul squeezed his eyes shut. *That's fine. I'll call Mabit. He has the fucking suit, and there is a murderer in the build-*

ing. I know I can talk him into it. I'm not just asking for it to stalk Tolina.

"Corver, open an emergency line to Mabit."

Seconds later he heard Mabit clear his throat, "Kortul? Do you need help? Has something happened?"

Kortul squeezed his eyes shut. "I have a problem. There was a murder on the seventh floor, and haven't caught the murderer. Lanute, a man I know from the city asked Tolina on a date today and I need father's chameleon armor so I can follow her to make sure she is safe."

There was a long pause before Mabit laughed, "Kortul, are you drinking? She is one of the most talented people I've ever sparred with. She is fine."

Kortul thought he might be sick. "Mabit, I don't think you understand. I need to follow her."

"Tyce already explained to me how worried he is about Tolina even being around you. I don't like this."

"Tyce is always worried about everything. Mabit, listen to me, do I sound like I am joking? I could love her. I think I already do." Kortul couldn't take a breath as he felt terror wrapping around his throat and cutting off his air.

Mabit sighed and Kortul heard him shuffling something. He hoped he was retrieving his father's chameleon armor. "Kortul, do not become your father. If you harm her, I will intervene."

"I just want to make sure she's safe. I would never hurt her."

Kortul could hear Mabit open his safe before ending the call. Seconds later, his father's old chameleon armor appeared folded on the couch cushion behind him.

"Thank fuck." Kortul slipped the armor on as quickly as he could, and for once, he was thankful his father was the same size as him. He could still smell his father in the material, and he closed his eyes as he blocked out the memories. Kortul had no time to deal with his trauma right now. He had a wife to watch over. He tapped on the arm to activate the suit and when his body went invisible, he sighed with relief.

"Corver, transport me to the restaurant."

He looked around the restaurant for Tolina and spotted her sitting at the bar just as Lanute came in. *Thank fuck. I arrived just in time. Why does she not have a drink? Does she not know how to order to our room? Fuck. I need to pay attention and explain things better.*

Lanute came up and greeted her, kissing her on her hand and helped her rise from her seat. *Take your fucking hands away from her.* Kortul clenched his fists. He hated he had agreed to allow her to date other people, but he had to know if she cared about him in return before he made any kind of move on her, and he knew not to test her that way, not yet. She would gut him like a fish. *Mabit would too, and so would Tyce. Fuck, I cannot let these dates go well.*

He followed them from the restaurant's side door and into the gardens. Kortul watched as Lanute creepily slid his arm around her and pointed to something he saw. *I will break your slimy arm, and I will kill you.*

Lanute moved his hand lower around her waist, and Kortul had to hold himself back from tackling him. He took several deep breaths before he passed by one of the few invasive mammals still on the planet, a small monkey. *Perfect.*

Kortul picked up a pebble and moved forward until he was close enough to ensure he would not accidentally hit Tolina. He watched, and the next time Lanute slid his arm around her, Kortul threw the rock, and it hit him in the back of his head. Behind Kortul, the small primate chewed on a bug.

Lanute whirled around and pointed to the monkey as he rubbed his head. "I think that little monkey hit me with a rock."

Tolina looked over at it and cocked her head to the side before Kortul watched her flip on her skills and scan the gardens. Kortul smiled when she looked right at him but couldn't see him. She stared at the place he stood for far too long. *Oh fuck. She talked about empath training. I need to back away. She might really murder me if she finds me here.* Kortul pranced away on his tip toes to avoid making a sound.

When he decided he was far enough back, he looked back as Tolina frowned and leaned closer to Lanute. She extended her antennae. "I thought I sensed something, but I guess I was wrong. I'm sure it was just the monkey. If it happens again, we should go back to the restaurant."

Fuck, fuck, fuck. She almost caught me. His heart was raging, and he moved to follow when they began walking again. *How can I follow them without her noticing me? Think.*

Lanute placed his hand on her back, and Kortul lost his cool. He sprinted through the soft ground cover to catch up, and when he did, he grabbed another rock from the ground. He aimed and threw it at Lanute's head, hitting him in the temple before Kortul moved behind a tree. This time Tolina was livid as she studied the area. *I need to ask about her empathic abilities. I could have ruined everything.*

He could hear Lanute, "It's not bad, but I think walking back to the restaurant is a superb idea. Maybe we can see the flying fish another time."

Who the fuck says superb? Lanute is too soft. They

wouldn't last a week even if I allowed it to happen, but I won't. Kortul followed them into the busy restaurant, and he was glad to see they picked a central booth surrounded by tropical foliage. He could watch her from around the plants and she couldn't detect him with so many people around. He hoped that was true and she couldn't differentiate individuals.

An overripe pear lay on the ground next to his foot, and he bet the gardeners must have missed it when cleaning the beds. *Perfect.* Kortul lifted the red pear, and it looked odd in his invisible hand. The pear melted between his fingers, and he smiled with anticipation.

When he checked on Tolina again, Lanute was leaning in to kiss her. Kortul's vision blurred as he jumped vertically from his position and nailed Lanute's back with the sloppy pear. The fruit made a slap as Kortul landed on his feet. Kortul peered around the foliage to watch Lanute rip off his nice shirt and slam it onto the table. Tolina was stunned and stood as she appeared to look around for an exit.

While Lanute fumed with anger and tried to clean his shirt, Tolina walked toward the beach. Lanute saw her leaving and shook his head before slamming his fist on the table.

"Corver, transport me to my room." Kortul fell over onto the floor holding in a laugh when he arrived in his room before he stripped off the chameleon armor. "Corver, transport the chameleon armor to my safe at home." The armor disappeared, and he slipped on some jogging shorts and comfortable shoes. "Corver, transport me in front of the crystal tours."

He stood in the entry of the crystal tour at the end of the beach and could see Tolina's form as she walked toward the water. Kortul ran toward the wet sand and kept a steady jogging pace as he approached Tolina.

When she saw him, she seemed to relax, and he couldn't help a devious grin. As soon as he was near enough for her to hear him without shouting, he asked, "How did it go?" It took every ounce of his willpower not to grin at her snarl. "That bad?"

Tolina wasn't discussing it. "Can we just walk?" Her words were quiet, quieter than she intended, and Kortul nodded.

They walked along the beach until Tolina's feet were caked in sand. Tolina stared off into the distance, watching a small rainstorm roll in. "I'm afraid I won't find what I'm looking for, and I made a mistake leaving my home."

"You didn't make a mistake," Kortul assured her, but she frowned as she eyed him.

Tolina couldn't believe what was about to spill from her mouth. "I think I even miss my old job."

She sat down on the sand, and Kortul sat next to her. "Being an assassin? You mean you miss killing people?"

She could tell Kortul was a little disturbed at her admission. Tolina drew her name in the wet sand as she answered, "I killed over three hundred targets. All of them were considered threats to the Vo-Pess, but they were also the lowliest people. It makes me sick to think the man who destroyed my leg wasn't really my target because he killed his wife. He was my target because his wife was an important person, and her murder was considered a threat against the Vo-Pess. Most of the time I was sent to eliminate any non-Vo-Pess targets who were close to finding out about my people. They were always involved in the worst kind of crimes, and I did enjoy taking them out. I don't think there was anything wrong with the work I did knowing the harm my targets were causing. I even miss the documenting."

Kortul didn't have anything profound to say to make her feel better, but he did agree with her. "I couldn't do work like that, but I don't think you're wrong for it." Tolina looked over at him and smiled softly. It wasn't a joyful smile, but one to say thank you for acknowledging her moment of vulnerability. The system stars were setting behind them, and Kortul stood and reached his hand out for her. When she took it, he lifted her to her feet. "Do you want to return to the room? We can sit on the balcony and have a drink while we look at the stars."

Tolina nodded as she brushed the sand from her bottom. "That sounds great."

"Corver, transport us to our room and transport a hot tub to the balcony with two bottles of O'Poinets on ice."

They arrived in the living area and a large clear tub with jets swirling the steaming hot water was on the balcony with a table next to it and two bottles of champagne with glasses hanging on the side. Without a word, Tolina pulled her clothes off as she walked toward the hot tub. Once nude, she grabbed a bottle of champagne and popped the top before drinking a fourth of the bottle.

Kortul hadn't moved as he watched her climb in and stare at the beautiful constellations of stars. She looked back at him and frowned, "What the fuck are you just standing there for?" Shaking his head, Kortul climbed in with her and handed her a glass before taking the bottle from her and filling her glass and doing the same with his glass. He set the champagne back in the ice and leaned back, looking at Tolina as she watched the sky. Her light fuchsia complexion was glowing in the warm light, and Kortul had never seen anyone more captivating. She was perfect, and he would throw away everything else in his life to have her, including what little morals he had. This woman was his and his alone.

Kortul smashed his hand against his slit and held himself together as she leaned back with her eyes closed and he could see the edge of her nipples peeking above the water. He licked his lips thinking about sucking on her breasts and burying his face in her pussy. His slit burst open, and his angry cock was hard as a rock. He grabbed the champagne and drank the rest of the bottle before he smashed his cock back inside of him. *Not yet.*

Chapter 14

Coconut

Long before Kortul woke, Tolina stood on the balcony admiring the bright starlight from the double system stars as they peeked over the horizon. The orange and yellow blended with the periwinkle sky, and her heart felt full as the warm light soaked into her skin. This planet's beauty was mesmerizing, and she understood why the people here were so protective of it. She didn't blame them at all. This place was a magical intersection with nature.

Kortul shifted in his sleep, and she couldn't help remembering his wanting eyes on her. The memory gave her chills in the best way. She heated inside and was tempted to release her wings and jump from the balcony to fly away as she heard his feet against the floor. He came up behind her, so close she could feel the heat of his skin on her back as he stretched.

Tolina tried to speak, but it came out quiet. Too quiet. "The two system stars here make for some entrancing morning light. I could have watched for hours."

Tolina froze as she felt Kortul place his hand against her wings which were folded against her back. With a gentle touch, he stroked his fingers along the swirls of her black wings, tracing the edges where her veins were. Her mind glitched as she felt fireworks of pleasure from his touch, and she almost forgot she hated him. It took all her strength to step forward, and the loss of his fluttering heat was a chill that curled her stomach. She turned around, and he was giving her a look that made her want to melt.

"I should remind you wings are sensitive, and touching them is an intimate act, but I think you know that don't you." Kortul smirked at her, and she hated how gorgeous this man was. He stole her breath, but his motives surrounding her freedom were still unclear, and as much as her body wanted to submit to him, she was far too stubborn to give in. She had killed too many abusive men to not see the warning signs in Kortul. The deadliest flowers are always the most beautiful to look at. "I don't trust you enough for that," Tolina admitted and she was not surprised when Kortul grinned at her.

He gave her a playful smile as he replied, "And you shouldn't. You should not trust anyone here not to pull a trick or go to extremes for what they want. Wendi, as a people, have one strong downfall, and that is we are bored. That means some of us tend to gravitate toward intense activities, and sometimes it leads to toxic behaviors. I have made my intentions with you clear. It's you who hasn't made your choice. Perfection is a fallacy, and searching for it in your life is naïve. I know you had some imagined plan for your future after you left your home, but that's over. You landed on *my* patio, on *my* building, and on *my* protected planet. You were and are the most stunning being I have ever seen, and protecting *you* is all I can think about. It's all I have thought about since I found you. I regret nothing. I would do it a million times over, and I don't give a fuck if you don't trust me." He paused and couldn't help a chuckle before he continued, "I don't believe you. You slept for hours in my arms. I know because I was awake, and I watched you." *If I didn't have to answer to Mabit I would have forced you to submit to me before I ever untied you. I would have made you beg for my cock in the first five minutes you woke up. The harder you run from me, the harder I will chase you. You are mine. You just haven't accepted it yet.*

Filled with hatred from feeling trapped and desire from the hunger in his eyes Tolina peeled her wings from her back and spread them before flying into the sky. She needed some air and space before she combusted and did something she would regret. *I can't fall for this game he's playing, and I can't fall for him. I don't care how my body craves him. I am not giving in. I know why he married me, but he has been possessive and I can feel his resistance to me dating. He's also been a playboy up until now, and these are screaming warning signs. He is just a good looking man, and there are lots of good looking men who live here. I just need to find a service or locate a place to meet single people. Maybe I'll date a woman instead. I really could care less what gender the person is as long as we make each other happy. Kortul does not make me happy. All he does is turn me on and piss me off.*

She looked back at the resort balcony to see Kortul watching her fly. A shiver rushed through her, and she flapped her wings quicker to keep herself in the air. *Dammit, that honey fucking man will be the death of me. He has me about to fall from the sky.*

She darted away and flew toward the top of the crystal

where the massive stone was cut and reflected the light. When she reached a high point overlooking the sea behind her, she balanced on one of the edges and warmed her wings in the bright morning light. She looked behind her and a giant shadow of her wings cast onto the sea below. She flapped leisurely, watching how the enormous shadow moved on the glittering water.

She adored her wings, and she knew she was a prize of a woman. Anyone would be lucky to have her. Kortul would need to find his place in line because she was not settling for anyone less than she deserved.

The intense starlight was too bright to look in that direction, and the rays were becoming hot, so she flew back to the balcony, where Kortul was still waiting for her. *Of course he's waiting for me. He's always waiting for me.*

She landed in front of him, and her wings curled and lay against her back in swirls. His heated gaze hadn't changed. "Is there anything you want to do before we return home this evening? You have a week of practice with Mabit before we have our meeting, and I need to visit the capital court building to register you as my personal protection tomorrow morning. It's not required, but it is encouraged for anyone who is in a residency waiting period to work for a Wendi business or individual. Once you have a registered job, along with the resort footage of the last few days, we shouldn't need to worry about the planetary authority questioning us. If they do, we should have the proof they want."

She wasn't sure what she wanted to do so she admitted, "I've never been to a resort before this, or a vacation. I have no idea what there is to do here."

Kortul thought about a place he hadn't visited in a long time and suggested, "When I was a child, I found a cave on one of the cliffs over the ocean, and I haven't been there since before my father died. It's a long cave that stretches through one of the larger crystals, and smaller crystal formations grew inside of it. The formations cause a symphony when the wind blows. I can show you if you're interested." Kortul imagined fucking her against the clear crystal wall while she moaned, and the wind whistled around them. His heart stammered as he willed his cock to stay in its slit.

She brightened a bit, and they went to the replicator for hiking clothes. Kortul stopped her when she was ordering her shirt and selected the winged option instead, something she had not noticed. "Remember, we have a planet in our galaxy where the people evolved from moths. They are called the Vitolas, and they have wings similar to yours. Clothing designers often have options for people with wings. He pointed to the screen and made the image larger. "See the slits here in the back? They're made with magnetic thread, so they slide open and closed along with your wings unfurling." Recalling his desire to know more about her empathic ability, he asked, "Are you long range empathic like them?"

Trying to place the feeling she had was distracting her until she realized it was comfort. Hearing there was another planet of empathic people who evolved from an insect like a butterfly, and that Kortul knew so much about her kind, gave her such familiarity it almost brought tears to her eyes. Something moved inside her, and it felt as if a spinning gear clicked into place. Her heart raced as she lifted her antennae. *Could my empath ability be developing? Why now? Is it the rest? Oh, fuck. I can feel so much.*

Her nerves lit up, and she felt more sensitive than she had ever been before. "I need to sit down." Tolina felt like her body was goo as Kortul eased her into a chair by the bed.

Kortul seemed more curious than worried. "Are you feeling alright?"

Tolina stared at the floor between his feet and cleared her mind before she used her antennae, and she reached for Kortul's emotions. She raised her antennae just above her hair when a wave of fierce desire, deep loving care, infinite curiosity, and intense possessiveness hit her like a storm wind. She slammed back into the chair and curled her antennae against her head before she whispered to herself, "I was so wrong." *This man is obsessed with me. How could he love me so quickly? Now that I know Kortul is being honest about his feelings, I guess I just need to figure out my own.*

She paused trying to sort out how he felt about her and Tolina was lost on a response. How could she tell him she just had a glimpse of his feelings for her? No. Not a chance.

Kortul stared at her with worried confusion on his face. "What is happening? Do I need to call a Vitolas physician? We can go right now. I can have us there in less than five minutes."

His urgency made her heart explode with tingly emotions she wasn't used to, and she slapped her hands to her face to hide her giddy smile. *Fuck me! No wonder I kept feeling so exposed at random times. It was waves of emotion because my empathic ability has been developing! FUCK! This just became a million times harder.* Having sensed his emotions convoluted things in her mind. His feelings were a sip of the most delectable nectar in the galaxy, and she wanted to jump on him to stick her antennae against his face to suck it all down. *I need to stop before I do something stupid. I have been trapped my entire life. I cannot fall for the first man who wants me!* She took a breath and assured Kortul she was not in need of medical intervention. "I am physically fine. I think I just had my first empathic experience. I trained for years at the Vo-Pess Military Academy trying to harness the ability. One fucking vacation, a few moments of fun, and the ability comes rushing in so strong that it's like I've always had it. The way my former leaders squeezed the life from us, it's no wonder none of us could use our empathic skills. It was the pressure and harsh life killing our gifts, not the bloodlines." Kortul remained silent as he listened, so she continued, "Thank you for giving me the chance to find this gift. It brought me closure I never thought I would have."

Kortul gave her a genuine smile and even with her antennae curled and hiding in her hair, she could feel some of his joy. *I am so glad I won't need to share a bed with him tonight. I'm afraid one touch, and I'll want him to crack me like a coconut.*

Chapter 15

Crystal Cave

Tolina was relieved when Kortul stood and held his hand out for her. She didn't want to discuss what happened. She had never had emotion threaten to overrule her mind. She was trained to resist it, and she used every ounce of her training to shove away her desires. She took his hand, but this time instead of standing not using his help and not fully touching his hand when she rose from the chair, she allowed him to help her.

He narrowed his eyes at her, noticing the change, and stared at her while they walked over to their climbing clothes he had set on the bed. Kortul seemed confused, and she wanted it to stay that way.

Tolina noticed there were no hiking boots as she stripped down and started with the cargo pants. "Where are our shoes?"

"Oh, right, you're not Wendi. You need actual boots." Kortul went to make her some at the replicator and came out with shoes that look more like socks within individual toes.

"What is that?" She grimaced as she held up the strange shoes.

Kortul laughed as he explained, "They give you the same grip as my feet. I have gloves like my hands for you too."

He handed the gloves over, and she set them next to her before she slid on the odd shoes, marveling at how they molded to her feet once she had them on. When the gloves were on, they did the same thing, molding to her skin. She wondered if it would work on any surface. The possibilities motivated her, and she ran for the wall and climbed it like it was second nature. Tolina looked back at Kortul once she reached the ceiling and laughed as she looked at him upside-down. "This is so much fun!"

Kortul hooked his finger at her, "Let's climb the cliff-side." Tolina flipped away from the ceiling and landed on her feet by him. "Corver, transport us to location twenty-five."

The blast of salty air and the warm breeze against her skin was divine, and she was in awe at how she could be transported into paradise. The clear water had hundreds of fish swimming in schools, sharks, octopus, and giant crabs covered the sloping sea floor. *They do have sharks here!*

Tolina stared up the cliffside. Kortul was already preparing to climb, and he looked over at her, "Are you ready?"

She was more ready than she thought possible. Doing something thrilling for the fun of it was new, and she wasn't sure how to react. The pure joy was overwhelming, and she rushed to climb alongside Kortul.

The clear crystal wall taunted her with the challenge of scaling it. Delight rushed her senses as she climbed with the warm breeze and crashing waves behind her. She stayed even with Kortul, and her muscles burned from intense exercise she had been missing. When they reached the crystal cave, she gasped at its beauty. The space looked like the cliffside had a mouth, and the crystal was its teeth. Tolina was enamored with the sounds of the wind as it whirled around the pink and orange crystals. The whistle created a song as she closed her eyes, and she inhaled the sweet smells of the flowers from the fruit trees around the island mixed with the salt of the sea.

She could feel the heat of Kortul's skin brush her ear, as he whispered, "This place has brought me peace for many years."

"I can see why." Tolina opened her eyes, and the view made everything all that much more spectacular. The caerulean of the ocean appeared endless, and she took it in with a satisfied sigh.

Kortul squeezed his eyes shut with the sound she made and stood back, giving himself space before he stuck her to the wall, ripped her clothes off, and buried his cock in her. *This woman is a test, and she better be the right answer, or I might not survive this.*

A pit formed in his stomach knowing he agreed to allow her to date. That thought became worse by the moment, and even his chameleon armor didn't set his raging heart at ease. He rubbed his chest and willed himself to calm down before he leapt from the cave and dove into the waves below. *That might not be a bad idea.*

Tolina felt desire hit her, and she whirled to find Kortul distressed. His blue blood trickled down from the top of the pink crystal he was grasping far too tightly. "Kortul?"

His wild gaze met hers. "Want to swim back to the resort through a cave?"

She knew she formed the word 'yes,' but all she could

hear was her own scream as Kortul grabbed her as he jumped from the mouth of the cave, and they slammed into the water below. In the water, he grabbed her and guided her arms around his shoulders and her legs around his waist. They broke the surface and both took a few deep breaths before he took them under and swam toward a cave opening. Tolina noticed several caves and couldn't wait to come back and explore them. Her clothes tightened against her skin, and she was astonished at the thoughtful technology of these recreational clothing. The clothes felt like a thin wetsuit. *I am dying to find out what kind of spy tech this galaxy has.*

Kortul swam her through the darkness where she could see a few bioluminescent crabs and anemone before a glowing octopus the size of an escape pod went shooting by them. After swimming over some vivid yellow coral, they broke the surface of an open chamber in the long cave system.

After quietly admiring the space, they took a few slow, deep breaths before Kortul took them under again. This time he swam much faster through the turbulent water. He tapped her arms, and she held on tight as he forced them into the current. In seconds they were being shot from a waterfall coming from the side of the crystal, just above the water on the resort side of the island.

Tolina screamed with delight and hugged Kortul, "Thank you. That was incredible!" He swam them back to the beach and helped her stand once they reached the shallow water. She turned and flopped into the wet sand and panted, catching her breath.

This vacation was the cleanest, most thrilling excitement she had in many years, and although she wasn't budging about dating other people, she considered this one hell of a date. She knew it would be hard for anyone to beat the effort Kortul had given her, but she knew Trel would be disappointed in her if she didn't follow through and extend her wings. It was what they both always wanted for *her*.

She spread her arms and legs against the sand as Kortul tossed sand dollars someone had dug up back into the water. When she was finished making a sand butterfly, she stood up and admired her work. Kortul laughed, "Are you planning on washing all that sand off before we go back to the room and change to go home?"

Tolina looked over her shoulder at her sandy backside and ran for the ocean before flopping onto the water. She spun around a few times and washed the sand off before walking back to Kortul. "I'm ready now."

He smirked as he stood. "Corver, transport us to our room."

Tolina had a chill from the abrupt change in temperature. Hooking a finger for her to follow, Kortul went into the bathroom and started the shower before he stood at the replicator and made them some clothing to go home in. "You can shower first. I saw that chill." When the clothing was ready, he opened the replicators cabinet door and handed her clothes. As he walked from the bathroom, she shut the door and quickly rinsed off before she dressed so Kortul could bathe next. When he was finished and they were both clean and dressed, he asked, "Corver, transport us to the front desk."

Tolina had no idea why they were visiting the front desk again, but she wanted to see Nire and hope she would be there. When she turned around, Nire was there but hadn't looked up from her work yet. Tolina came to the counter with Kortul but didn't say anything. She smiled and waited for Nire to look, and when she did, Nire threw her arms up and ran around to hug Tolina. Nire squeezed Tolina as she squealed, "Thank you for everything. You are the most amazing person I've ever met. I hope you come back soon!" Nire paused when she saw Kortul, "Oh, bye, Kortul."

Kortul stood stunned as he looked at both women and had no idea what just transpired between them. Tolina gave him a sweet smile. "We can go now."

When did Tolina have time to make friends with Nire? Also, why did Tolina make friends with Nire? He narrowed his eyes at Tolina. "Corver, transport us to my ship."

"Are you planning to explain that?" Kortul's heart steadily beat quicker as Tolina sat down in her chair and leaned back, ignoring him. He sat down and turned his entire body toward her before he asked, "Tolina, do you plan to explain when and how you and Nire became friends?"

Tolina flashed him a dazzling, devious smirk and replied a flat, "Nope."

Kortul's face fell, and he cringed inside, but he knew Tolina saw it or felt it. "Corver, transport us to Saltic Tower ship hangar." Wanting to be with an empath who doesn't trust him may not be his brightest idea, but he couldn't force himself to do anything but *want* to be with her. *It's so far beyond sex. This woman makes me want to go to war and kill things. I might kill her dates. Fuck. I need to calm down before I end up in prison for murder. Who the fuck can I explain this to? Tyce. Wait, no! He would call the authorities. Mabit would lock me in my own room. Damn. All three of my other friends I fucked, and I didn't want a relationship with them, so they don't talk to me anymore. No wonder Tolina is hesitant. I'm killing her positive dates though. Wow, I went right back to murder.*

"Kortul?" Tolina was staring at him as she stood in front of her seat. He looked up at her before looking around and standing up. *How long was I sitting there lost in my own thoughts?*

Tolina giggled to herself as she waited for him to ask the computer to send them to their apartment.

"Corver, transport us home."

They stood in the familiar space, and Tolina paused before walking toward her room. "Are we having dinner together?" Tolina stopped before the hallway and was staring at him wanting an answer, but she could tell Kortul noticed the softness to her tone, and it stole his attention. It was one she knew she didn't have before. It was a tone of comfort and belonging. She felt like she was home, whether she wanted to admit that or not.

"I'll tell everyone to meet here in an hour." Kortul watched her disappear down the hallway and into her room.

It's working. Fuck, it's working. Fuck! Why am I so nervous? His hands shook as he grabbed his tablet from the counter where he had left it before the vacation and sent messages to Brock, Mabit, and Tyce. Within seconds, Brock was coming to greet him.

Kortul met him halfway, and he patted his back as his little companion hugged his leg. "Where is Tolina?"

"She's in her room, and before you ask, she had a great time. I'm sure she will tell everyone over dinner."

Brock nodded and waddled off to start cooking and preparing a meal for several people. Kortul went to his room and jumped into the center of his bed from his doorway. The covers flew and landed everywhere around him as he paused. *Fuck! I almost forgot to block the sound.* "Corver, silence my room."

Kortul screamed at the top of his lungs and beat on his bed with his fists for several extended seconds before he finally calmed and went to splash cold water on his face. *I need to exercise after dinner, or I will never fall asleep.* His cock was straining inside of his slit, and he was tempted to take a freezing shower. A taunting image of Tolina on her knees sucking his cock burst into his mind, and he couldn't hold his cock in anymore as he ran for his shower and tapped the coldest setting before walking in fully clothed and lying on the floor in the icy stream.

Chapter 16

Dinner

Tyce was sitting at the round dining table when Tolina came out in warm sweats. "It's good to see you!" After she hugged him, she sat down by him, and Brock brought them water.

Tolina looked over at Brock confused. "You don't need to bring me food and drinks. I can get them for myself."

Tyce burst into laughter and patted her arm as he reassured her, "Eckolie and Wendi evolved together, and our symbiotic relationship remained strong throughout the process. He can't change wanting to help with what Kortul is bad at, like cooking and cleaning the windows, as much as Wendi can't help spoiling their Eckolie and giving them unconditional love and protection. Every Wendi has a companion."

"What do you mean spoil them?" Tolina was so fascinated she failed to notice Kortul had taken a seat beside her, and he had his hand on her knee. Now nothing mattered except that hand. *How do I move it off without being dismissive?* It was too late to shove him off, so she tried to ignore it.

Fucking honey balls! If he does not stop moving his fingers I might die.

Tyce ignored Kortul as well and answered, "Have you seen Brock's room? It's filled with whatever Brock wants. Kortul has fish and ornate puzzles from all over the galaxy imported for him. Eckolie vary in their tastes. Mine is named Hanes, and he is obsessed with these little red worms from a moon circling a giant gas planet in our solar system. They come dried with salt on them, and he can eat a case a week. He takes care of my finances, which I hate, so he can have all the worms he wants."

Mabit appeared and sat down on the other side of Kortul as Brock set plates in front of everyone before sitting down with a plate for himself in the last open seat between Mabit and Tyce.

Tolina felt Mabit studying her, and when she looked back at him, he asked, "How was your vacation?"

She knew what he was searching for, and it was confirmation Kortul had behaved. She chose to omit the part about the two different people who approached Kortul about ignoring their messages and focused on the positives. Her mind was still scrambled from Kortul's hand on her thigh, and she swallowed her dry throat as she did her best to answer. "I was able to fly, oh! And he stomped on the back of a giant crab, and it walked off into a crevasse. We went climbing on the crystal cliffside and swam through the caves under the island. It was by far the most fun I've ever had." Mabit was quiet, and she wondered how much he knew. His flat expression said nothing which she knew enough about soft interrogating to know that meant he was waiting for her to continue. *Maybe he wants me to admit Kortul behaved when I went on my date, even if it was awful.*

I bet he called Mabit. "Did Kortul tell you I went on a date?"

Mabit smiled at her as he replied, "Yes, he called me."

Tapping his foot, Kortul fidgeted with his fork as he stabbed a piece of white bird meat and a long green bean. Under the table, Tolina reached over and she smashed his knee down to keep his foot still. "That date was a disaster, but I am excited to start dating more now that we're back."

Mabit seemed moved by her words as he slowly panned his gaze from Kortul and back to Tolina before he asked, "Oh? Please tell me what happened to make the date so disastrous?"

After the painstaking process of prying her fingers up, Kortul shoved her hand away from his knee as she answered, "There was a rambunctious primate who kept tossing small rocks at my date, and it agitated him. When we went to eat afterwards, there was a group of younger men gathered at the bar. I think one of the rowdy drunk men threw an overripe pear and it landed on my date's back. It made him furious. I was finished with the date after his reaction and went to walk on the beach. It's fine though. I'm sure I can find plenty of people to date in a city like this."

Tolina pinched Kortul on the leg as the tapping started back, and he glared at her. "What was that for?"

"Will you hold still? Your foot tapping is obnoxious." Tyce and Mabit both laughed and Kortul scowled at them.

Kortul tapped his foot when he was nervous and if either said a word, he would stab them with his fork. "Both of you can fuck off." He stabbed another piece of meat and ate it as the rest of them refocused on their meal.

It was only temporary because Mabit a few minutes later asked, "Are you sure it was a rowdy drunk man?"

Kortul flared his eyes at Mabit, and all Mabit could do was hold a knowing smile as Tolina shrugged and admitted, "I don't know who else it could have been? I wasn't paying attention, and that's my fault. I'll stay more focused next time."

Mabit shifted his grin, and it became genuine as his eyes fell on Tolina. "I think being more observant in times of leisure is wise."

Kortul's head would explode if Mabit didn't shut his mouth. He rose from his seat in a rush. "Drinks?" *I don't know if chugging straight liquor right now would even take the edge off.*

Tolina wasn't saying no to a drink. "Sure. I would love one."

Kortul grabbed a savory drink mix from his ice box and a stack of glasses from his cabinet. He set the items on the table and began pouring drinks before passing them around. Kortul drank his and refilled his cup before anyone else had more than a few sips. He plopped back in his chair, and everyone ate quietly until they were finished, and Kortul collected the plates.

Warm and cozy feelings were new for her and Tolina couldn't get enough. "Can we do this regularly? I would love to do this more often."

Mabit hugged her and she basked in his aura of kindness. "We come to Kortul's for dinner at least once every two weeks. We will see you soon."

Tyce and Mabit left, and Brock went back to his room, leaving Kortul standing at the table drinking another glass of savory liquor. *Fuck, I should have known Mabit would pull that shit.*

"Is there a reason you're so nervous?" Tolina was concerned as she came up and refilled her own cup again.

Fuck, she knew because she's a fucking empath! I know I cannot be this stupid. I'm nervous because I am a toxic wreck over you. I can't help it, and I'll fucking die if you find out! He bit the inside of his cheek to stop his descent into chaos and once it subsided, he sighed and tried to change the subject. "We need to program your translator for my meetings coming up. I sent you music with subliminal language training so it can learn all the galaxy standard languages in a few hours. The music files are in your tablet, but I'll need you to add your alphabet and comparable words to the language software so it can create translations for you too."

"My tablet?" *My language? My written language?* It had only been a short time since she had seen her people's language written, other than her name in the sand. Her thoughts stopped when Tolina wondered when she was given a tablet.

Kortul lifted his brows knowing she had not seen that he had her drawers filled with everything she could need while they were gone. "Check the drawers in your room. The written translation software is easy to run, and I set it to start from the opening screen."

Tolina went to her room and opened drawer after drawer filled with everything from wing cream with an applicator stick to reach the top of her wings all the way to a collection of digital games, planet guides, and destination advertisements. *Is he trying to convince me to be with him through vacations? Because that might work.* She lifted one of the planet pamphlets, and it looked like a dark forest paradise. The first page featured a sprawling glass hotel built over the top of a forest. Jutting treetops in between the rooms created privacy which mystified her. She flipped to the next page with a waterfall canyon tour. *Put the damn vacation brochures down and stop falling for his fucking bait!* She stretched as she checked outside, and the moons were high in the sky. *How long have I been in here checking out products I can't even read the labels on? Wait. He said I had a tablet somewhere around here.* She checked the last drawer, and there it was, a tablet just like his with a holoscreen.

Perfect. Once I can read things, I will have more freedom. Thank fuck that was one thing I was actually good at. She failed her spy classes in hacking and keeping a straight face. She failed her hacking class by a small margin the last time she took it, but her face ruined it all for her. She could not force her expressions to cooperate, and she had no idea how she was able to keep her face in check all weekend with Kortul. She giggled to herself a bit as she realized the difference might be determination. Tolina was dead set on not settling for anything, so maybe she didn't need to keep a straight face because that was how she felt, and it wasn't fake. *That also means I still suck at hiding my feelings. How fun.* She rubbed her neck a bit with that realization and looked around at the gifts he had given her as she recalled their wonderful time together on vacation. *I know this is real for him, but I need to make sure it's real for me.*

On the tablet, she entered the words of her language on the screen with her finger as it showed her pictures of various creatures and items. It took a few minutes of entries, and a written message asked her if she could read it. She felt nostalgia and grief as she read her own language for the first time since she had been there.

She answered by selecting the 'yes' button on the screen, and when the tablet lit up seconds later, everything was in her language. She gasped and began flying through program after program as tears gathered in her eyes. Tolina sniffed and brushed away the tear. *How silly to have tears right now? What is wrong with me?*

After she went through the program list, she discovered one she could use with the transparent glass tablet. It gave her the ability to hold it over something and read her language superimposed, but readable on top of the Wendi word. *How genius! I can learn how to read the Wendi language like this. Why the fuck am I crying?*

Tolina wiped her face as she set the tablet down and tried to assess why she was shedding tears. This was not normal for her, and she was starting to panic. It started with her feelings of being exposed, and now she's crying over reading her language. *What if something is wrong with me? What if this is an empathic disease? Fuck. What do I do?*

She felt heat erupt inside and placed her hand on her chest trying to feel for a fever. She was warm, but it was not a sick type of fever. Her antennae were stuck straight up, and she couldn't make them curl back down into her hair. *What the fuck is happening to me?*

Feeling more tears slide down her cheeks, she succumbed to her panic and ran from her room straight for Kortul's room and was shocked his door opened for her when she walked up. Her heart was beating in her ears, and she didn't have time to think about it. Tolina rushed to his bed and lay her hand on his shoulder. "Kortul?"

He cleared his throat and turned over, blinking each one of his four eyes before blinking them a few times together. "Tolina? What's wrong?"

She sat down on the bed and tried not to pant as she

explained, "I'm crying, and I don't know why. I think something is wrong with me."

He sat up slipping his arm around her. He reached around and tapped her on the nose as he whispered, "I'm naked."

"Oh." Tolina turned around and shut her eyes for Kortul to slip on his sleep shorts.

She opened her eyes when she heard him rustle the covers. He moved to sit next to her and wrapped his arm around her. He was as gentle as possible as he asked, "What were you doing when it happened?" Tolina wiped her river of tears as Kortul asked, "Corver, dim the lights." When the dim lights came on, Kortul saw her puffy eyes and rubbed her arm as he pulled her closer and asking softly again, "Can you tell me what happened when this started?"

She swallowed the lump forming in her throat and answered, "I was just teaching the tablet my written language, and my eyes started leaking." Her voice cracked when she said 'leaking,' and he eased her head onto his shoulder.

"Do you miss your former home?"

Tolina paused a moment before answering. *Why am I scared to hurt his feelings? I wanted to cut his ears off mere days ago and now what? Why is this so fucking difficult?* "Yes. This is more, though. Something happened on the vacation. After my emergence, I was forced to spend my life suppressing all my emotions. On our vacation I allowed myself to feel again, and that was when my empathic ability turned on. It was like a switch in my head. I can't explain it, but I think I'm having an overload or something."

Kortul narrowed his eyes at her. "Corver, take what Tolina said and compare it to Vitolas medical information on empathic research. Send all relevant information to my tablet." His tablet lit up seconds later and he retrieved it. He seemed relieved when he read the screen.

"It's normal for some Vitolas teenagers to experience random bursts of emotion when they emerge from their cocoon. This can happen at any time in a Vitolas' life when the empathic gland in the brain develops, but it is most common in children who are raised in a safe and nurturing environment. The stronger the waves of emotion, the stronger the potential range of the empath. It is imperative to allow the emotions to flow or the empathic range could be suppressed." Kortul looked over at her and she was sobbing and shaking with her arms wrapped around her middle. He dropped his tablet and rushed over, wrapping her in his arms and pulling her into his lap.

Tolina could feel Kortul holding her, but the rush of profound grief and sadness was so great she couldn't comprehend anything other than the gripping pain wrapped around her heart. She felt a hand around her neck and fingers feeling for her pulse before the hand was flat on the top of her chest. *I know it's Kortul. Why can't my brain understand anything except sadness right now?*

Chapter 17

Superhero Caterpillar

Kortul stayed awake all night on the side of his bed with Tolina in his arms as she went through a long stretch of sobbing before she passed out. Her eyes were moving under her eyelids, and he watched her wake and realize she was still in his arms.

In a scratchy voice she asked, "Kortul?" as she blinked and tried to focus on him through her narrowed, swollen eyes. "Why am I in your bed?"

He gave her a reassuring smile as he watched her antenna bounce up and down in her hair. "I bet you were an adorable fuchsia and black caterpillar."

Tolina laughed under her breath as she climbed from his lap and stretched, "Where did that come from? Why did you say that?"

Kortul smiled at her and explained, "You had an emotional overload last night and rushed in here. I looked it up, and it mentioned something about the event happening after emergence so that led to thoughts of you as a caterpillar. I can just imagine little you rummaging around your parent's greenery house. I bet you were a cute little worm." Tolina tried to smile at his joyful thoughts, but her face told on her. "What's wrong?"

"Where I was from, we had a spawning forest. All Vo-Pess had to give their eggs to the forest as a cultural practice, but it was just a way for the elite to tag and track the females with the wing types they desired. The only people who raise their own eggs are in the Van-Well elder family." Tolina watched Kortul's face turn from joy to horrified and she came back over to sit down next to him. "I'm sorry to ruin your fun thoughts. That would have been a nice reality, but it wasn't mine. Our time as caterpillars was so stressful many of us don't remember much of it at all. What we do remember are moments of terror and unending hunger."

"You mean you don't have parents or a family? As a child you were loose in a forest and alone?" He became quiet as he continued, "I don't think I would be able to cope with a childhood like that. I thought mine was bad."

Tolina leaned against him and corrected, "You can't compare experiences. It doesn't work that way. Do you understand now why I'm not giving you an answer about anything? I have never had a choice in my life."

Kortul hated every second of this. Tolina was his, and he would do anything for her, except one thing, and that was let her go. He couldn't fight who he was, and his father haunted his reasoning, but his intentions were different. *I want to give her the world, not control her with it. I want to watch her heal and thrive. I want to see what she looks like when she's old and has years of joy on her face.*

He recalled the poison he ordered a few days prior and hoped it arrived soon. He would need to call the delivery company and put a rush on it if it didn't arrive in the following days. It was only a matter of time before her next date, and he needed to be prepared. The image of her date choking on his food was glorious, and he had to hold back a smile.

"What are you so stirred about? You went from sad, to fury, something I can't identify, and now pure conniving joy." Tolina's antennae were straight up, and she could feel her empathic range had widened to the entire floor they lived on and at least two below them. She could sense Kortul, Tyce, Brock, and even Hanes. *If I had my old nano tech armor, I could read empathy for a mile. This feeling is so overwhelming. I need to keep it blocked off.*

Kortul grinned at her and stood to dress for his day at the courthouse to file her employment documents, but he wasn't leaving her if she needed him. "I have plans at the courthouse today, but if you need me to cancel them, I can move them to next week."

Tolina shook her head. "No, I am through the wave of emotions for now. If it starts happening again, I'll tell you." She went back to her room and prepared for her day with Mabit. She had her tech training with him, and she wanted to be prepared for it. She began with stretching before she changed. She reached for her tablet to send him a message to let him know she was ready.

He responded quickly and told her to transport to his apartment. "Corver, transport me to Mabit's living room."

Tolina looked around at the various boxes in front of her and smiled. Mabit had wrapped each and all the bows were tied like black butterflies. He was standing behind the gifts seeming stoic, and she didn't need empathic skill to know how happy he was to give her the gift. Beyond his statuesque form was the strength and safety only a loving parent can covey. She reached for him anyway and could feel his delight. It was genuine, and she could tell they came from his heart. "Start with this one." He had her open a large box and inside was a tiny floating orb on a small disk. It reminded her of her former nano tech armor, and she slowly raised her eyes to Mabit.

"Is this what I think it is? I had nanotechnology armor back home which integrated with my antennae to extend my range. Is this the same thing?"

Mabit chuckled a bit under his breath before he explained. "It's better. I looked into a Vitolas armor company and discovered they have a nanotech line which has new crossover tech with a chameleon armor company. I used Kortul's banking information and bought you the best suit they have. It has site to site transporting, integrates with your antennae to extend your range, rolling force fields, it's space ready, and has full chameleon capabilities. It absorbs nanotech based tools or weapons you can retrieve at any time. You have the option to download Corver, and I believe the model I bought also has resuscitation, wound sealing, and microbe filtering."

Tolina reached for the orb, and it crawled up and spread over her arm before enveloping her body. When it reached her antenna and covered them with the nanotech, she shivered at the tingling down her nerves. When it connected itself to her nervous system at the base of her skull where her port was found, it amplified her empathic range so far, she whistled. The various controls displayed as a hologram in front of her face, and she selected the chameleon option.

It didn't feel like anything happened. She hopped over to a mirror, but she was unable to see herself whatsoever. "This is incredible!"

"The suit conceals your voice too. Come open the rest."

She selected to download Corver and turned off the chameleon setting. Tolina returned the armor to black before she waved her hand in front of her face, and the nano-tech receded from her head. She was so happy she felt like skipping as she walked back to Mabit for her next gift. She opened it to find a pair of sleek guns. She picked one up, and it was lightweight yet balanced in her hand. A little holo-screen popped out from the side and top with sights and a list of settings.

"Rest the weapon on your armor by your hip."

Tolina briefly met Mabit's gaze before she watched the weapon melt into her suit at her side. "Well fuck a beehive. How does it reform?"

"Grab it. The weapon will reform in your hand. It uses a laser burst and can be fired like a physical firearm or hold the trigger to create a solid beam. It penetrates flesh and bone without the possibility of breaching the hull in a space altercation."

Tolina gasped when she moved to grab the weapon and the gun became whole in her hand in an instant. She placed it back against her armor, and it melded together before she did the same with the second weapon on the opposite side.

She opened the next gift and inside it was a tiny rectangular metal box. She reached down and lifted it in her hand before opening it. Inside were two contact lenses. She narrowed her eyes at them and peered over the box at Mabit.

He grinned at her, "They are bio-tech which dissolves permanently into your eye like a translator. They will synchronize with your tablet's language program so you can read any language in our galactic database. It's painless, and if you completed the program on your new tablet, the lenses will work right away."

Tolina didn't wait as she popped them in her eyes. They were cool as they dissolved, and she could read everything around her after a brief moment of fog. "This is so far beyond the tech I had back home. I am not sure what to say. I don't see how thank you is enough. This must have cost you a fortune."

"Kortul bought it. I didn't pay for a thing." Mabit grinned, and Tolina remembered him mentioning Kortul's banking information.

"Does he know about this?" She wondered why Mabit's eyes seemed so devious.

"Of course not. I thought this would be a nice surprise for him when you walk out in it the day of his meeting. I think it might boost his spirits."

Tolina stared at Mabit and felt nothing but pure joy from him, not the emotions of someone with a nefarious plan. *Forget it Tolina. Maybe he always has that look on his face, and you're being judgmental.*

Mabit's face dropped, and he quieted, and he seemed to be finding his words. "I may have told Kortul that we needed to practice all day while he's gone, but I have no plans for that. I did make plans for you to spend a day relaxing at the pool though because I've been reading up on Vitolas people and their empathic development. I hope you don't mind. Kortul sent me a message last night when you were asleep. He was very worried about you and asked that I look into it."

She beamed, "Are you joining me?!"

"If you would like. I was planning on joining you for a bit because I have a dating service I found which I think you would like to see. I haven't mentioned anything to Kortul yet, but I have been dating, and I've had a bit of luck with this service over others."

Kortul is still growing on me. Mabit however, I love him and will probably love him forever. "I'll meet you there. I need to change. Corver, transport me to my room."

Back in her room, she wondered if the new armor could be stored away like her old armor. She tapped her hip, and the armor receded into a tiny fingertip point which adhered flat. *I might be obsessed with this armor.* After she grabbed her tablet, she went to the replicator in her closet and found a black swimsuit. Once she was dressed, she asked, "Corver, transport me to the pool patio."

Mabit was lounging in a chair with his tablet propped on his legs, and he greeted her with a smile as she sat down in the lounge chair beside him. "I'm sending you the dating link. Select your species as Vitolas since they have similar biology."

A screen popped up on her tablet with a Wendi couple embracing. It had a ring of mathematical and scientific symbols circling behind them. She tapped on the center, and it led her to a questionnaire. It took a while to read the numerous questions, but she understood the importance of compatibility. When she was finished, she selected submit, and it notified her that her matches would be available for her to select from in the next few days.

Expecting to feel relaxed and reassured, Tolina instead felt a pit form in her stomach. She needed a change of subject. "When is Kortul's first meeting, and who is it with? Kortul told me a little, but I need to be able to see what you're talking about."

Chuckling under his breath, Mabit sat up and answered,

"I don't know whether he received the message this morning in time to tell you or not, but his first meeting was moved to a few days from now. It is with Vespuc S Cobbles. He is a Ukirostir lithium refiner."

Tolina searched what a Ukirostir looked like, and then she snarled at the image of Vespuc. He was grey skinned, bald, and had neck gills like all his people, but he had an expression of superiority, and it made her want to spit in his face and then skewer him in the eye with her knife. *Oh, or I could blow a hole through his face with my gun. That would be fun too.*

"I want to be clear. Saltic, the company, is trapped in these contracts with these men *specifically*, correct?"

Mabit paused for a moment and gave her a knowing smirk as he answered, "Saltic, the company, is in long term binding contracts with the men, *specifically*."

Feeling a cruel delight wrap around her heart, Tolina grinned at Mabit. "That's so, very interesting."

Chapter 18

Doctor Joistifles

After a day of chatting and laughing together, Mabit and Tolina were too locked into one another's attention to notice Kortul now standing behind them.

Tolina's antennae began bouncing and she whirled around to look up at him. "How long have you been standing there?"

"I transported in a few seconds ago. You noticed me quickly." *I need to remember that.* "I didn't receive the message in time to tell you this morning, but I trust Mabit told you our next meeting was moved. You have tomorrow to review the information, and we leave in the morning the following day."

"Mabit gave me a few items to help this morning. I'm ready. What are we doing tomorrow?" Tolina asked as Kortul he tapped his foot.

He sat down next to her and quietly explained, "I booked an appointment with a Vitolas physician to make sure you don't have any residual problems after everything you went through in your former life. With your emotions fluctuating, I thought you could use a listening ear who understands. It's a woman physician, and you can speak to her privately or with me there. You could even bring Mabit if that's more comfortable."

Tolina considered it and appreciated his thoughtfulness. "I do think I need to speak to someone who knows what's happening. I don't want an emotional fluctuation during a meeting when I need to be focused."

She stepped toward him and Kortul asked, "Corver, transport us home."

When they were back inside the apartment, Tolina and Kortul quietly sat at the table for the meal Brock laid out. A bowl of honey for her, and some left over bird meat and vegetables for him. After dinner they started down the hallway, but Kortul stopped Tolina before she went in her room. "If you have any more emotional waves, you can come wake me again. I don't mind at all."

Of course you don't mind. You got to snuggle with me all night. Honey fuck Tolina, he's trying to be sweet. Be nice back. "Thank you. I promise I'll wake you if it happens again."

He smiled at her and went on to his room as she went into her own. She slept through the night this time and woke to an alarm blaring by the door. Tolina ran over and shut it off before showering and dressing in a T-shirt and leggings.

She met Kortul in the hallway and he seemed much more refreshed. He was wearing a fitted T-shirt and a nice pair of slim cargo pants. He wore tall, laced boots, and held two black hooded jackets. "Is it cold today?"

"We have another cyclone coming this afternoon, so the temperature dropped. It formed quickly overnight though so it doesn't seem to be quite as strong as the one before which formed farther out. We may not even need to tilt the buildings."

He handed her the coat he had resting on his arm, and she slid on the long black coat before he pointed to some boots by the front door. When she had her boots on, he asked, "Corver, transport us to the sidewalk in front of the building."

A hovering bird egg shaped transport vehicle had its double back doors open, and the assistant stood next to them waiting for Kortul and Tolina. Kortul helped her inside and followed her in, sitting next to her. After their door closed, the assistant opened the front door and sat next to the driver.

The vehicle rose in the air and zoomed away at speeds far too quickly for her to tell which direction they were moving. They arrived at a tall, sleek, metallic building, and it felt like gliding through butter as they came to a stop. Kortul helped her out of the transport and wrapped his arm around her. "Corver, link with the medical building's computer and transport us to Doctor Hyvenic Joistifles waiting room."

They appeared in a solid white room with a single flowering plant in the corner, a long white sofa, and a window showing a broad view of the city. As Tolina peered from the window, the vast skyline seemed to stretch forever.

"Kortul Voutin Saltic the Fifth and wife Tolina?" A beautiful, smiling Wendi nurse with a bright green face and blonde hair so light it was almost white stood in an open doorway with a tablet in her hand awaiting an answer.

Kortul guided Tolina toward the nurse with his hand in the center of her back. "Did you need to say my *entire* name?" He hated hearing his full name. It reminded him of his father.

The nurse shrugged at him as she gestured for them to follow her down the hallway. "It's protocol. Too many Wendi have the same names."

Kortul huffed under his breath as they followed along. She took them to a room with a round circle marked on the floor with a podium and a control panel a few feet away. The nurse positioned Tolina in the center of the circle and began pressing buttons at the control panel. After a few minutes an image appeared next to Tolina, and the nurse's mouth dropped open. She briefly looked over at Tolina with sorrow before she rushed from the room mumbling, "Fetching the doc…"

The door slid shut before she was finished speaking, and Tolina groaned, "Fuck. I forgot about my leg." She started looking closer at the hologram next to her and whispered, "Oh, no." The scanner had an arrow pointing to her healed gunshot wound with a warning notice flashing with the words, 'possible gunshot' written in bold.

The hologram showed everything that had ever happened to her. The nurse was not running for the doctor because of her leg. The nurse was running because Tolina was covered in deep scars, and some of which were on her internal organs. She shivered, remembering having to have the gash in her digestive tract sown back together *before* the external wound could be closed. It was on the practice mat after she had been stabbed by her sparring partner. Her clumsiness had caused far too many accidents.

The doctor wearing a long flowing lab coat slid into the room and studied Tolina and Kortul with her antennae straight up. She had thick black curly hair, which made a halo over her head and her milky mint skin glowed in the lights. With piercing black eyes and a stunning face, Tolina thought she looked like a midnight moon goddess. "Mr. Saltic, I am afraid I need to know why you have brought a woman into my practice who has been through extensive trauma, a gunshot wound, and who knows what else."

Tolina cringed and explained, "In my former galaxy, I was an assassin. I left that harsh life and found a new one here. I am now Kortul's bodyguard, and we are here because I need to make sure I am healthy enough for the job. I have had recent emotional waves related to developing my empathic range, and I need to know that it will not affect my ability to work.

"I am doctor Joistifles and I'm at a bit of a loss for words. I need Mr. Saltic to leave the room for a moment so I can ask Tolina some questions privately."

Kortul understood and nodded at the doctor before he walked to the door and into the hallway to wait. The door closed, and the doctor swiveled on her heals to stare at Tolina.

"Are you safe with your husband?" Dr. Joistifles could have burned holes in Tolina with the way she was looking at her.

Tolina smiled at the doctor, "I am safe with him. You can let him back in now."

Still seeming concerned, the doctor opened the door and waved Kortul inside before she addressed them. "Tolina, your body has been through more than any person should ever go through, but essentially, you are healthy. As for emotional fluctuations, did you just begin to develop your empathic abilities?"

Tolina was thankful to have a doctor with similar

empathic abilities and answered, "Yes. I was used as a pawn for my government to take out people they deemed lesser than acceptable. I believe the stress and depression from suppressing my emotions caused my empathic ability to be held back. We just recently went on a vacation, and that was the first time I had ever experienced any peace. That was when I felt my empathic ability growing."

"Fascinating. You endured the deep emotional wave. It's usually an overwhelming sadness and it signifies your empathic ability is in the final development. It doesn't always happen, but when it does, it can be jarring."

Tolina was relieved as she looked over at Kortul who seemed to feel the same. "Yes, it was. I won't have another episode like that?"

The doctor shook her head, "No, your range will continue to increase over the next year or so, but that's the only change. If that is all, I appreciate you coming in. If you need any type of services outside of business hours, don't hesitate to call me privately. You should hurry if you have far to travel. The cyclone is approaching." She seemed panicked over the storm and Tolina understood too well. She knew her own distress over the storm would be arriving the moment she spotted it in the sky.

Kortul's tablet chimed, and he nodded at her before he led Tolina into the waiting room. "Corver, transport us to the sidewalk in front of the building."

They climbed back into the transport they arrived in and Tolina was anxious to return home. As they were stepping from the transport in front of Kortul's building, he pointed to the sky. "I wanted to show you around the city today, but that will need to wait. It looks like the storm is rolling in much quicker than I expected. We need to move inside and have the replicator make you a leaf cigar. Corver, transport us to our living room."

Tolina heard the 'our' in his request and sighed. She wished it were that easy. She approached the window and gawked at the sky. She didn't know what she was expecting but seeing the massive storm front moving toward them caused her heart to rage. Her stomach dropped to her feet when she watched the first wave of water and wind slapped the window. "I should not have looked at the storm."

Kortul was there quicker than she expected and guided her to the couch before she could think twice. "Thank you." He helped her sit down and rushed back over to the replicator before jumping over the couch and landing next to her.

He stared off into nothing for a moment before he closed his eyes and whispered, "I forgot the lighter again. Corver, I need a flame at the end of my leaf cigar."

The end of the cigar burst into a tiny flame, and he puffed on it before handing it over. After a few drags, she felt much better and relaxed into the cushion. "Maybe I won't pass out so quickly this time."

Kortul chuckled as he rested his arm on the back of the couch behind her, "I give you five minutes."

That was the last thing she remembered before she woke up in her bed in the middle of the night. The raging storm was now soft rain against her window, and she climbed from her bed to watch the droplets slide down the glass. She raised her antennae and sent her empathic ability as far as she could stretch it.

She noticed a curious sensation, but she couldn't quite identify. A warmth spread through her, and she was confused as she felt the need to rub her thighs together. A tingling began and she squirmed, trying to place what was happening.

Oh no, is Kortul in his room having sex? Her heart was squeezed so tight she struggled to breathe. She rushed from her room and into Kortul's room, but he wasn't there, and she saw steam coming from the bathroom, so she crept forward low to the floor. Pleasure flowed through her, and she could hear Kortul moan under his breath.

I will murder him if there's a person in there with him.
"Tolina..."
Did he just say MY name? Oh fuck.

She was far too heated and curious to turn back now, so she hid outside the bathroom door and peeked around the corner. Kortul had his cock in his hand, and he was stroking himself. He whispered "Tolina" once more before he groaned and shot cum across the shower.

Tolina scrambled from his room, rushed through her door, and dove into her bed, covering herself with her blankets. *That was the hottest thing I've ever seen in my life.*

Chapter 19

Can You See Me?

Kortul fell over onto his bed and intended to fall asleep, but as he closed his eyes, he detected a sweet scent in the air. It was brief, but he swore he smelled Tolina in his room. *I know I didn't imagine my Tolina so hard I can smell her. Was she in my room?*

He didn't finish his thought as he slapped his hand onto his tablet next to his bed and selected the surveillance option to access the cameras in his room. He would rush her room and fuck her right now if she were in his room and showed any interest at all. *I have never been this desperate for anything. I need her.*

His stomach twisted as he watched her rush from his room. Not a hint of how she felt. He tossed his tablet across the room and rubbed his face before he grabbed his hair and resisted the urge to rip it out. Knowing he would not sleep now, Kortul slid from his bed and went into his bathroom for a sleeping pill. They only had a few hours before they had to be up, so he picked one which was fast acting and didn't last long.

In seconds he was drowsy and dosing off. It felt like minutes had flown by when his tablet alarm blared across the room. He huffed as he crawled from the warm bed and tapped his tablet with his toe, ending the alarm. After dressing in one of his galactic travel suits, Kortul checked himself in the mirror, and he wanted to strike his own image with his fist. The black, sleek, form fitted attire with tall black boots, which was made specifically for galactic business, made him cringe no matter how badass he knew he looked. He looked *identical* to his father when he wore one of the travel suits. The travel suits were technically armor and designed for safety, but he still hated it. He hated his father so much he had thought about surgery to alter his own face. He hated being forced to look at the man who shattered the heart of the little boy he once was. His father had broken his spirit long before the day he broke his body.

Forcing himself to calm, Kortul styled his hair before he checked the time. He needed to meet Tolina in the hallway soon, so he grabbed his tablet from the floor and stood by her door while he confirmed his galactic travel route. It was approved with a chime as her door slid open and she came out wearing solid black Vitolas made metallic nanotech armor. *What the fuck? Is she wearing the newest model?*

"Did Mabit give you that? Fuck. That's a Vitolas top model nano-suit." Kortul checked his banking accounts and whistled. Mabit had spent a *fortune* of his money on the armor. Tolina deserved the best, and he wasn't upset about that part, but the amount of the armor was so high it was suspicious. *I bet he bought her fucking chameleon crossover tech. Fuck me in the ass with no lube. I think Mabit loves her more than me.*

"Tolina, is there chameleon tech integrated in that

armor?" Kortul watched her light up with enthusiasm as she waved her hand over her face and disappeared before his eyes. "Oh. I'm glad he bought you the best." *I don't know whether to laugh or cry. I might do both.* Kortul checked the time and if they didn't transport now, they would be late. "Corver, transport us to my ship."

When they were standing on the bridge, Tolina watched Kortul as he walked ahead to the captain's chair. *Is that what he's wearing to every meeting? His looks are interfering with my judgement. It should be a sin to look that good. Why do I want to spank him?*

Tolina was ready to stomp on her own foot as Kortul leaned back in his chair. "Corver, transport us into orbit and open a wormhole to B'Otipe. Land at the planetary coordinates entered. Override to land on a restricted, low atmosphere planet approved."

Tolina watched as their names Kortul Voutin Saltic the Fifth and Tolina Saltic displayed on the screen. "Did you change my name?"

Kortul had changed her name, and it was intentional. "No. I didn't know what your full name was, and I needed to add it to the employment form."

She stared at him and replied, "You spelled my first name wrong. My name is Toli-na Pa-Frelep. You could have asked."

"Your name is Toli?" Kortul was far too thrilled about that as he smiled at her, and she glared back at him. Tolina combined her first names to sound better to her when she left her home planet. Now she regretted telling him.

"Toli is much better, but I won't call you that if you don't like it. I'll change your name when they send the confirmation." Kortul smiled to himself as he watched the wormhole open like a shiny bubble in front of the ship.

They rode the wormhole for a few minutes in silence. When they were on the other side, Tolina was struck with sorrow over the dead, glistening white planet before them. The once saltwater dominate world was now a dry salt bed with no atmosphere. Three high tech, space station rings the width of a moon rotated around the dead planet. She could spot lush forests between large lakes taking up most of the surface of the rings.

"The rings are where the owners of the remaining mining companies live. The rings started as a terraforming project. The water began to evaporate from just eight hundred years of unchecked pollution, and once the seas almost completely evaporated, it caused a cascade of environmental failures until the planet surface fully dried. Once the surface dried of all moisture, the mining companies who caused the pollution problem to begin with extracted the planet's core and sold it off. This made the magnetic protections for the planet fade with the atmosphere, so now the mining companies are stuck with a salt covered planet shell with no atmosphere. The only thing left to sell is the lithium and salt. We are here for the lithium."

Tolina grimaced as she understood what he meant. "These people are sounding super nice, and this little trip should be fun, right?" *This is why Corbatton has such strict laws. Mining operations won't stop until a planet is in ruin.*

Kortul laughed under his breath as the ship transported to the surface and he waited for the building to signal the airlock would be open for them. He was not standing there like an idiot like last time. *Assholes took forever to open the airlock, and I'm not falling for that again.*

He slipped on his black spacewalk helmet from the hallway storage cabinet leading to the ship airlock. They stood inside the ship, and Tolina asked, "What are we waiting on?" She waved her hand over her face to spread the nanotech. She loved how her armor was spacewalk ready.

"Clearance. Last time I had to stand outside the airlock. I'm not falling for that again. They can tell me I have clearance before I transport from this ship. I initiated it manually from the captain's chair so Corver should respond soon."

A few seconds went by and Corver spoke, "Clearance approved for two. Airlock sixteen is now open. Transporting now."

The ground shook as they appeared, and they grabbed onto one another to steady themselves. The airlock opened, and they climbed in. It shut behind them, and the air whooshed as they pressurized to the station atmosphere. When the doors opened, Tolina's skin crawled. It was a white and tan salt tunnel, glittering from the bright lights. Something about this place made her feel sick.

After walking for several minutes, they came up to a doorway with two double doors. Kortul pushed them open, and he went inside before he removed his helmet. Tolina remained concealed in her black armor as she followed Kortul. They approached a small round table with three Ukirostir seated, two men and one woman. The man in the middle was Vespuc S. Cobbles, the man Kortul's company Saltic had a forty-year contract with.

"Saltic, sit." Vespuc snarled as he pointed to the seat in front of Kortul. Tolina watched Kortul as he stared at the man, and she approached Kortul's chair before pulling it out for him and sending her antennae above her head as Kortul briefly blocked her from their view.

They are planning something. I can feel it like its yelling loud and clear. Tolina was furious, and she recalled a moment of her empathic training which she had forgotten to that point. *We had records showing strong empathic ability could be used to push emotion as well as sense it. The moment the fuckery starts, I'm testing it. Those old books considered sensing across a room powerful. I can sense for a mile or more without my tech.* Tolina was thrilled but held it in and erased all her emotions like she was trained to do.

Vespuc slid a tablet over to Kortul, and he read it over before he slid it back. "That's not to contract."

Vespuc laughed and smacked the man next to him on the shoulder. "What will you do? Have your new little Vitolas wife slap us around. You're a joke."

Sharky fun time is over. It's my turn. Tolina imagined her rage, anxiety, and pain and concentrated it into dreadful terror. She recalled a moment where she was held down as her shoulder was dissected by her classmate to find a bullet. Moments of pure horror and pain spun at her core, and she grinned to herself as she found a reason to be thankful for all the agony she endured.

She wanted them to look her in her eyes as she made them squirm, so she waved her hand over her face, and they all stopped to stare at her. In that moment she blasted the three with her volatile bundle of dread and watched their faces fall at the same time. She smirked at them as she waved her nano-tech to cover her face.

Vespuc snarled as he grabbed the tablet and altered it before sliding it back to Kortul. This time Kortul agreed and signed the documents before setting it down.

"Don't insult me." Kortul stood and Tolina followed

him from the empty room, and they started down the long hallway back to the airlock.

Once through the airlock and back on the ship, Kortul paused before he took them home and looked over at Tolina with wonder. "Toli, what did you do back there?"

"You are kidding. You are really calling me Toli right now?" She sighed at his rapid blinking and answered him, "I tried something I learned my people were able to do long ago, and it worked. I concentrated my dread and blasted them with it."

That's unheard of, rare for a Vitolas. Kortul's mouth hung open for a moment before he quietly asked, "Corver, transport us home."

When they arrived at Kortul's apartment, Brock was at the top of the windows, stuck on by his toes and the fingers of one hand as he whistled and cleaned the window. Tolina smiled at Brock and went straight to her room for her tablet. She wanted to check if the dating service approved her and if she had any matches.

She checked her tablet and the message in her inbox said she was approved. She swiped through some of her matches. A handsome man by the name Bonnay Valtteri was the second match listed, and she enlarged his photo. He had a turquoise face with a black neck and blue-black short hair. She read he owns a medical tech company, and his interests were climbing, visiting remote places in the galaxy, and spending time with family and friends. *That was easy.*

She selected the match option on his profile, and it stated the service would notify him of the selection. She read the top of the file for those who had matched with her, but she ignored the number. The number was eighteen thousand, and she knew that could not be right.

Chapter 20

True Love

After swiping through her dating matches for a few hours, she noticed the system stars were low in the sky, and it would be time for Kortul and Brock to eat. She was feeling bored and decided to join them.

She came out and Kortul seemed depressed. "What's wrong?"

"Asshole sent me dirty lithium. I need to refine what he sent which means he shorted me by about a quarter. This will cost me over half of what I paid for the refined ore. He still found a way to fuck me." Kortul took a big bite of his sandwich and chewed as he stared at the table. *My father made sure if he died early, I would be punished in his absence. What a nice parting gift.*

Tolina sighed and was thankful her armor had chameleon tech as she sat down next to him. "Are there no galactic laws against bad business contracts?"

Kortul scoffed at that and didn't meet her eyes as he replied, "That would be impossible to enforce without a galactic takeover. There is a multi-planet enforcement group for freedom or ecological protection, but that's the limit. I'm taking a sleeping pill, and I'll be over it by tomorrow morning."

Brock slipped his arm by Tolina and set a bowl of nectar in front of her before he sat back down. "Thank you, Brock." She understood why Kortul loved him so much. He was the sweetest being she had ever met. She bet Kortul would roast someone alive if anyone ever hurt this little man's feelings.

Kortul rose from the table and quietly went to his room. The fact Kortul had been screwed over twisted her insides, and she felt a force she couldn't control growing. *I'm afraid I may need to do something about this tonight.* As much as she loved keeping Kortul at bay, the idea of someone wronging him was so infuriating she felt as though she would burst into flames. The joy of murdering an awful person swirled through her, and she bit her lips together as she deposited her bowl in the dishwasher.

As she stood in front of the door to her room, just out of range for it to open, she raised her antennae to search for Kortul's emotions. He was embarrassed, furious, and filled with self-hatred. No, not self-hatred, but something close. *His father is still managing to harm him. This ends tonight.*

Tolina went in her room and patiently waited with her antennae tuned to him until she could tell Kortul had fallen asleep. She tapped her armor tab. "Corver, transport me to Mabit's living room."

Tolina stood in front of Mabit who wore a facial mask while wrapped in his robe watching a romantic comedy. "What's wrong?"

"I need a way to B'Otipe so I can kill Vespuc tonight."

Mabit dropped the bowl of mixed nuts he was munching on, and they spilled over his floor. He stood up and brushed the crumbs from his robe before he approached her. "Right. A moment please."

Mabit walked by her and into his bedroom where she heard him open an airtight safe. He appeared with a small device between his fingers and handed it to her. "I trained the people who run the planetary authority academy. They have ship cloaking tech and don't use it or release the development of it because they don't want anyone else obtaining the tech." Tolina stared at him as she tried to process how this man had the tech in his hand. "I was testing chameleon armor they planned to issue to operatives, and I found the tech. I copied it. It's on this drive, but Tolina, only upload it to your armor. Do not upload the cloak to the ship or they will detect your ship when you land. Use your armor programming to run Kortul's ship, and the sensors won't detect anything."

Tolina vibrated with delight beyond what she could contain as he pressed the chip to her armor, and it downloaded the software. Tolina gave Mabit a bright smile. "Do you have any fun knives? I can't lie. I enjoy the process."

Mabit screamed with laughter as he half skipped back into his room to come back out and presented her with a high-tech cutting device and a bundle of button restraints. "This is a particle separator. You can do substantial damage with this. Corver is set to answer to you as an owner, so it's not Kortul's ship when you're using it. It's yours."

Tolina took the items and set them on her armor so the nano-tech would embed it. She waved her hand to cover her face. "Corver, transport me to my ship."

She sat in the captain's chair and set the armor to control the ship. She enacted the cloak software before she turned on her armor's chameleon feature. She and the ship became invisible in a matter of seconds. Giggling to herself, she submitted the coordinates Kortul had used earlier in the day.

It didn't take long before she was parked on the desolate planet surface. She jumped from her seat and passed through the ship airlock before walking toward the salt mine airlock. When she reached the thick, reinforced glass, she retrieved her particle separator from her suit and flipped the switch while concealing the handle with her hand. When she had a large circle cut into the glass, she lay on the ground below the airlock and raised her legs before she slammed them into the pane. The airlock burst open, and the glass panel went flying away along with the two people she remembered at the table with Vespuc. They both crashed into her cloaked ship and their heads burst with the impact and lack of atmosphere. They must have been close to the airlock when she depressurized it. She grinned at her luck as she flipped to her feet and waited until the last of the air pressure had been released.

Climbing inside, she could see who she presumed was Vespuc running to the room where they had their meeting with Kortul. He had a respirator pressed to his face and his movements were frantic as he slid the strap over his head. Tolina ran with her separator gripped in her hand, and she was so thrilled she thought this might even top scaling the crystal cliff with Kortul.

Halfway to the meeting room, she remembered she needed to be collecting feelings of impending doom, dread, and incredible suffering. By the time she reached the meeting room, she was brimming with emotional agony. The door of the meeting room was off the hinges, and she saw Vespuc gathering papers from the floor. He was hunched over, and she could sense he was more than aware this was no accident.

Tolina ran toward him and right before she slammed into him, she jumped and tucked her legs to kick him with her running momentum. He rolled with his paper plans sliding across the room and hitting the wall from the lack of atmosphere. He growled as he found his footing and scanned the room for who had struck him. "Show yourself!" He screamed into his respirator, which was now smashed against his face with his hand. He had broken the strap.

Tolina struck him in the temple with her fist, and he slumped to the ground. She took the button restraints from her suit and secured his ankles and wrists behind his back. The restraints were secured with just a tap of the button tab.

She searched the room for his tablet, and once she found it, she approached him and scanned his face before she spread his hand on the tablet, and it accepted the biometrics. When she was inside the tablet, she transferred half of his monetary assets to the account Mabit had uploaded to her armor along with the cloaking tech. The account number changed every five minutes, and she assumed it was an untraceable account.

Tolina began to set the tablet down, but something chimed and she clicked on it. It was a message. She read that the girls he ordered were ready to be abducted on his orders, so she clicked on it to read the rest. The picture showed surveillance of four girls of his species at a young age. They looked around eight to ten years old.

She dropped the tablet on the ground with the message still open before she approached Vespuc. After she tied his respirator on so it would not slip from his face, she started the particle separator for its most brutal purpose.

I'll make him eat four of his own digits. One for each girl.

Tolina used her separator and sliced four of his fingers from one of his hands. Vespuc awoke screaming into his respirator and thrashing against the bonds. She laughed to herself as she bombarded him with feelings of terror and dread. The horror in his eyes brought such joy to her heart that it threatened to burst. "Oh, this is better than I ever could have imagined!"

Vespuc screamed at the sweet feminine voice coming from the seemingly empty room, and she took the opportunity to stuff all four of his fingers into his mouth. She forced his jaw apart and slammed her small hand into his mouth, shoving his fingers down his throat. When she yanked her hand free, her nano-tech armor became snagged on his sharp teeth. His teeth broke against the hard surface.

His eyes bulged as he gurgled, fighting to breathe and cough to dislodge his fingers from his throat. Tolina slapped his respirator on his face, and he struggled through a couple of shallow breaths around the fingers in his throat before she removed it and tossed it away. *He can still breathe. I guess that means I can keep going!* He whimpered and shook as she continued to blast him with intense feelings of endless doom.

With her hand wrapped around the handle of her separator, she held his arm and sliced a long ribbon of skin from it. He was crying now, and his tears flowed around his gagging mouth as he fought for air.

Tolina admired her work before she wrapped his skin around his neck and tied it in a knot and then a bow. Stepping back to watch him die from the lack of oxygen, having too many fingers in his throat, and being strangled by a tacky skin bow tie, she grinned in pride. Tolina was so enthralled by her work she began wiggling her hips and dancing to a rhythm only she could hear.

Her heart sang with imagined sweet chirping birds, double rainbows, and bright starlight. After he was dead, she kicked him to be sure, and then Tolina skipped and danced all the way back to her ship. When she was aboard, she shrieked and sang like a bird as she sat in the captain's chair. *Who knew I just needed some gruesome torture and well deserved murder to bring back my spark!*

Tolina was back in the apartment building hangar within an hour. "Corver, transport me to Mabit's living room."

When she looked round the room, she saw Mabit reading at his dinner table. She turned off her armor before she waved her hand over her face. "I assume you succeeded. You look like you've just kissed the love of your life."

"I think I did. I loved every second of it, and I cannot wait for you to see it on the news." Tolina grinned at him, and he chuckled under his breath as he shook his head.

"Goodnight, Tolina. I hope you're able to sleep without needing to slaughter anyone else. Try not to kill Kortul next, will you?" Mabit joked as he looked back down at his book.

Tolina giggled, "Corver, transport me to my bedroom."

When she was in her dark room, she tapped her hip, and her armor receded into a small tab. She danced into her bathroom and turned on the shower before she twirled herself into the stream and rinsed off. After prancing around her closet, she dressed in a loose crop and comfortable shorts.

How the fuck am I supposed to sleep? She sat down on the couch by the window and began scrolling through visual media options. She had already listened to all the subliminal music he had given her, and she wasn't in the mood for music. Trel would listen to her gush about her kill, and he would always be affectionate with her after an exciting kill because he knew she craved it. *I want to watch something about love.* She found a romance movie category and couldn't select a movie fast enough.

Chapter 21

Do You Dance?

Groggy from his sleeping aid, Kortul shuffled in the living room and plopped on his couch. He often turned on the news while he woke up, and he lay back against the cushions to watch. He needed to stay current with galactic events in his position of power over his company.

The top planetary Wendi news anchor Yenalo with her curly red hair and brown skin caught his attention. She was the main evening news host. *Why is she broadcasting the morning news?* "Headline news: An investigation is underway on B'Otipe where there appears to have been an attack on Vespuc S. Cobbles and his mining operation. Vespuc was discovered in his decompressed salt mine brutally murdered with his fingers inside his throat. A strip of his own flesh was cut away and used to strangle him to death. Authorities believe Vespuc was aiming to abduct young girls and reports indicate one of their parents appears to have been made aware of his surveillance of the children. The parents are being held and questioned for any connection. B'Otipe authorities are requesting any information about the murder, yet no reward has been set. Surveillance recordings provided no evidence. If you ask me, the B'Otipe authorities don't seem too concerned with this brutal murder. Viewers, what do you think? Send in your opinions, and you could have your comments read on air during our follow up this evening."

Kortul turned it off and rubbed his eyes. *Vespuc is dead? That means I'm free from the contract.* He took a deep sigh of relief and turned around to find Tolina behind him in a delightful mood.

"Vespuc is dead." Tolina beamed, and he wanted to jump over the couch to grab her and fuck her until she screamed for him in the middle of the kitchen. Kortul licked his lips. "Why don't we celebrate?"

"Sure, what are you thinking?"

Kortul wanted to see her dressed up. "How about a nice dinner with me tonight?"

"Can Mabit and Tyce come too?" Tolina didn't want him having any ideas. She saw his hungry eyes and knew what he was thinking about.

He smiled at the idea and agreed. He always enjoyed when Tyce and Mabit came along. "Sure. We should visit a place Tyce has mentioned. It's a clear platform restaurant, bar, and club out in the middle of the ocean. Dress for a nice club, but warm."

Tolina squealed and ran to her room to watch makeup tutorials. When she was ready, she had the replicator make the cosmetic hues she needed. After several hours and washing the makeup off twice, she managed to do it well the last try. Satisfied with her make up, she slipped on a revealing black dress and black heels. She stepped back and admired herself in the mirror. The halter maxi dress accentuated her hips, and it made her legs look longer. The closed toed heels were comfortable, not taking away from the dress. *I know he said dress warm, but I don't care.*

She sprayed herself with a pheromone perfume she had seen on an ad advertisement during the romance movie she watched. The movie was terrible, and she regretted picking the first thing she saw. The woman complained the entire time and the man was as soft as pudding. She wanted to turn it off halfway through and wished she had.

She slipped a long black coat over her arm, knowing the nights on this planet were frigid, and walked from her room to find out when they were meeting everyone. Kortul was in a nice dress suit, and it reminded her of the military dress suits her people wore for ceremonies. It had a high tight collar and buttons down one side with a straight bottom hem. The fitted black slacks made him look even taller than he was, and by the time she reached his face, she realized she had been caught checking him out. *Fuck. Say something smart!*

"I like your suit. Your people have good style." She watched him narrow his eyes at her and she ignored it. The door opening and Mabit arriving stole her attention, and she held back a laugh at his knowing grin.

When he hugged her, he whispered, "You did well. I'm so proud of you," and her heart swelled with his affirming words. She would have passed all her classes if she had that sort of support when she had been in training. She felt unstoppable now.

Tyce appeared and didn't even greet them with a smile before he asked, "We are really visiting the Platform? You've been brushing off that idea for months."

Kortul laughed as Tyce stood next to him waiting for an answer. "You wanted to go for no reason. We are not spending an astronomical amount of money on dinner and drinks for no reason. Now we have a reason. Are you ready?"

Everyone took a few steps toward Kortul. "Corver, use long range transports and send the four of us to the Platform Club and Restaurant."

After a warm few seconds, they appeared inside the entryway of a glass structure. Tolina was starstruck by the massive glass platform on stilts above the waves and the giant glass dome over the top. In the center was a club, surrounding the club were various bars and people mingling, and a wall was around the edge separated the tables of people eating and conversing.

A host led them to a table, and Kortul guided her to sit by the glass dome and sat beside her. She was so interested in the glass structure and being able to see the nighttime starlit waves that she knew Kortul was ordering something for them to drink, but she couldn't force herself to pay attention to what he was ordering. Everywhere she looked stole her breath. *I never want to leave this world. I never dreamed anything like this could be possible.* When she realized discussion was moving along without her, she knew she needed to pay better attention. She had no idea what they were discussing.

"I think it's the parents," Tyce announced as the server dropped off their drinks.

Oh, lovely. They're discussing my kill which I must pretend wasn't me. What a precarious situation. I wish this was not the area I failed in spy school. She couldn't keep her face neutral, and she knew Mabit was watching her, so he changed the subject, "The time for the sky dance is near. Are you planning to have a rooftop viewing this year? They say it could last a few days."

Kortul peered over at Tolina and hoped she would join him for it. When he was a child, it was one of his favorite activities. Sharing it with her would mean the world to him. If any of the nights landed on one of her dates, he would kill the person to keep her from missing it. "I am. I'm sure the rest of the building occupants will be coming too."

Tolina met his smoldering eyes and didn't look away as he asked, "Have you looked at the menu?"

She had not, and when she tapped on the table hologram to read it, she noticed her menu was nothing but the sugars she could eat. "Did you call ahead about a menu for me?"

"This planet doesn't have a lot of outsiders except a few Vitolas, so anywhere we visit, we will need to call ahead and let them know about your dietary requirements. Vitolas are the most common species to marry Wendi outside our own species, but most of them eat anything." Kortul didn't act like what he did was special, but Tolina thought it was.

Tolina was beginning to wonder if she would ever be able to find a better man than Kortul. She could feel herself falling for him. She selected her dinner, a type of honey, and she sipped her drink as she watched the people dancing in the center through a gap between two long bars. Kortul finished ordering and saw where she was looking. "Have you ever been dancing before? Did they do anything fun where you came from?"

Tolina had been bored to actual tears many times during her old life because there was nothing but work to do, and that was it. Occasionally, when one of the head spies killed an important target, the leading Van-Well family would have a limited gathering where only select males were invited, only the most loyal and dedicated. Other than that, *fun* was unheard of. *Sitting around with a bunch of rotten old assholes celebrating doesn't sound like much fun anyway.*

Kortul rested his hand on hers and leaned in close as he whispered, "I didn't mean to bring up anything uncomfortable."

Tolina smiled at him and shook her head. "You didn't say anything wrong. There was rarely anything positive about my old life, and sometimes life here is so different that it almost doesn't seem real. To answer your question, I shouldn't discuss when I dance before we eat."

Mabit burst into a laughter which gripped him to his core, and he had to drink something to calm himself. Even then his giggles still took a while to trail away. Confused, Kortul slid his gaze to Tolina, who was shrugging and smiling at him like she had a treat hidden behind her back. "What is that supposed to mean, and what do I not know?"

Mabit laughed a bit again as he tapped his fingers in a rhythm on the table. "Kortul, that's a discussion for later."

In front of Tolina, Tyce chimed in with his eyes flared, "How about we don't discuss anything gross tonight, and you three can take that up later. If you even mention something disturbing, I am leaving." He pointed to Mabit and then Tolina, "You and you scare me to a point of nightmares. I just want to make that clear."

Tolina was a bit offended, and she gasped as she placed her hand on her chest, "Not me!"

Kortul and Mabit both laughed as Tyce gave everyone scathing looks. A smiling Wendi server with a gold face glided over like they skated on ice with a tall stack of glass covered plates. They passed out the covered plates and collected the covers before drifting off to deliver the next order.

They ate quickly and Tyce announced, "I am dancing. See you three when it's time to leave," and disappeared in a crowd as Kortul shook his head.

"How long do you think it will be until he realizes he accidentally drank too much, and he comes waddling back to the table to ask us when we're leaving?"

Mabit chuckled as he answered, "You and Tolina have about two hours, maybe."

Kortul stood up and held his hand out for her, "I am not wasting any time then."

Tolina took his hand. "Go where? Are we dancing?" His hand was strong but gentle, and she felt tingles rush down her spine with his touch.

"Yes, but not in that mess with Tyce." Kortul grabbed their jackets, and he led them outside where softer music played and only a few couples danced. He slipped her jacket on her before he put his own on. The stars made a band across the dark sky and the soft light of the moons made the glass platform shimmer.

Kortul wrapped his arms around her, and they danced for a while before he asked, "Are you cold?"

She was freezing, but she wanted to keep dancing with him, so she lied, "I'm not."

"Liar." Kortul tapped her nose, and he lifted her hood over her head. They kept dancing until Kortul shivered and decided he had enough of the cold. "It's colder than I thought it would be. Let's order a hot drink and sit with Mabit."

She smiled and agreed, "That sounds great. It's beautiful, but it is freezing." He interlaced his fingers with hers, and he noticed she didn't brush him away. *Tolina is mine.*

Chapter 22

Bad Bonnay

After an intensive stretch and exercise, Tolina felt refreshed. She had a late night with Kortul and Mabit. Tyce did just as Mabit predicted and drank too much within two hours. They left early, but she Kortul and Mabit had played an adventure holo-game when they returned to their apartment until late in the night.

She came around the corner of the hallway into the kitchen, and Kortul was deliberating over his tablet, but he didn't seem distressed. There was a steaming cup sitting on the counter, so she grabbed it and warmed her hands as she sat next to Kortul.

He looked up and took the cup from her. "Not a fucking chance. You are not drinking coffee. You will turn into a vibrating rocket." *I should not have said that.* Kortul's imagination was far too vivid, and he was already fighting with his cock to stay in its slit. The image of her shivering on his cock with her wings spread nearly caused him to wheeze. He guzzled the rest of the coffee and set the cup down before explaining, "Coffee has caffeine, and with you being close to a Vitolas, I bet you have a similar reaction."

She was captivated by this news. "You mean vibrating like when I want to dry my wings quickly?" She did not often vibrate her body to dry her wings only because she ended the habit when she had her leg surgery. She was not able to shake off to dry for months, and it was something she never regularly did again. Kortul's focused became locked on what he was reading, so she asked, "Has something happened?"

"I would say so. Saltic had someone deposit a hefty sum of money into one of our main accounts. There is no record of what it could be for or why it was deposited. I have a meeting with the head of the Corbatton Planetary Bank to see if we can trace it, but I can tell by the numbers it's a hacker's account. They won't find who sent it, but it doesn't matter. I'm still required to investigate it because of the amount." Kortul stared at the screen and tapped his fingers on the table.

"Isn't a deposit a good thing?" she asked, and he focused on her. She loved that she could tell where he was looking even though he had solid black eyes.

Kortul leaned back and explained, "A large deposit like this can be to force a hit. The person who wants you dead has first stolen it from someone I'll call the bad guy. The bad guy will come looking for where the money went and kill whoever took it. It's a way to have someone high profile killed without having much of a trail. Once they're dead, the person who deposited the money steals it back with hackers. There are certain people in this galaxy who fear nothing and no one. I know a few of them personally, and they are not people I want to be entangled with further."

Tolina bit her own cheek. The desire to smile was uncanny and to avoid busting herself, she rose from her seat and went to the replicator for a bowl of honey. She wanted the same kind as the night before at the nice restaurant. She couldn't find what she was looking for, and Kortul must have noticed. He came up behind her and he was so close she could feel his warmth. "They don't have everything. What are you looking for?"

"The same honey I had last night at the restaurant." Kortul nodded and sat at the table by his tablet.

It took a bit of scrolling before he answered, "I found some, but it won't be here until tomorrow. It's a galaxy away on a moon the Vitolas own."

She laughed and waved her hands at him. "No. No, way. That sounds so expensive. I will just pick another one."

Kortul narrowed his eyes at her. "I do not care how expensive it is. If you want it, I'm buying it."

"It feels strange relying on store credits to survive my whole life while here you are always offering to buy such expensive things. It's a bit of a shock." Tolina wasn't sure the feeling would ever fade. Comfort and care were not something she thought would affect her this way.

Checking the time, Kortul only had a few more minutes before he needed to dress for his meeting with the old women who ran the bank. They were terrifying in a godly way, and he avoided the bank if he could. "As much as I don't want to leave, I need to be on time for this appointment at the bank. The last thing I want to do today is upset the bank owners. They're delightful until you step one toe out of line. Fuck, I hope this doesn't take all day."

Kortul went to his bedroom to change, and Tolina sat at the table with her bowl of honey. She was still feeling awkward about all the expensive gifts, but she knew it was nothing to complain about. She just needed to get over it. *I'm not used to having so many tingly feelings. Negative feelings are a lot easier. These positive feelings are weird.*

Kortul came back a few minutes later and Tolina couldn't look away as he walked over in a sleek suit. *No one should ever be so attractive that I lose concentration. I hope he doesn't expect words.*

"I'll see you in a few hours. If you need anything Brock is here, and you have Mabit and Tyce's contact information." Tolina just nodded and continued slurping honey through her tongue.

He grinned at her, and she wanted to slide off her chair and onto the floor in puddle. "Corver, take me to the sidewalk in front of the building." Tolina slumped in her chair when he disappeared, but she sat back up when she looked over and realized Brock was staring at her, preparing to take her empty bowl.

Brock took the bowl and deposited in the sink before he teetered off toward his room. Before he went in, he looked back at her, and in his childlike voice, he reassured her, "Eckolie keep secrets forever."

When his door shut, Tolina held a hand over her mouth and grinned. If Brock was similar to other Eckolie, she understood well why Kortul and the Wendi loved them so much. She loved them too.

Tolina saw the date by the door and remembered she had made plans with Bonnay Valtteri. She forgot and didn't tell Kortul before he left. *Honey fuck me. Now I don't want to go.* Seeing the time by the date, she needed to start her makeup after how long it took her before. She went to her room and showered before she started. *Moisturizer, goopy stuff, and wait. What was next? Why is this so complicated? Shit.* She went to turn on the holo-screen in her living area and wished she could watch it in the bathroom. *I wonder.* "Corver, is there a holo-screen in my bathroom?"

"Yes. Any mirror or window surface of the home has holo-screen technology. The options can be accessed by tapping on the surface."

Thrilled, Tolina went back to her bathroom to tap on the mirror to find the same video. The option popped up to transfer the video, and she selected it. *This technology is directed at flawless convenience. I love it here and it just makes me hate Hyret even more.* Learning about this innovative technology was fun, but everything wonderful she learned just reminded her of the awful place she came from.

All the Vo-Pess technology focused on warfare and espionage. Meanwhile, their homes were low tech and rudimentary at best. Everyone lived in tall, bland towers. She hated knowing what her people could have had.

Several hours passed as she worked because one slip of her hand resulted in starting over. When the tedious work was finished, she sighed at her image. She looked beautiful, but something felt off. She checked her messages and Bonnay confirmed he would be there in two hours.

"What the hell should I wear?" Tolina tapped away at the holo-screen and accessed a few fashion magazines. It was all high fashion, and she tilted her head trying to decipher what she was looking at. *Is that tall pants or is that a romper?* Tolina turn off the hollow screen and went into her closet to access her replicator. She found a basic long sleeve, floor length black dress. It was cold from a recent storm, and she would be wearing a jacket. He said to dress warm, so she added some tall, warm black boots.

She twirled in the mirror and was happy with how she looked just as she could hear Kortul was home. She was aware he didn't know she had a last minute date planned tonight. She knew he wouldn't be happy, but she had her mind made up about what she wanted, and she wasn't changing it.

Tolina left her room and came around the corner to Kortul in grey lounge clothes smiling as he stood and watched the news, which had just started, and the intro was playing. When he saw what she was wearing, his face fell. "Do you have plans?"

"I have a date tonight, but I won't be long." Tolina hated the way he looked at her when she mentioned her dates.

His gaze devoured her whole as he approached her, and she felt the urgency to run, but she stood still. She didn't run from anything. He brushed some of her hair from her shoulder and his knuckles caressed her neck, "Be careful." That touch sent blazing heat and urgent need through her.

"I'll be careful," she assured him. She was squirming as she fought to stay in place, and this was the last thing she needed before she went on her date.

Kortul seemed unconvinced as he stared down at her. "The bottom right corner of your tablet can be removed and used as a portable communicator. Take it with you."

She agreed and went to her room for the communicator. When she came back out, Kortul was still standing in the same place in the living room, but instead of watching the news, he was watching for her.

Something occurred to her, she had no money. "What happens if I need to pay for something?"

Giving her a genuine smile, Kortul answered, "If you

need to pay for something, you can use your communicator."

She nodded as she checked the time, and it was time to go. She slipped on her jacket and looked over at Kortul. "Thank you. I'll see you later."

Kortul watched her disappear, and he sprinted to his room for his chameleon armor. When he had it on and activated, he asked, "Corver, transport me to the sidewalk in front of the building."

In seconds he was looking at the back of Tolina's head as she climbed in a transport with a man. Kortul rushed over to the transport and slipped inside with them right before the assistant shut the door. *I need to remember to keep my fucking emotions in check, so she doesn't detect me.*

Bonnay was seated next to Tolina, and he carried on a conversation with his communicator at his ear with what sounded like a business associate. As they traveled, the conversation continued, and Tolina seemed more annoyed by the second. *I don't even think I need to intervene this time. I bet she calls me.* Kortul knew from the outside his suit was silent and was thankful for that. By the time they arrived, Kortul had spent the journey cussing at Bonney who had been on the phone the entire time. *My Toli is pissed. Perfect.*

Bonnay climbed out and didn't wait for Tolina. She followed behind. and Kortul followed too, but not too close. Tolina reached into her pocket and retrieved the communicator. She looked at it as she walked behind Bonnay toward the city gardens.

I need to have a transport available nearby. This man is an asshole. Bonnay turned around and noticed Tolina looking at her communicator and scoffed at her. "Corver, request a transport to wait for me at the city gardens."

Kortul knew Tolina would be calling. *Fuck! I need clothes too!* "Corver, transport my workout clothes and my black long coat into the back of the vehicle." He followed them inside and watched as Bonney approached the counter and bought their tickets. He thrust her ticket at her and Kortul wanted to strangle the man. Tolina seemed like she was genuinely hurt by the way he was acting, and it made Kortul want to murder the man even more than he already did.

They climbed in an open touring vehicle, and Tolina sat next to him as he pointed to a few things, but when he answered another call and started chatting, Tolina studied him. The moment he leaned his communicator on his shoulder and began digging in his pocket, she stood, hiked her dress, and jumped from the slow tour vehicle before slipping between two bushes. Tolina had slipped away from the man unnoticed. Kortul followed her and watched as she lifted her communicator from her pocket, and he could hear a vulnerable softness in her voice. "Kortul?"

"Yes?"

He waited for her to answer as he watched her look around and sink her head. "I need you to send me a transport to the city gardens front gate. This man is awful."

"I'll be there soon. I'll call when I arrive."

The moment she hung up, he rushed toward the city gardens gate and jumped into the transport. The door was thankfully unattended, and the driver's assistant didn't see anything. In the seat, he found his clothes folded, so he crouched where he was concealed from view, and he peeled off the chameleon armor before he slipped on his gym clothes and jacket. When he was dressed, he scoffed at his bare feet. "Fuck. Oh, well."

He folded his armor and did his best to squeeze it in the

inside pocket of his jacket, but it created a weird bulge, and he smashed it down with his arm. Kortul climbed from the transport and startled the driving assistant as he pulled his communicator from his pocket and dialed Tolina. The man whispered, "Where did you come from?"

Tolina answered, "Kortul?"

"I'm out front. Do I need to come in there and get you?" Kortul took a few steps toward the building next to the front gate. She came running from around the corner and passed through the gate before moving straight for him. He wrapped his arm around her and helped her inside the transport.

Once inside, she glared at the city garden gate and huffed before she paused as curiosity struck, and she looked over at Kortul. "Wait. How did you make it here so quickly? Didn't I just call you?"

Chapter 23

In Deep

Silent and annoyed, Tolina went to her room to wash her face and dress in a comfortable loose sleeping crop and shorts. She wanted to ignore life and watch a movie, but not an awful romance like the last one. *Maybe Kortul will know of something to watch.*

In the hallway, Kortul was just coming from his room. His shirt was off, and his shorts were so low, she bet one light tug, and they would fall off. *Do I want that? Fuck. He is growing on me like a mole. I didn't want it, but it's stuck on me whether I like it or not.*

He watched her eyes roam him and wished with every fiber of his being she would cave. He would wait as long as she needed, but the moment she slipped and admitted she cared about him? He planned to make up for lost time, and at this point, he would need to spend several days catching up.

"I watched a movie the other day, and it was terrible. Could you show me some good visual media shows?" Kortul's eyes seemed to glitter when he felt thrilled, and she loved it. He jumped over the back of the couch, and she walked around to sit next to him. He moved through several shows on his tablet before he found one and as it began, he explained, "This is a show about a team of explorers looking for a shipwreck near the Corbatton south pole. It is a true story, but the expedition happened several thousand years ago, so who knows how accurate it is."

Tolina nodded, and they spent the rest of the evening watching a crew of sailors and explorers freeze to death. It was a tragic story, but she enjoyed it, and it was successful in distracting her from spiraling thoughts about her bad date.

"We have a meeting on Blifordat with a Warest copper refiner tomorrow. Get some rest tonight. He is a fucking asshole. It will take some willpower to not kill him on the spot. I want to every time I face him."

Tolina laughed as she followed him until she reached her room, "Goodnight."

"Goodnight." Kortul disappeared in his room as Tolina did the same.

Tolina climbed in bed and fell into a deep sleep. Her tablet alarm blaring by her head sent her tumbling from her bed. Sprawled on the floor, she stretched and jumped to her feet with a thrill when she remembered what the alarm was for. *I meet my next victim today!* Delightful memories of painful screams and begging filled her mind and she sighed. *I can't wait to meet him.*

Once she was showered and dressed in comfortable underclothes, she pressed her armor tab, and it covered her body in the protective nano-tech. Tolina left her room and came around the corner ready for the day, but when she saw Kortul in his solid black galactic travel suit, she was overcome with tingling butterflies in her stomach. *Just don't look at him.*

Tolina failed and held his steamy gaze. It left her wanting to run and hide when he neared. "Are you ready?"

"Yes." It came out breathy and sexy and that was not something she meant.

Kortul lifted a brow. "Corver, transport us to my ship in the hangar." Once they were seated, Kortul asked, "Corver, transport us into orbit and open a wormhole to Blifordat. Land at the planetary coordinates entered. Landing clearance is on file."

Tolina watched as their names Kortul Voutin Saltic the Fifth and Toli-na Saltic displayed on the screen. *He didn't change my last name back. I didn't like it at first, but now I don't know how I feel about it. Do I like him? Honey fuck, I think I do. Is that what the tingles are?* The warm swirling feelings rushed through her, and she bit back a smile.

The ship indicated they had arrived at their destination. and Kortul stood next to her. "Corver, keep an emergency lock on us. If you detect any major changes in vitals, transport us back to the ship, take us home, and alert Mabit and the Corbatton Medical authority. Transport us outside the ship."

Tolina looked all around at the astonishing natural brick red walls of the giant cavern. It was well lit and filled with parked spaceships though most she couldn't imagine in space at all by the level of rust. She followed Kortul to a lift, and he selected a number she knew could not be correct. "Are there six thousand stories in this building?"

He scoffed as he rubbed his brow. "There are, and this is not a building. This is how the entire planet works. They live underground in enormous bunkers. Some levels are commercial, and most are residential which you need clearance to visit. We are heading for the bottom level to the copper dealer's office in the refinery district. They use the planet's molten core for the heating portion of their refining to cut cost."

"Why don't they live on the surface?" Tolina was beyond intrigued and wanted to know more about this planet.

Kortul frowned at her as he answered, "It's nothing but volcanoes and rivers of lava. Several thousand years ago, the planet exploded with volcanism, and it hasn't stopped since. All life which was able escaped underground, you'll see when we stop."

The lift was still moving and didn't come to a stop for several more minutes. When the lift door finally opened, Tolina gasped. The cave was just as tall as the ship hangar, except it was narrower. There was a long road in the center with businesses built from dilapidated rusted metal on either side. It was steamy even with the giant air ducts overhead. They provided air from tall vent stacks on the surface with ash filters, but without a way to pump away the core's heat, the level remained humid.

Any foliage was black instead of green, and she bet their system star gave off a different range of light than an average white star. "They didn't have a white star when they were on the surface did they?"

Kortul pointed to one of the plants as they passed by. "Right. They had a red dwarf star. They're lucky the plant life evolved in dim, red light or their plant life would not have survived the transition."

A reddish orange Warest woman wearing loose fitted clothing was standing in front of an office building with tax preparation written above the door in flashing green lights.

Her sharp horns were as tall as her head and stuck straight up between her temples and pointed high-set ears. She had a wide bottom jaw with an indentation down the center of her chin, no nose, and large round black eyes. Her segmented black tail whipped back and forth, and her curved antennae went straight while she watched Kortul and Tolina pass by.

Kortul pointed to a tall building which stood apart from the rusted buildings around it with its shiny copper plated exterior. The walls of the boxy, filigree etched building sparkled like it had just been polished. There were steps leading to the front doors, and the banister swirled at the ends. The dim red lights shining onto the steps gave the area an eerie feel.

Kortul stood at the end of the steps and waited. Tolina could sense someone coming to the door. When it opened, it was a timid Warest woman with a bright rusty orange complexion. She waved them inside and led them to a staircase. They went upstairs and she brought them into a large room with natural copper formation statues on either side of a tall, curved copper chair. There was a copper table in front of the tall chair with filigree legs and feet. In contrast, the chairs they were provided seemed as though they would fall apart once they sat down. The rust had eaten holes in the seats.

Kortul stood behind the rusted chairs with Tolina at his side. *Where the fuck is this asshole?* She knew from his file that Hewditch Ripecairns would be her next target. They waited several long minutes before Hewditch came in and sat down.

"Saltic."

"Ripecairns, I expect you to deliver on time. A week late

is not acceptable." Kortul glared at the copper refiner, and the man snarled back at him.

Hewditch rose from his seat and pointed at Kortul, "You're no threat like your father, boy. You'll receive the fucking copper when I send it. Your time schedule is not my problem. You are not Saltic the Fourth, and you can't make demands of me. You're stuck with me for forty more years, and if you break contract, you know what happens. Leave my sight."

Kortul stormed out and blew by the woman in the hallway before he made it outside and looked back at the building. "Fuck this place, "Corver, emergency transport us to the ship."

They were too far down, and Corver responded, "Transport failed."

He took off in a near run toward the lift at the end of the long underground road. "Fuck. I hate that man."

"Your dad sounded like a real fun guy." Tolina couldn't help thinking that Kortul's father would be on her hit list if he were still alive.

Kortul scoffed and looked over his shoulder at her, "He planted bugs everywhere and would uncover everything I wanted to keep secret. Growing up with him was a nightmare. He even tormented me with my own innocent childhood questions. He loved to bring me here to embarrass me in front of that fuck." He continued quietly after a short pause, "I live in constant fear of ending up like him."

Tolina wasn't sure what to say, and they rode the lift back to the ship hangar in silence. She was fearful of him ending up like his father too, but was cruelty something from within, or is it something made? *I know all too well most monsters are created. How far does a person need to be pushed to reach that point? I wasn't born loving murder, or was I?*

Kortul was watching her, and she could feel his eyes on her. "I don't want to be like him."

Tolina met his pained eyes and remembered how he felt, warm and caring, and even something more than that. It was a feeling she didn't want to name yet. She wasn't ready to accept those feelings from him yet. *He loves me. Honey fuck! Shut up, Tolina!* "I don't think you are. I don't think you're anything like him." She whispered and wasn't sure Kortul heard her over the windy sound of the lift, but when his shoulders relaxed, she knew he had.

They went back to the ship as quickly as they could, and Tolina tried to think of something to cheer him up as he signaled the airlock to drop the staircase. The cocky Kortul she was used to wasn't shining as usual, and she hated that. Before she could move onto that though, she had to know the consequences of him breaking contract. "What happens if you start buying copper from somewhere else?"

"My father signed a legal document allowing Ripecairns partial ownership of Saltic if copper was purchased from anywhere else. All the contracts are the same. He set it up this way so that his crooked best friends could inherit his company instead of me if I didn't continue doing business with them. No one knew about the contracts until after he was dead. The only way I am free is when the contracts expire, they die, or I die, and my company is sold off." Kortul sat in the captain's chair and manually entered their return course.

Tolina was not giving up on trying to make him feel better and suggested, "My tour of the city gardens was ruined, and I had been thrilled to see it. Do you think you could take me?"

Kortul looked at her as though she had tossed away the sad blanket he had been wrapped in, and he brightened up. "I would love to."

She grinned to herself as he took them home. She couldn't wait to see the gardens with him. *Am I reconsidering my feelings? Is he winning me over? Fuck. I think I will go on one more date, and I'll stop trying after that if things with Kortul keep improving. I hate to admit it, but I was so wrong about him. This is a good man, and he loves me. One more date, and I'll admit to Kortul I'm not looking anymore.*

Chapter 24

Personal Growth and Murder

Stunning flowers from all over the galaxy had been cultivated in the city gardens, but Tolina couldn't care less because Kortul was stroking the exposed skin of her shoulder with his fingertips. The air had warmed, and she was wearing a sleeveless dress. They had been chatting about silly looking violet trumpet flowers when he slipped his arm around her. *How could such a small touch make me want to grind on the seat? Why is this the second hottest thing to ever happened to me? I might fall from my seat when we stop.*

Kortul watched Tolina squirm as she tried to keep a straight face. *She will snap her control, and then she's mine. Mine to keep forever. Funny how 'forever' was a word I never dared to say before, but here I am desperate for it.* He had never once dreamed he would imagine himself growing old with someone. He imagined how she would look with fine lines after years together, and how gorgeous she would be. *I need her. I don't care how many dates she has. I'll sabotage them all until she's mine.* Tolina smiled and pointed to some red flowers with hundreds of petals and a bright yellow center. He wanted to remember this moment forever. Every moment with her was better than the last, and he didn't want the tour to end, but he could see the gate approaching, and their transport on the other side.

Her skin felt chilled with the loss of Kortul's touch, and she reached for him when he held his hand out to help her from the vehicle. He didn't let go of her hand as he led her to the transport. Tolina was enjoying herself, but she kept seeing flashes of Kortul's distress over Hewditch. *That man is dying tonight.* As the system stars began to set on their way back home, she planned how she could go to bed early and just transport from her room before Kortul fell asleep. In the time she had been there he had not bothered her after she went to bed. *What is the risk in him finding out? He's been excited about it every time. Would it be so bad?*

When they return to the apartment, she was lost in thought and headed to her room. "I'm going to bed early. I want to study up on the next planet and people."

Kortul smiled at her, and she was relieved to see he was much more content than earlier. "Sure. I'll see you tomorrow. Goodnight."

Tolina went to her room and leaned on the wall next to her door. She had no idea dating would be so complicated. One thing she knew was not complicated was murder. She changed and tapped her armor tab before grabbing her tablet and asking Mabit if he was home. He responded that he was. "Corver, transport me to Mabit's living area."

Tolina appeared before Mabit who was grinning. "Off to take out another one? Hewditch Ripecairns?"

She smiled back at him, "I cannot wait to gut him. Any advice?"

"Warest do not mingle outside their species besides the worst of them, so unfortunately, I do not have much information for you. The only thing I have heard is they might have empathic senses, so be careful and try to remain a void. Make this one quick."

Nodding, Tolina set her chameleon suit to invisible and waved her hand over her face to raise the nano-tech over her head. "Corver, transport me to my ship."

She stood in front of the view screen. "Corver, engage the cloak and follow the flight plan from earlier today."

In seconds she was in orbit, and the ship was opening a wormhole to Blifordat. Once she was parked in the ship hangar on the Waret's planet, she climbed onto the lift and started the long journey down. Her palms tingled, and she wiggled her fingers as she anticipated her next kill. The thrill was building, but she shoved it down and instead cleared her mind, using her training to wipe away her emotions. She emptied herself of all feeling as she stepped from the lift.

She didn't want to waste time, so she ran toward the building and saw the woman from earlier sweeping with the door open. *I didn't even need to wait for someone to open the door. What a score.*

Tolina tiptoed up the stairs and peaked into the room where she and Kortul met Hewditch. She saw Hewditch standing in the center of the room chocking a Warest woman with her feet dangling under her while she fought for air.

"If you are late again, I will kill you." He threw the woman onto the floor, and Tolina waited until he turned around to face her.

He stopped and stared at her position in the room and narrowed his eyes. "We have an intruder. Ring the alarm, bitch." She scrambled off, and Tolina grinned as she pulled her guns from her suit and opened fire, shooting him over and over in the chest until he landed on the floor. She knew better than to come near him with that sharp tail. Setting her weapons back against her armor for storage, she approached him to finish the job. Knowing Warest were tough, and bullets might not be enough, she reached for her separator as he swung his arms out and grabbed her. She turned the separator on just as she felt something pierce her side. It was his sharp tail. The pain didn't distract her, and she reached up to plunge the separator in the back of his neck and severed his spine. He went limp, and she expected to hear an alarm any moment, but she looked around to find several women staring at his dead body.

Tolina was bleeding, and she held her hand against her side before lifting it and seeing her own clear blood appear to float in the air against her invisible hand. It was deep, and she knew she needed to patch whatever he cut. A few gasps came from the women, and Tolina had a strong feeling she was safe to reveal herself.

She waved her hand in front of her face and showed the women she was also a woman, and they all knelt around her. The oldest woman spoke first. "You are injured. How can we help?"

"I need something to keep it closed so I can make it back to my ship without bleeding out. If you have a needle and thread that will work too." Tolina flipped on her particle separator and cringed as she waved the suit away from her injury. She took a few slow breaths before she began cutting the wound longer so she could see the internal damage. She gagged as she cut the skin on her side just below her ribs enough to see that he had sliced one of her main arteries. "Fuck!" If she didn't repair this quickly, she would die.

She snarled and shouted, "I need that thread and needle now!" One of the women pushed her down and shook her head at Tolina as she held up the needle.

"I will sew you. What flesh should I take to mend it?"

Tolina pointed to the flap of skin she just cut. "There, you can graft it with that skin, and I can have it fixed when I get home. My nano-tech will block the remaining blood flow. It doesn't need to be perfect, just enough that blood isn't squirting out. The armor will hold the rest."

Tolina felt her take the separator from her hand and slice away a bit of her skin. The pain made her nauseous again, and she held back bile from spilling from her throat. The sewing only took a few minutes, and it wasn't perfect, but the bleeding drastically slowed. The woman had sewn her skin over the vein tight enough to reduce blood loss but not prevent blood flow. She put a few stitches in Tolina's skin to hold it together before putting a bandage over the area. "Thank you. I need his personal tablet. I need to make sure my client's funds are transferred back to him."

"I have access, but we will be taking over the business as Hewditch had no male heirs. We would rather honor a mutually beneficial deal. I am his daughter Hewlan, and I have awaited this day for many years. Your agreement would be our first step in a positive direction for our level."

"Agreed."

The woman stood, and all the women gathered and helped Tolina to her feet. Tolina waved her hand over her face. *Fuck, I don't think I can walk far.* "Corver, emergency transport me to the lift."

When she looked up and saw the lift door, she could have cried. *Thank fuck that worked.* One step inside was excruciating, and she tapped the options to take her to the top level. By the time she arrived, she was fighting to stay conscious as the site of her injury began to swell, and her pain was increasing by the second. Once she reached the top, she swallowed a gag. "Corver, emergency transport me to the ship and take me home. When we arrive in the ship's hanger, transport me to Mabit's living room."

Corver complied and within a few minutes she was lying on Mabit's floor and tapping her armor tab. Mabit rushed to her and peeled away the bandage on her side before he whistled. "I have tissue bonders and great pain medication." Mabit rushed away for a few seconds and was back at her side before she could take three breaths.

He took her face in his gentle hands, and he was careful as he tilted her head over and injected her spine with a painkiller. She slumped against the floor. "Thank you. He's dead, but he stabbed me with his tail. I don't think he emptied his venom though. I think I would be dead already if he had."

He began the repair to the skin on her side after he had her artery bonded. "I'm giving you a blood multiplier to counteract your blood loss. I should have gone with you for this target."

Tolina couldn't help but laugh, "One little scratch, and you're having second thoughts?"

"A scratch? This injury could've killed you." Mabit sighed before he continued, "There is only one more, and he will be much easier. He is a lazy fuck who runs his father's company. I have never understood why his father gave him the company last year, but Kortul has made it clear that although he's not as threatening, he is just as much a problem."

Mabit finished repairing her side and helped her to her feet. "I have an intrusive question, and forgive me if you feel I am prying, but I need to know if Kortul is still treating you well."

"I don't mind if you ask. I know it's because you care, and you were both hurt for so long by his father. I haven't noticed Kortul doing anything wrong." Tolina wanted to reassure him further, but she wasn't assured of anything herself. She knew people often hid their true nature for selfish purposes of entrapment, and that was her only remaining fear with Kortul. Would he become someone else if she allowed herself to be with him, or would he still be the same man she was falling for?

Mabit dropped his gaze to the floor before he looked back up at her, almost concerned. "How have your dates been?"

"The last one was so bad I snuck away from him and called Kortul to come get me."

Mabit's demeanor shifted to curiosity. "Oh? Did something happen?"

"He ignored me and kept talking on the phone. It was obnoxious. I jumped out of the tour vehicle at the gardens and ran through the bushes to hide. Kortul picked me up at the gate. He was there faster than I thought possible."

Mabit briefly bit his lips together. "I'm glad he could be there when you needed him. That's good to hear. I have always thought Kortul could be a great man. He just needed a reason to try. Your presence has now given him a reason to strive to be better. I hope, if you choose to move on to another relationship, that you will consider remaining friends with Kortul. He does care for you, and you make him want to be a better person."

Tolina was touched by the sweet sentiment, but she cringed inside at her own train of thoughts. *I make Kortul want to be a better person, but he makes me want to murder people.*

Chapter 25

Last Chance

A ding on her tablet stole her attention from watching Brock smile to himself as he cleaned the giant windows in the apartment living room. She looked down, and it was a reminder for something on her calendar. *I don't have anything scheduled today, do I? I thought the planetary lights were tonight. Kortul wanted me to watch them with him.*

Tolina open the notification to read a reminder for the day, and she saw the plans she made with a man named Otso Kesonen. He was taking her to a play after dinner, which would take hours. Guilt strangled her and she cringed. Kortul came from his room and sat next to Tolina at the table. She wasn't one to hold back when it was necessary, so she admitted the truth, "I fucked up."

Concern was written all over Kortul. "What's wrong? I'm sure I can help you figure it out."

She slid her eyes to him and felt terrible as she admitted, "I may have accepted a date a few days ago not realizing it would be on the same day as the planetary lights tonight."

Kortul did a great job hiding that he was crushed, but she could tell as his gaze fell. She didn't need empathic ability to see hurt all over him. "They happen all night. Maybe you can catch the end with me when you come home." *I can't waste any time tonight. I refuse to watch the sky dancing lights without her beside me.*

Relieved, Tolina smiled at him and assured him, "Thank you for understanding. I was afraid you would be upset. I'm honestly upset I accidentally overlapped it. I know this is important to you."

Kortul smirked at her and reassured, "It's not a problem." *Don't worry my love, I'll waste no time ruining your date. You'll be mine soon enough.*

She went to her room and when she reached for her makeup, she didn't feel like doing much and decided to keep it minimal. She picked out a dress like the one before, uninterested in trying to find anything new. *I can't believe I did something so rude. I assured Otso I was coming, and he bought expensive performance tickets. I cannot cancel even if I want to now.*

She dressed quickly and sat on the end of her bed, staring at her tablet. She pulled up the messages with him and debated on canceling even after she decided that she couldn't cancel on him. Tolina wanted to wash all the makeup from her face and watch the lights with Kortul.

No more dates after this. I don't want to do this anymore. It doesn't feel right dating other people anymore. Tolina huffed when she saw the time and went to her door hoping Kortul wouldn't be waiting for her. She already felt bad enough, and if she had to look at him again, she might not go. She finally went into the hallway and walked toward the living room. Brock was sitting by the kitchen sink soaking his feet in steaming water, but otherwise, the room was empty.

She waved to Brock, and he was groggy as he waved back at her. *That must be one hell of a foot soak.*

"Corver, transport me to the sidewalk in front of the building."

In his room, Kortul was ready in his chameleon armor, and he heard her request, so he quickly asked, "Corver, transport me behind Tolina."

Kortul spotted Tolina searching for her date and she saw him waving at her. He had a deep green face and brown hair with a brown neck. He wore a nice dress suit and held his hand out for her to help her into the transport. Kortul slipped in and sat across from them.

Tolina smiled, but Kortul could tell her heart was not behind it. "Otso? I am Tolina. It is nice to meet you." She didn't want to be on the date, and Kortul sagged in the seat with relief.

Otso was kind and attentive as he shifted to face her. "Tolina, I have been looking forward to tonight. I have reserved a table at one of the highest demand restaurants in the city. It's called Kiener's. It's on the rooftop of a building a few blocks away."

"That sounds delightful." Tolina seemed to be pleased with his plans, and she relaxed into the seat. Kortul frowned as he mouthed 'that sounds delightful' to himself before he recalled the open style kitchen of the restaurant. *That does sound charming. Fuck, I should have thought of that.*

When they arrived at the building, Otso escorted Tolina from the transport. Kortul had to dive and roll on the ground to avoid being slammed in the door. *Fuck, that was close.*

Kortul was not squeezing in a lift with those two, so he waited for the next group of people. When he arrived at the restaurant, he spotted them at one of the viewing tables and made his way over, finding a seat on a bench surrounded by foliage.

He listened as Tolina giggled and chatted with Otso. *Should I just kill him? I could strangle him in the bathroom when he's there to vomit from the poison I brought.* A Wendi man with a purple face approached the table and Kortul came up behind him to find out what Otso's order would be.

"I would like the daily fish special, and she would like the syrup I asked to be made available." *He stole my move! Fuck this guy. I would have just added a little, but you just earned yourself the rest of the bottle. I hope you shit your pants.*

Kortul took off for the kitchen and waited for the special, which was spicy pasta with fish to finish cooking. He watched the server check an order and take it over to another table before coming back and waiting for Otso and Tolina's food. Kortul kept his eyes on the Chef to start to slide the plates over to the server, and he knew he only had seconds. He pulled the poison from his pocket as the plate appeared and popped the cap open before sloshing it in Otso's plate. He yanked his hand back as the server grabbed the plate. *That was too fucking close. This poison better work as quickly as the company claims.*

He returned to his spot on the bench and watched as Otso devoured his food. *Perfect, eat it all.* Kortul read the poison only took around five minutes to start the nausea, and around ten to start the vomiting. He watched the time on the wall at the opposite end of the restaurant, and a few seconds before the five minutes was up, he heard a gag.

Kortul looked over, and Otso had his napkin over his mouth. Tolina's back went straight, and he wished he could see Otso's face better from his spot, but people were moving around too much for him to shift. Otso gagged again and stood up before trying to make it to the bathroom. Instead, he spewed vomit onto the floor and Tolina flew from her seat and sprinted from the restaurant. Kortul ran after her and judging by the direction she ran, he knew she was running home. They were close to home, and he wanted to be back in their apartment in time to beat her there. "Corver, emergency transport me to my bedroom."

The moment he was back in his room, he stripped off the chameleon armor and shoved it in his safe before he dressed in black lounge pants. He came from his room and sat on his long grey couch before selecting the news since it was on. A few minutes later, Tolina transported in, and she was silent as she walked to her room. As much as he knew he should feel guilty, he didn't at all.

She came back out in a loose t-shirt and sleep shorts with her face freshly washed. When she came around the couch to sit next to him, she fell over onto the cushion.

"You were gone less than an hour."

"He threw up on the *honey fucking floor* of the restaurant. It was so bad I ran. Is it bad that I don't feel guilty about leaving him there?" Tolina grimaced as she looked over at Kortul, who was having a hard time holding back a smile.

"No. I don't think you should feel guilty about leaving him there. He should not have gone out if he felt sick." Kortul bit down on his own tongue to the point of drawing blood to keep from laughing. *If I laugh right now, she will know and hate me forever. Don't fucking laugh dumbass!* Kortul forced himself to calm and they quietly watched the news until the sky outside darkened. "The planetary light show will start soon. We can slip on coats over our lounge clothes, and I have a hot spiced apple drink queued up in the replicator."

"That sounds great."

Kortul grabbed their coats and made their hot drinks, and she met him by the table after she slipped her shoes on. He slid her coat on before sliding on his own, and he grabbed both drinks. "Corver, transport us to the pool patio."

There were a few other people on the rooftop, and the wind was increasing. "Corver, turn on the rooftop wind shielding." The wind abruptly stopped, and although the air was still cold, it didn't seem that way with their coats. Tolina followed Kortul as he sat down on the outdoor couch by the steaming hot tub, and she sat beside him. Mabit and Tyce appeared one after the other and joined them in the small seating area. After a few minutes, several more people were on the rooftop, mingling and chatting.

Kortul and Tolina sat quietly as they sipped their drinks. She couldn't help thinking about her awful date. *Am I a bad person for being glad the date ended quickly so I could come back here and watch the planetary light show? I am convinced I should feel bad, but I don't.*

There was a flicker before intensely bright colored light was painted across the sky. She wasn't sure what she was expecting, but being able to hear the sounds from the explosions made the experience all that more incredible. The volatile gases of the nebula were detonating as they met the atmosphere of the planet, and just like lightning, the sound waves were delayed like thunder. The thunderous sound combined with the rainbow of color from the various elements mixed into the nebula made for a stunning experience.

Tolina wasn't sure when it happened, but she felt Kortul pressing her against his side with his arm around her. She didn't want to admit how good it felt. She felt at home with him.

When the show was over, and everyone had said their goodbyes, Tolina went to her room and fell face first into her bed. She remained face down as she willed the heat gathering deep in her belly to fade. *Stop it right now. This is the worst timing.*

She screamed into her covers and ran to her bathroom to splash cold water on her face. *I want to burst in there and tell him the truth. I've been lying to myself. I care about him, and I don't know when it happened. I think he loved me from the moment he first saw me, and I've been so wrong about everything.*

She groaned as she tried to block the heat brewing inside when she realized Kortul probably had his cock in his hand again. She couldn't help but imagine she was sitting on that cock. She gasped and splashed more chilly water on her face before she ran to the replicator and had it make her a sleeping pill. As soon as it was finished, she swallowed it and lay down in her bed. She stared at the beautiful colors of the sky as the sleeping pill began to do its job, and finally drifted to sleep.

Outside her door, Kortul was leaning on the wall in the hallway after his shower, and he squeezed his eyes shut as he rubbed his face. No amount of making himself cum would work. He needed Tolina, and his cock ached inside of him. When he went back to his room and climbed in bed. He heard his door open, and he shot his head up to see who it was.

It was Brock, and he teetered over to Kortul's bed. "I had bad dream. You were gone."

This is the worst timing ever. I know I'll wake up with a hard cock and him perched on my back like a barnacle. Dammit, he looks so sad. Fuck. I could never send him back to his room. I can't believe I'm about to let a two-foot tall fifty year old man sleep in my bed with me, again. I know some Eckolie do this, and its normal, but this would be better ANY other night. He knew he shouldn't be surprised. Brock had been doing this for years. "Come on." Kortul felt Brock crawl over him, and he didn't start the night on the other side of the bed as he usually did. No, Brock stuck himself to Kortul's back and made himself comfortable.

I guess this is payback for all the times I went to Mabit's scared in the middle of the night when I was a kid. Kortul remembered as a child once frightening Mabit so badly he fell from his bed, and he smiled at the memory as he tried to ignore the snoring old man stuck to his back.

Chapter 26

The Calm

Scowling, Tolina huffed at her tablet as she snuggled in a blanket on the couch in the living room. She was the only one awake and had just received a message from Otso. He apologized in a long formal note and begged her to give him a second chance. *Not happening. I'm not looking anymore.* She thought she should reply and say no at least, but she set her tablet down when she saw Kortul come from his room. He seemed exhausted and when he saw Tolina, he chuckled a bit under his breath and turned around.

Brock was asleep in a huddle stuck to his back, and it was so cute she wanted to squeal. Tolina giggled as Kortul made himself some toast and joined Tolina. In a serious whisper Kortul explained, "He had a bad dream."

There was no way Tolina was messaging anyone else in a romantic sense ever again. Brock looked so peaceful and safe, and she felt the same way. The idea of setting aside her freedom made her want to sob, and she decided she would spend part of her day grieving and moving on from it. Tolina's greatest fear was losing her freedom. She only had it for a single day of her life. No matter who she handed it over to, it was still not *hers*. It would never be hers, and that stung so deep to her core she felt her skin heat. *Maybe Kortul will spend the day with me. The more time I spend with him the easier this becomes. If I'm choosing him, I need to be sure this is right. So much has happened, and it's been such a short time. I think I just need a little more time to see what a good person he is because I think that if I had met Kortul under different circumstances, I would have chosen him without a second thought.*

"What are you thinking about?" Kortul took a bite of his toast and chewed as he waited for her to answer.

She didn't answer. What could she say? Tolina would tell him the truth, but she knew the moment Kortul was aware of how she felt, he would seduce her within an inch of her life. She sensed depraved feelings in him more than once, and it was always when his wanting eyes were on her. *Or when he was whispering my name in the shower.* She imagined him in the shower and had to fight the urge to climb on his lap and straddle him. *I need to stop before I jump on him. I can't do that with Brock on his back! It's too early. I need to calm down.*

Kortul swallowed his last bite of toast. "How are you feeling after what happened yesterday?"

She kept cycling from desire to fear to grief, and right back to desire. Tolina wondered if she was experiencing a fluctuation due to her empathic ability developing and admitted, "Not great. My mood keeps cycling. Maybe I'm having another emotional wave. It's not as intense, but the moment I think of something bothering me I become wound in my thoughts."

"When Brock wakes up, let's go to the pool and sit in the

daylight. Darkness helps Vitolas, so I assume since butterflies are daytime creatures that you could use some daylight."

Tolina felt her brewing feelings burst like a bubble in her chest and hid her face in her hands as tears erupted in her eyes. Kortul put his arm around her and rubbed her shoulder as she admitted, "This is so embarrassing. I was taught my entire life crying and emotion makes you weak and vulnerable. Our leaders were truly cruel to do this to us. We were not meant to be cold; we were meant to be free. We need to allow our deep feelings to exist so we could develop our empathic ability."

Kortul knew that feeling and he thought maybe if he shared his own experience, she wouldn't feel so alone. "My father gave me a pet lizard as a young child, and I loved it so much I must have drawn a of picture of it every day. I had it for a few years until one day I said I didn't want to go with my father on a business meeting because the man he planned to meet was a disgusting child abuser and I didn't want to be around him. My father either gave the lizard away or killed it, but I never saw it again, and I cried for months. He recorded me crying and would threaten to play the recordings when I would have Tyce over to visit as a teenager. I know it's not the same, but I can understand having to bottle up who you are to protect yourself."

"What happened to the drawings? Do you still have them?" Tolina asked and wished she hadn't as Kortul seemed even more sad than he had moments before.

Kortul took a slow breath and replied, "He was mad about a bad progress grade and burned them. The patio had a fire pit where the hot tub is now."

"Did he ever follow through on showing the recordings?" Tolina knew it wasn't nice to pry, but she had to know the extent of this. Kortul's detached behavior before made more sense the more she learned about his childhood. He was terrified of something he loved being used to hurt him, as he chose to avoid love altogether. *Until now.*

He smiled, and his entire mood shifted in an instant. "He did show Tyce. We were seventeen, and Tyce didn't say a word to him. Tyce waited to say something after my father left the room, and he told me my father reminded him of dirty, smashed chewing gum on the sidewalk. He's not that great at insults, but the disgust on his face told me who my real family was."

"What about Mabit, I mean before your father...?" Tolina didn't want to say the rest. She meant when his father almost beat him to death.

"My father hid it from Mabit. Mabit was the only person in the universe my father ever cared about, and Mabit never saw the truth until my father almost killed me." Kortul's mind flashed to that day. Mabit rushed in and hit his father so hard he landed several feet away. Mabit emergency transported Kortul to his apartment and that was all Kortul remembered. He woke up some time later in Mabit's bed with Mabit slumped in a chair asleep beside him. Kortul never saw his father alive again.

Tolina leaned into him. "I'm so glad you have Mabit. I see why you are so close."

"Life has been peaceful since my father died, other than the contracts I'm trapped in."

He doesn't know about the murder yet. Kortul turned on the news as usual and adjusted the volume low, and Tolina watched the screen knowing the news may not report the story. She knew from her research Ripecairns was not as well known as Vespuc, but she wasn't sure how wide Ripecairns's copper production reach was on the galactic scale.

Tolina bit her lips together as a headline ran across the bottom announcing the Ripecairns's company was under new ownership following his death of natural causes. She turned and watched Kortul's mouth drop open, and he climbed over the couch to grab his tablet from his room. When he came back, Brock was walking alongside him rubbing his eyes. Brock went to the kitchen as Kortul came back and sat next to her to check his messages. She watched as he scanned through a message, and she could see it had been sent by Ripecairns daughter.

"Hewlan Ripecairns wants a holo-meeting as soon as possible." Kortul tapped the option to connect the meeting, and Hewlan answered quickly as her face appeared above his glass tablet.

"Mr. Saltic, I am Hewditch's daughter Hewlan and I have assumed ownership after my father's *fortunate* death. I would prefer to continue supplying you with premium copper for your chip production. Your copper delivery will be above previous contract specifications so that I may work to regain your trust."

Did she just say fortunate death? "Fortunate? I will skip condolences for congratulations then. I look forward to receiving the new shipment. Thank you." Kortul was confused, but pleased, as the call ended, and he looked over at Tolina. Curiosity was burning a hole in his head, and he blinked each of his eyes individually as he tried to understand what just occurred. "That was fucking weird."

Tolina was glad for her current somber mood because she wasn't sure if she would be able to hold a straight face. "I don't think it's weird at all. She just wants to make sure you will still do business with her."

"No. Not that part. The part about how the second man Saltic had an unwanted contract with was murdered, is weird."

Kortul stared at her with his glossy black eyes, and she shrugged, "Doesn't it mean you're closer to freedom? Who cares. I bet everyone they knew wanted to kill those two."

"You are right about that." She was right, but it didn't matter. Kortul felt curiosity sink in further. He needed to know what was happening because *something* was happening. *This is too many good things in a row. My Toli appearing, Vespuc was murdered by a rightfully angry parent, and now Ripecairns is dead? Hewditch was not old. I'm sure he was murdered, and by his daughter if I had to guess.* He huffed under his breath knowing he would probably never have the answer. "Go put on a bathing suit. I guess it's time to celebrate. It might be confusing, but it's a win."

Tolina smiled at him and went to her room to change as he did the same in his room. They met in the hallway, and Kortul asked, "Corver, transport us to the patio and turn on the wind shielding."

Tolina loved how tall the building was with its stunning view of the city. The air was still cold from the night, and she resisted a shudder. Kortul handed her a drink, and it smelled floral and light. She sipped it then narrowed her eyes in disbelief at Kortul. "Does this have alcohol in it?! It's not even mid-morning!"

Kortul laughed as he sipped his drink. "Who is here to tell us we can't?"

Tolina frowned and lifted her drink to her lips again. He was right. *Who cares?*

She gave in to the cold and trembled a bit, and Kortul noticed. "We should sit in the hot tub until the air warms."

She almost tripped on her own feet as she ran to the steaming water while she tried to force away another shiver. She stepped onto the first stair, but it was too late, and her exuberant tremor was so violent her drink sloshed from her cup as water shot up around her ankles. "Fuck!" She jumped down into the hot water trying to stop the shaking and caused splashes over the edge.

Kortul shook with laughter, and he dumped his drink on the ground. He had to sit down on the side of the hot tub with his hands over his mouth trying to regain composure. "I knew I would eventually see it, but I was not prepared for how funny it would be. You should see your face!" Kortul scrunched his face trying to mimic her expression and laughed all over again while she scowled at him and crossed her arms.

"Quit laughing and make us new drinks!"

"No, I'll never stop laughing about what you just did, but yes, I will make us new drinks."

She rolled her eyes as he pulled his legs from the water and made them new drinks at the replicator. When he had two new drinks in his hand, he climbed back in and sat next to her.

Tolina had just begun to relax when Mabit appeared and came over to sit in a chair by them. "Did you see the news?"

Kortul held his drink up. "Why do you think we're celebrating?"

Mabit smiled and winked at Tolina. "Well, you two have fun celebrating. I have a busy day. Corver, transport me home." He disappeared, and Tolina had to hold back a laugh.

Kortul peered over at her with a sly gaze. "You must be good luck."

Tolina bit her cheek and sipped her drink to avoid busting herself. *I need to change the subject.* "I know we are not sitting in this hot tub drinking all day."

Kortul acted as if he were offended with his hand on his chest. "And why not?" He waited a few seconds, and when she just stared at him, he continued, "What do you want to do?"

"How am I supposed to answer that when we are a transport and a wormhole away from almost anywhere in your central galaxy?" Tolina snarled at him and sipped her drink.

He shrugged as he thought for a moment. "I know I will regret this, but do you want to play night-ball with me? Our people have intense color vision and over a thousand years ago someone created a two-player game played in a blacked-out court with bright, colorful obstacles. It's popular on Vumenko too. It has one small fluorescent orange ball, and the object is to move around the obstacles on the court and arrive with the ball in between the opposite player's goal posts. The best part is you're allowed to use full body contact to prevent the opposite player from scoring."

Tolina grinned to herself as she thought about how fun that would be, but she remembered they were meeting her next target the following day, and she didn't want to be exhausted for it. She also had a stack of documents to sift through for the meeting so she could be prepared to take him out afterward. "As incredible as it sounds, we will need to postpone those plans. We have your meeting with Pollard tomorrow, and we both need to rest today." *I will enjoy kicking your ass in that game when we can play it.*

Kortul leaned back and tipped up his drink before admitting, "I forgot about that fucking meeting. I hate that guy the most. He is disgusting and I find him so repulsive even thinking about him makes my skin crawl. If he tried to touch me, I would scream like a child and not be ashamed about it."

Tolina cringed as she drank a few gulps of her drink. "I'm sorry I had to ruin the fun."

Kortul slid his arm around her and pulled her close. "You didn't ruin anything. You couldn't ruin my fun if you tried. You would kick my ass in night-ball."

Chapter 27

Pollard Gondek Tweed

Following Kortul from the ship's airlock and down the stairs, Tolina understood why they didn't request a direct transport to the building. The planet Delvianit was more beautiful than any of the descriptions from the information she received.

Four hundred foot evergreen trees lined a river so wide it looked like a lake from where she stood on the giant wooden ship landing deck. Giant snowcovered mountains peeked between the trees taunted her to fly over them, but she knew the ice would freeze her wings. She and Kortul walked to the edge of the landing deck and peered down the river where the line of trees seemed to stretch forever.

"This planet would be wonderful to visit for a vacation, but when you meet Pollard, you'll understand why I don't come here. He is too nasty. The thought of him being on the same planet as I am is not worth it. He eats cups of cold butter and always has candy stuck to him. He smells like a giant crab shit on a candy store before someone bulldozed it and let it rot for a few days. You're lucky your armor filters smells." Tolina was glad the nano-tech was covering her face because her lips twisted up in disgust as she held back a giggle. "Let's get this meeting over with." Kortul turned around and led her to a pathway between the trees and they walked for a few minutes before coming upon a enormous cabin. The logs used for it were as wide as the shift they arrived in.

The trees used to build this cabin are wider than the trees growing around us. That's unreal. I should kill this guy just so we can visit this planet. We need to come back here. Something about the place made her heart sing. *I wonder if this is what my ancient people's planet was like before my people were killed off there. If that had never happened, our people would never have turned toward the military to take over and lead us.* She watched Kortul walk up to the door for it to scan him for entry, and something occurred to her as they went inside. *If my people had never lost their planet, I wouldn't have ended up an assassin, I would have never met Kortul, and I wouldn't be here right now. So many things to think about later. Right now, I need to pay attention because, armor filter or not, I can tell this place smells terrible.* The dining room table was covered in a rotting hog feast and rodents scurried about devouring the decomposing scraps. Kortul startled when he saw it and rushed to a hallway with a door at the end.

When Kortul opened the door, Tolina had to resist grabbing him and dragging him from the cabin. There was a gaunt Zaerini man in a torn plush chair with stacks of what appeared to be heavy crystalline drugs on a table in front of him. A holo-movie was playing, and Pollard curled the edge of his big round ears and grimaced at them as he turned his volume down. "I assume you're here to confirm your silicone contract for this quarter, but I'm busy so you'll need to come back next week."

Kortul wasn't playing his game. "Last time I needed the confirmation from you, you made me come back three times. Confirm it now with a tap on your tablet. I can leave, and I won't need to return. You are not busy, you're just ready for another hit. That drug is not addictive, and your people don't have genes for addiction. You are choosing to sit here and turn yourself into a raisin because your father isn't here to tell you otherwise. Confirm the damn shipment, Pollard."

Pollard stood and his wide flat, brown tail slapped the chair as he pointed a bony finger to the door. "Get out Saltic! I don't need to do shit for you. Too bad your own home planet won't give you the silicone you need, and you need to come here to beg for it. Oh wait, you don't have a choice because your father bound you to my father and we have the same fucking name, so you're trapped! I'll squeeze you until you break and watch your company crash before you'll ever reach the end of your contract with me. Now get the fuck out before I call my cats."

Kortul whirled around and grabbed Tolina before he half ran them from the cabin. The moment they were outside the front door, he asked, "Corver, emergency transport us back to the ship and take us home."

They were back in their apartment in just a few minutes, and when Kortul looked around at the familiar surroundings, he grasped his hair in his fists. "Fuck! I want to kill him! I need that damn shipment! The factory has run out of our entire back supply of silicone."

Tolina would take immense pleasure in this kill, but first

she needed to know what the cats meant. "What did he mean by the cats?"

"He has four trained mountain lions for protection."

Tolina nodded in understanding. *I love cats, too bad I won't be there long enough to see them, or will I when I come back?*

"If my father would have had the name on the contract listed as Pollard Gondeck Tweed the first, and not just Pollard Gondeck Tweed, I wouldn't be stuck with his son. When Pollard the first gave his company to his son Pollard the second last year, I had to find out the hard way I was still fucking trapped. I spent a small fortune trying to be free of that contract, and I still can't understand how the Wendi court didn't rule in my favor. I would've had him killed by now, but I'm trying not to live up to my father's image."

Tolina could tell his anger was lingering. "What can we do to help you feel better?"

His shoulders relaxed. "We should watch a horror movie."

She had never heard of that before, but it sounded fantastic. "Great. I'll change and meet you back out here."

Kortul seemed a bit lighter as they went to their rooms, and they changed into comfortable clothes before sitting on the couch together. He flipped through movies and stopped when he found two he wanted to see. "Weird horror killer slugs or serial killer who targets crooked politicians."

"The second one sounds amazing."

He smirked as he turned it on and Tolina didn't mind when he tugged her closer and wrapped his arms around her. She enjoyed the movie, but Kortul wiggling next to her as he watched the brutal murders was making her giggle to herself. His hand was resting on her side, and he could feel her holding in her giggles. By the second murder he whispered, "You hush, not everyone has killed people. This is fucking disturbing even if they do deserve it."

The moment he finished whispering, the killer burst out and stabbed a man in the stomach, spilling his guts and Kortul shook his head. "Bleh. That's so nasty, but this is helping though, so we're finishing it."

Tolina couldn't hold her amusement back and laughed and Kortul squeezed her sides, causing her to laugh harder, and before she knew it, they were on the floor wrestling. Although Kortul was twice her size, he stood no hope against Tolina. He only won when she allowed it. Over the course of half of the movie, Kortul was beaten by Tolina to the point of him tapping for release eleven times. She was consistent like clockwork, and it took her less than four minutes to win each time.

He lay on the ground panting. "Do you turn into a noodle when I grab you? How do you slip away like that? You're like an oily, wiggling noodle!"

Tolina collapsed next to him laughing. "How does it feel to be beaten by someone half your size?"

"I can honestly say I don't mind because you're on my side, but if you weren't, I would be very upset right now," Kortul admitted, and Tolina was giggling all over again.

She tried to think about ways to cheer him up, and Tolina remembered all the drawings of his lizard. "Will you show me what your old lizard looked like?"

A scream erupted on the screen and Kortul tugged her close during the brutal murder scene, and something about that was endearing. He whispered over her hair, "I would love to. There is a habitat center with one, and it's short a walk down the street, but it's cold and we need to dress warm."

They quickly dressed in warm street clothes. Kortul handed over her coat before he slipped his own on. "Corver, transport us to the sidewalk in front of the building."

Tolina pulled her hood over her head when she felt the wind from the street, and this time when Kortul slid his arm around her, it wasn't around her shoulders. He wrapped his hand around her side, and she melted into his warmth as they walked. The sidewalk was busy, but Tolina didn't mind. She loved watching all the chattering people as they went by. Everyone seemed so happy here.

They approached a tall building with Reptile Preserve and Rehabilitation Center written above the tall main door. When they went inside, she was expecting some kind of front desk, but it was more like walking into a swamp. Kortul lead them down a central stone path and to a lift at the back of the building.

They rode the lift to the third level, and when the lift door opened, Tolina was again introduced to an environment which was stark in comparison to the last. It resembled an arid desert, and he brought her over to a small section with a lizard which walked on two legs and had a fleshy pointed protrusion around its neck. It moved its head back and forth at them before running off. "That one was like mine." Kortul spoke softly, and Tolina could tell he needed this.

"This environment doesn't look like anywhere on Corbatton."

He shook his head. "No, it resembles a moon circling our system's largest gas giant. We have a few moons with basic microbial life, but this moon has bugs and lizards. My people tried to build on the planet, but there was a bug which burrowed into other insects, and it loved the taste of Wendi feet. The only thing we have left from their project were these lizards they brought back."

"They are so cute. I see why you loved yours so much."

They went around and looked at a few more habitats before they started back to their apartment. "Can I ask you a personal question?" It had been gnawing at Kortul, and he couldn't hold it in any longer.

"Sure." Tolina had a feeling she knew what he would ask as she watched him tapping his foot.

Kortul paused for a bit and asked, "Do you have any more dates planned?"

"I knew that was coming. No, I don't." Tolina could sense his relief, but she wasn't ready for more, so she didn't elaborate. She still had a target to eliminate first. Being with Kortul and killing someone behind his back was not something she wanted on her conscience.

He seemed content, and when they returned to their apartment, Mabit was there with a box. "Someone delivered this to my front door, and it has your address on it. I didn't read the date, and I don't know how long it's been sitting there, but it's been a while."

He handed it to Kortul and when he opened the box he laughed, "Tolina, it's the honey I ordered for you. I forgot all about it."

The box came apart at the seams and slowly opened to reveal a perfectly round glass container with a tall cork stopper. The front of the glass was etched with the company name, but it was written in the Vitolas language, and the translator lenses she had in her eyes didn't have a word to replace it with. "I can't believe you ordered this for me. How much did it cost? Wait. I don't want to know. Don't tell me." She opened it and held the cork while Kortul poured her a bowl of it. To stop the thick flow, she had to cork it before they lifted it away from the bowl. She didn't want to spill any of it. Tolina unraveled her tongue and tried it. The sweet viscous liquid was better than she remembered. "This is so good." She watched Kortul stick his finger in her bowl to taste it, and when he stuck his finger in his mouth, he seemed much more shocked than she anticipated. Kortul sucked the honey off his finger, and she had to fight the urge to rub her thighs together.

"Until now I thought only you would be able to tell the difference in the quality honey or syrup, but I was wrong. That tastes like fucking heaven." *I bet this is how your pussy tastes.* Kortul fought a groan and his mouth watered as he swallowed the honey.

Chapter 28

Murder and a Mud Mask

When Tolina was sure Kortul was preparing for sleep, she slipped on her chameleon armor. "Corver, transport me to Mabit's apartment."

"Hello, Tolina, my dear. I knew you would be stopping by tonight. Be careful and make sure Pollard receives what is due. He is now rumored to be involved with trafficking his planet's neglected populations. Interesting enough, the story came out a few hours ago. What nice timing, don't you think?" Mabit chuckled as he bit down on a piece of fruit from his plate. He was sitting at his dining table facing her, and she sat across from him for a moment before she left.

"I've been lucky every time. That's the only thing that concerns me with this one." Tolina admitted, and she watched as Mabit smiled at her, his warm fatherly demeanor always made her feel loved and safe. She adored him.

"I have no doubt you will be home soon with news of your efficient kill."

She grinned at him before she stood by her chair and waved her hand over her face to cover her head with the nano-tech armor. She turned on the chameleon feature and wiggled her hips. "Corver, transport me to my ship."

She sat in the captain's chair and turned on the cloak through her armor. "Corver, take the same route we took earlier today to Delvianit."

The computer complied, and in a few minutes, she was on the wooden landing deck of the heavily forested planet. It was dark, and according to the synchronized planet time listed on her display, it was close to midnight. *It must've been early evening when we were here.*

She wasn't wasting any time, and she ran down the trail toward the giant house. She watched patiently until she saw a Zaerini guard come out for a bathroom break. When he finished relieving himself, she walked close behind him and followed him inside. She counted just two guards, and they were seated in a room next to the front door of the cabin watching surveillance screens for the entire house. She came in and studied the feeds before she saw arms reaching out from an animal transport cage behind the home. *I wonder where his cats are. Feeding him to his cats might be better than making him eat his toes. I think I need to find out.*

Tolina pulled her silent guns from her hips and shot both the guards in the head at the same time, and they slumped over onto one another before falling on the floor. She watched for several more seconds to be sure there were no more guards, and she shook her head. She knew there were mountain lions here, but did he sincerely have the rest of this home unguarded?

Checking under the surveillance screens, she noticed an unlocked tablet and tapped on the screen. The controls for the home security system had been left open on under the view screens. She turned off everything. *A fresh assassin could have handled this job.*

Tolina went straight back to the room where she knew he was, and the door was open when she came down the hallway. Before she even reached the doorway, she could see all four of his sleepy eyed mountain lions lounging around his chair and she eyed the chandelier of antlers. *Oh, this is too perfect.*

She crept toward him and hoped she didn't fall as she climbed the chair to perch above him. *Don't fucking fall off, Tolina. This is not the time to be clumsy.* Once she was in position, she lifted her separator from her armor and hid the handle in her hand as she leaned over his head. He was groggy and half asleep and lolled back in the chair with no shirt on.

Tolina turned on the separator and sliced it across his lower belly dumping his intestines onto the floor. He shook and gurgled as he screamed, and Tolina grabbed his tablet from the arm of his chair before she jumped onto the chandelier above her to hang on and watch. All four of the mountain lions pounced and began devouring him. He screamed and thrashed as they ate him, and she was shocked at how long it took him to die. This was by far one of her favorite kills, and technically, she didn't even do it. The mountain lions did.

She tapped on his tablet menu and found his banking account, but a security notification came up, and she needed a facial scan. His face was below her, and though it was frozen in a permanent scream, it was close enough, so she tried. It chimed and allowed her into the account. She transferred half of the money from his account to Mabit's rolling account before she broke the tablet and tossed the pieces.

When the mountain lions became full and slowed their movements, she swung from the chandelier and landed in the doorway. After she shut the door behind her, she moved toward the back of the home and into the kitchen where she found a pantry with fruit, vegetables, and all sorts of dry snacks. She filled an empty box with as much food as she could and went through a door leading behind the home. Tolina walked down a long dirt path until she reached the cage filled with emaciated Zaerini people. She set the box down in front of the cage, and a few people gasped 'ghost' before an annoyed voice announced, "It's someone in chameleon armor. Don't be stupid."

She turned on her separator to cut the lock as she explained, "This box is filled with food. There are lions in the home, so do not go there for any reason. Get away from here and run as quickly as you can for help."

A few more gasps rang out as well as a few 'thank you's' before she set her separator against her armor to store it and dashed through the woods toward her ship. *It's over. Kortul is free!* Tolina was so thrilled she shouted, "Corver, transport me to my ship and take me home."

When she made it to the hangar and transported into Mabit's living room, he was wrapped in a blanket on his couch, reading something on his tablet. She turned off her chameleon setting and tapped her armor tab.

"It's done? He's dead?" Tolina nodded and Mabit gave her a bright and beautiful smile. "You did well. I'm so proud of you."

Tolina felt so loved in that moment she could have jumped on him to hug him, but he looked comfortable, and she didn't want to disturb his peace. "Thank you. Corver, transport me to my room."

Tolina was tingling with joy and she wasn't sure if she would be able to fall asleep anytime soon, so she decided to dig under her bathroom cabinets and find out what Kortul had stored away in there. She pulled mud masks, floral creams, and all sorts of makeup removers from the cabinet and set them on the counter. After opening the mud mask and slathering it all over her face, she stripped off her under clothes and rubbed *all* the floral creams over her body. *It smells so good.* She sniffed too close to one of the creams and some of it ended up on the tip of her nose, as well as some mud ending up in the cream container. *Damn.*

She danced around a bit before she rinsed off and dressed in some lounge clothes, a loose crop and shorts. One boring ocean documentary later, and she was asleep on the couch in the little seating area in her room. She woke a few hours later and looked around confused before collapsing in her bed to sleep the rest of the night.

When she woke up in the morning, she might as well have been flying as she leapt out of bed and rushed to her door. She came around the corner to see if Kortul was awake, and he was already sitting on the couch watching the news. It was just financial updates. She eased around the couch and sat next to him, but all he did was look over at her and back at the news with his mouth hanging open and his eyes wide.

She narrowed her eyes at him and asked, "What's wrong?"

He smiled at her with his brow furrowed and shook his head before he barked a laugh. "He's fucking dead! They just aired a brief segment on it. Pollard, that disgusting piece of shit is dead. It's over. I'm not trapped anymore. His fucking cats ate him. I don't know how the fuck this could have happened. Happiness and confusion are such an odd combination."

Tolina tried to act surprised. "Really? He's dead?"

"There was a story about him being involved with trafficking. I wonder if this mysterious murderer is a new vigilante. Do you think it could be the same person killing all these people? I know his cats didn't just eat him. Someone set this up."

She shrugged, "I have no idea," as she heard Brock come from his room with cleaning supplies.

After waving and smiling at Brock, Kortul moved down the couch closer to Tolina and wrapped his arms around her with his eyes full of wonder. "I just wish I knew who was killing them. I would find a way to thank them. I feel like they deserve it at this point." Kortul chuckled a bit and they watched the rest of the news with his arms wrapped around her. With her in his arms, he couldn't help it, he had to touch her more. He needed to feel her. He started by stroking his fingers along her side, but when she didn't stop him, he rested his hand against her exposed belly.

Tolina was dying inside. She froze in place as Kortul began brushing his thumb against her flesh. *Please don't stop.* He slid his hand into the band of her shorts to move it down a bit, and he began tracing his fingers along her side before he trailed his fingers just above the band of her shorts. Her pussy was soaked, and she could have cried when she realized the news was ending.

When the news was over, he stood up and reached his hand out to help her up. "We should plan some trips off world. We need to visit Vumenko where the Vitolas are from. They have taller trees than Delvianit, and most of them live in homes at the tops of the trees. Their planet only has a few hours of daylight because its orbit is behind binary gas-giants, so everything has bioluminescence. Visiting is like taking drugs without having to take any drugs."

Tolina loved the idea of traveling, but it didn't feel right to be accepting all these lavish gifts. "That sounds magical, but also so expensive. Don't you want to go somewhere that you would like? Or maybe something not so expensive sounding?"

Kortul laughed as he walked off to his room and came back with his tablet. "Enough talk about cost. Anyone on my planet can afford to go to Vumenko for a month or more. Let's book a trip right now."

Tolina felt little bees tumbling around in her stomach because she knew what this trip would mean. A planet of almost complete darkness, beautiful bioluminescent creatures, empathic beings like herself, and this loving man who was making it clear he would stop at nothing to have her. She didn't regret waiting though. She was sure of what she wanted now, and what she wanted was Kortul. He had become her best friend, and now she knew she was ready for more. The guilt was fading, and she didn't feel so trapped anymore. She felt cared for and safe.

She sat across from him at the table, and he pulled up a holographic image of the resort he was booking. "I want to stay in this room here in the canopy. This says the rooms are built over the original nesting ground of the lunar moths which eventually evolved into the Vitolas people. There is a cave with ancient drawings from the original protectors of the sacred area beside the resort. The revenue from the resort goes to maintaining the space and keeping it safe. See, it's perfect. We should go. I am booking us a few days there, and we can leave tomorrow." Kortul tapped away on his tablet, and when he was finished, he smiled at her, but this time it was different. There was so much more behind that smile. She could see the flames flickering in his eyes as he watched her from across the table. "This is a place I have wanted to visit, but I didn't have the right person to take."

The way he looked at her, she was considering jumping over the table and fucking him right there on the kitchen floor. Tolina wasn't sure how much longer she wanted to wait. She had already decided she wasn't looking anymore. All she ever needed was right in front of her the entire time.

Kortul scrolled through the menu on his tablet and Tolina couldn't help watching him. Seeing him happy was giving her joy, and she never wanted it to end.

His face fell and his eyes widened as he lifted his tablet to see better. "That cannot be correct. Where the *fuck* did all that money come from?"

Tolina looked away and grinned to herself. She tried to bite back her smile before Kortul saw her. When she dared to look at him, he was staring at her like she was the next course on his lunch menu. *Oh, fuck. He caught me smiling. He knows I killed them.*

Chapter 29

Snapped

Remaining silent as he held his searing gaze on the woman he loved, Kortul tapped his fingers on the table before he stood. He went to the kitchen island and grabbed something she couldn't see from a drawer. He came behind Tolina and brushed her hair back with his fingers and braided it before he secured it with a tie. The way his fingers caressed the skin of her neck, she could have moaned. *What the fuck is he doing?*

He came to her side and lifted her from the chair. The next thing she knew, she was upside down and staring at his lower back and ass because she was hanging over his shoulder. "Kortul, what the fuck are you doing?"

He responded only by slapping the side of her ass, and she pressed her hands into his lower back to lift and see where he was carrying her, which was his room. *Wait. Is he about to do what I think he's about to do?* She could feel him wiping his hand on his wall and she tried to look at what he was doing but as she leaned around, he slapped her ass again, hard. "Kortul! What are you doing?!" Her question became a shriek as he yanked her pants off and slapped her ass again, but this time it was her bare skin, and her ass was now stinging. He was smacking her on the side of her ass and nowhere near her wings, and her pussy was soaked with that revelation. She felt him lean her forward, and he stuck her lower half to the wall where he had placed his sticky webbing. With her still hanging on around his shoulders, he ripped her shirt in half. She sucked in a sharp breath as he pressed her back and arms against the wall. He dropped his shorts and climbed over her without a word.

Tolina was speechless while he stared into her eyes, and he clung to the wall hovering her nude form. He was so close she could feel his heat. His face was inches away from hers. Kortul whispered over her lips, "It was you, wasn't it? You killed them all didn't you?"

Kortul brushed his lips against her jaw before he whispered in her ear, "I know it was you. Admit it, Toli. Admit you did it. I need to taste you, and I need to see your face when you cum. I've thought about this moment since the day I found you. Toli, please tell me you killed them." He kissed her under her ear, and she clenched her core as heat exploded deep inside.

She could have moaned at that tiny kiss, and when Kortul was facing her again she couldn't hold back as she admitted, "Yes. It was me. I killed them."

"You killed them for me?"

"I killed them for you." Tolina did kill them for him. She may have had a list of other reasons, but she couldn't deny the main one.

Kortul brushed his lips against hers before he kissed her, and she had never thought something like kissing could be so wonderful. He took her face in his hands and made her feel so much more than just tingling butterflies. This time the butterflies had jackhammers and blowtorches as they made a wriggling mess of her.

He explored her mouth with his tongue before he kissed along her jaw and down the side of her throat. When he reached her breasts, he kissed her nipples before kneading her full breasts and sucking on each nipple. The way he licked and sucked on her nipples was drenching her pussy so thoroughly she could feel a trickle down her inner thigh. He pressed a kiss between her breasts before he faced her and licked the tip of her nose. "I need you to remember to breathe."

She released her held breath and took a few deep slow breaths. "I have no idea what I'm doing."

Kortul grinned as he chuckled under his breath. "I know. You're shaking like you're terrified. I can't wait to make you cum." He brushed his thumbs over her nipples, and she gasped as he studied her face.

She felt him touch her pussy, but both of his hands were stroking her nipples. "How are you doing that?" Whatever was touching her was slick and wet, and she couldn't help but look down to see.

Kortul's cock was moving on its own and stroking her pussy, and she shot her eyes back to him, curiosity burning in them. "I need you to explain. I am so confused."

Capturing her lips in a seductive kiss, Kortul left her panting as he whispered, "You'll understand soon."

She felt his cock change shape to reach her clit, which was a strip of nerves at the apex of her pussy. His cock began stroking her the way she needed for so long and she whimpered with the delicious heat and gathering pleasure. She felt the thrilling warmth of her orgasm building as she gasped for breath and banged her head against the wall as she came with a high pitched, "Oh!"

Kortul gently rubbed her nipples and kissed the tip of her nose as her hips trembled with pleasure. He stroked her pussy with his cock until she shrieked, and he grinned with triumph. "You look like a goddess when you cum." She was speechless at his compliment. He crawled from the wall, and he spread his sticky webbing on the wall stretching out from her hips. *What the fuck is he doing now? I thought my side of things was finished. Is there more?*

"Why do you look so confused? I am nowhere near finished with you. There will be days of this."

Oh. Wait, does he mean sex? Kortul was careful with her wings curled against her skin as he peeled her legs from the wall where he had them and stuck each one of her legs straight out where he placed the new sticky webbing. All she could do was blink with her mouth hanging open as he began kissing her along her inner thigh.

She looked down as he nipped at her skin by her pussy, and she whimpered at the sight. He ran his fingers down the center of her pussy and slid them inside of her. She felt his fingers stretch her as he reached down to taste her for the first time. Tolina had never felt anything so wicked and wonderful, and she banged her head on the wall again as she felt his tongue run against her clit. Kortul licked his lips and whispered, "fucking delicious," and she looked down to see him part her pussy with his other hand and tilt his head to the side before he leaned in and sucked on her clit. Tolina would have screamed if she could have taken a breath. He reached up and pressed on her chest to remind her to breathe as he ate her pussy like it was his last meal.

After he teased her to the edge a few times, he began

tapping the fingers he had hooked inside her at the same pace he sucked and licked her clit. The blend of the perfectly mixed rhythm forced another orgasm to the surface, and at the same time she felt Kortul run a single finger along the bit of her wing peeking under her spread legs.

Tolina felt an exuberant shiver developing alongside her growing orgasm. Her mind was so scrambled with the dual pleasure she screamed as the two converged. Her orgasm crested just as her body began to vibrate, and her scream came out as though she had yelled through a fan. When Kortul heard her, he gently bit down on her clit to hold it in place so he could press his tongue against it. The moment his tongue touched her trapped clit, with her body shivering and her already cumming, she burst into a second orgasm. She screamed and her heart felt like it would rupture. Her core clenched so hard she felt sweat form on her brow.

When Kortul released her clit and pulled his fingers from inside her she thought she might pass out trying to catch her breath. He licked his fingers clean and smiled at her before he reached down to suck on her nipple. "You can't be serious. I don't know if I can handle another one." Her words came out chopped and breathy.

Kortul faced her and grinned as he kissed her under her ear and down her neck. With his lips caressing her skin, he replied, "You can. And you will. My beautiful wife." Once he said the word wife, he reached down and trapped her nipple between his teeth and flicked it with his tongue. Tolina's pussy was ready all over again with the word 'wife' and his tongue, and she felt herself falling for him so hard she had sweet emotions welling up inside.

He noticed her shift, and he faced her, nipping at her bottom lip. "What are you thinking about?"

"I'm glad my dates didn't work out."

Kortul gave her a devious smile, and she studied his face, wondering why he seemed so sly. Her face fell, and she asked with devastation brewing, "Did you ruin my dates?"

Kortul could tell she was upset, and he whispered, "fuck," as he gently removed her from the wall and carried her to his bed. He sat down with her in his arms and admitted the truth, "I did. I couldn't stand the idea of you with anyone else."

Tears burst from Tolina as she shoved him away and tried to grab her shorts and what was left of her shirt to go back to her room, but when she reached for her shorts, she felt Kortul grab her and flip her around. "Where do you think you're going?"

Fury blasted through her as she cried out, "How could you? You knew I was fucking trapped before! All I wanted was to be free and find love the right way. How could you do this to me?" Tolina slipped from his hold and ran toward the door, but he caught her halfway. She pried herself from his grip and fell to the floor sobbing and crawling from him. He pounced on her and had her wrists wrapped in his silk before she could blink.

Kortul flipped her over and she tried to kick him, but he squeezed his legs around hers and pinned her down. Tears streamed down the sides of her face as Kortul gently wrapped his hand around her neck to force her to look at him. He stared down at her with possessive dominance. "You are mine, Toli-na Saltic. You've been mine since the moment I laid eyes on you. You can be angry all you want, but no one can make you feel like I do. No one could ever love you as much as I do."

He says he loves me, but does he? Was this all a lie just to fuck me and move on? Tolina had to know the truth. She sniffled and tried to blink away her tears as she stretched her antennae toward Kortul, and he didn't move as she placed the curled tips against his cheeks. He held his burning eyes on her as she felt the intense loving desire, care, and possessiveness. Underneath the fires of his lust, she felt a warm, protective, and unending need. He did love her. He loved her more than his words or actions expressed. This man would do anything for her. His hunger for her alone ran so deep she gasped as he wiped away her tears. She knew he could see her eyes shift from anger to understanding. He didn't do it because he's cruel; he did it because he loved her. It may be a poisonous, obsessive love, but it was real, and she wanted it all. "Fuck me. Fuck me *now*."

He released his hold on her bound wrists and grabbed her face, kissing her with a feverish passion. She moaned around his kiss and his hands moved to roam her body. His hands settled around her hips, and he sat back on his knees as he lifted her to line himself up with her. Kortul kept his eyes on hers as he constricted the size of his cock to be able to fit inside her. Her eyes widened as she saw how his cock could move and reshape itself any way he wanted. Easing inside her, he reached for her waist and lifted her to slide her down onto his cock. Her pussy was tight, and she groaned with the sting. He paused with a flash of concern in his eyes. "Toli, baby, have you ever had sex before?"

She didn't know how to answer, she wasn't sure. "I don't know. We tried, but it wasn't like this at all." Kortul pulled her closer and held her to him. His movements were slow as he eased her down onto his cock, but she wanted more, so she pushed herself down further onto him. He grabbed her braid to force her to look at him as he warned her, "Toli, listen. I would love nothing more than to pound your pussy across this floor, but if this is your first time, it could be painful for you."

Tolina hooked her bound wrists behind Kortul's head and watched his eyes widen as she forced herself further onto his cock. "Do you think I'm afraid of pain? I want you to make me bleed."

Kortul's mouth dropped open, and he caught her mouth in a searing kiss before he lay her on the floor, and he wrapped his hand around her neck before he began pushing further inside of her. She clenched and whimpered in pain and pleasure as he thrust all the way inside.

Tears sprouted in her eyes as his movements increased, and her pussy was stretched so far, she felt a tear and she screamed, "Harder!" Kortul let himself go as he thrust in her, and she cried out as he slammed his cock into the perfect place inside sending her into a different, thicker orgasm. Kortul groaned as he emptied in her, and as he pulled his cock from her, he lifted her into his arms and took her straight to his shower and waved the water on.

"There is blood. I need to make sure you don't need repair." Tolina grabbed his chin with her still bound hands and made him look at her.

She grinned at him and assured, "If I tore, I need to heal naturally so you will fit next time."

Kortul scowled and sighed, "You're right, but I'm checking anyway." He lay her on the warm shower floor and grabbed a salve and a soft cloth from the cabinet before returning to her. He moved her legs and parted her pussy to wipe his cum from her with the cloth. When she was clean, he checked her carefully and saw minimal tearing. "I need to check inside. This will hurt. Are you ready?" She nodded and she didn't move as he inserted his fingers and felt for any more tearing. "Do you feel anything inside?"

"No, but your fingers are making me want more."

Kortul removed his fingers and leaned down to kiss her lower belly before he rubbed her hip. "You need to heal first. I have some salve which will have you healed enough for more by tomorrow afternoon."

Chapter 30

All Day

Kortul and Tolina showered, and they dried before she lay on his bed. He climbed between her legs to apply the salve around her sore entrance. When he was finished, he closed the salve lid and growled before he gently bit her inner thigh. Tolina was still furious with him for ruining her dates, but she couldn't deny she was glad he did it. That was something she was not anywhere close to admitting though. He came back and wrapped himself around her before he kissed the top of her head.

She couldn't help but giggle when she realized her one fault which caused her to flunk from spy school was the same fault which tipped the scales with Kortul.

He squeezed her in response to her giggle. "What's so funny?"

She wiggled around in his arms to face him, but ended up with her face pressed against his chest. "I need to work on keeping my thoughts from showing on my face."

Kortul laughed and her head jostled with his chest shaking. "I thought it would take some heavy seducing when we were at the resort on Vumenko. I'm glad it happened here though."

Tolina was confused. "Why here?"

"Because I know *exactly* how soundproof it is. I've never stayed in those rooms before, and I didn't see any information about that on the booking page."

Tolina laughed in his chest as she recalled her screams. "Oh."

She didn't remember falling asleep, but she woke on her back with Kortul drawing circles on her chest with his fingertips. He went from her belly to her breast and back down, stroking her sides and then twirling his fingers around the edges of her nipples without touching the tips. She squirmed and tried to pull her arms down, but he had bound her wrists with silk and tied her arms somewhere behind the bed. She tried to lift her legs, but they were tied down and spread. She didn't open her eyes as he traced his fingers down the center of her belly and down her inner thigh before coming back up and circling her nipple again.

Kortul moved to straddle her, and he stroked his fingers over her breasts and down her sides before he gently brushed his knuckles against her nipples. She gasped and arched her back with his touch. Her eyes flew open as he reached under her arched back and lifted her to suck one of her nipples between his lips. She moaned with the contact, and her core burst with need. He moved to her other nipple and sucked it into his mouth before he twirled his tongue over the tip. She felt tingles rush down her spine and settle in her lower belly as Kortul nipped at her chest. He grabbed his pillow and shoved it under her ass before he crawled between her legs.

Kortul dug his fingers into her hips and using the tip of his tongue, he licked her along her clit and only her clit, while avoiding her healing entrance.

Tolina sucked in a sharp breath, and her heart soared as she felt herself nearing the edge. She tried to keep her breaths steady as she felt Kortul kneading her hips. She had never felt more craved and loved as her orgasm washed over her and perfect heat spread from her core. Kortul licked her through her delicate waves before he released her ankles and wrists. Tolina stretched and he wrapped himself around her.

"When do we need to be up by?"

Kortul's face was buried in her hair, and he didn't move as he answered, "A few minutes ago."

Tolina giggled as she tried to wiggle from his arms. "Are we traveling to Vumenko or is this bed as far as we're moving today?"

He nuzzled his face in her neck and kissed her under her ear before he grumbled, "I'm getting up. I do plan to have some fun with you tonight after our dinner, and that's the only reason we are leaving this bed."

"Are these plans a surprise?"

Kortul rolled from the bed and reached for her hands to lift her as he explained, "We will be discussing sex plans during dinner?"

Tolina bit her lip in anticipation and Kortul led her into his closet to make her some clothes with the replicator. As she walked, she noticed her entrance had healed enough that she had no more pain. He handed her a soft, light dress, and she slipped it on, noting he did not give her any underclothes. She lifted her dress and pointed to her bare pussy. "Am I going like this?"

He smirked at her, "Yes. I want easy access."

Looking down at her dress, she realized he picked it out so he could touch her anywhere he wanted without taking her dress off. To prove his point, he hooked his fingers in the neck of her dress and pulled it down, revealing her breast. He wrapped his hand around her throat and pressed her against the wall to suck on her nipple. The action sent heated sparks straight to her pussy. She rubbed her thighs together as he fell to his knees and freed her other breast before kissing and sucking on her nipple. Tolina was panting and her thighs were soaked when he pulled away and lifted her dress to cover her breasts.

He faced her and licked her bottom lip. "We need to go."

Tolina could have cried when he took her hand and led her from the bathroom. "Are you fucking serious? You sucked on my nipples like that, and you're just stopping?"

Kortul grinned at her and bit his lip as he pulled her close. "My beautiful wife, you have so much to learn." Tolina felt him reach up and stroke her nipple over her dress before he led her into the kitchen. He grabbed her big container of honey and held it under his arm. "Corver, transport us to the ship."

When they appeared in the ship Kortul gave her a knowing grin. "You took this ship, didn't you? How did you avoid the travel sensors?"

She noticed he said *this* ship and not *his* ship as she took the honey from him and went to sit in her seat beside his. "Mabit gave me cloaking tech."

"He must have had it from when he worked with the planet guard. I should have known the two of you were behind it. I was wondering what was happening with my accounts because the money in and out was outrageous compared to normal. I'm not sure if you understood this at the time you made the transfers, but you doubled our wealth."

Shrugging, Tolina had no clue and admitted, "I had no idea what they owed you, so I transferred half of what I could see."

Kortul slumped in the captain's chair and couldn't contain himself as he laughed with tears gathering in his eyes. "That's the best thing I've ever heard. Look, you made me laugh so hard I have tears. You stole so much money." Kortul wiped his eyes and showed her the smeared droplets.

Tolina giggled at him. "Mabit didn't say anything!"

"Of course he didn't. I'm sure he still has some money held back to make the deposits staggered and spread the transfers." Kortul didn't want to waste any more time. "Corver, take us into orbit and request clearance for our booked trip to Vumenko."

The ship landed on the moonlit planet within a few minutes. Kortul took the container of fancy honey from her and helped her from her seat. He held his hand at her lower back as they went through the airlock and down the stairs toward the resort's main desk. The soft green glowing leaves of the tall trees illuminated the forest floor. Bioluminescent toadstool mushrooms grew from rotting logs and scurrying bright white beetles moved along the underbrush. Glowing moths fluttered by as they aimed for a bush of pink florescent flowers, shimmering in the soft green light from the trees.

Tolina was mesmerized by this environment, and Kortul had to direct her as he headed toward an open archway of bright white flowers with petals as large as her head.

Through the archway there was a Vitolas woman with creamy mint skin, white hair, and fluffy antennae. Her floor length, flowing white dress seemed to float just above the ground as she walked toward them.

Tolina was smitten with her, and the woman greeted her with the same energy. "You must be Kortul and Toli-na Saltic. I am Resitari, and I will be giving you a short tour before I show you to your room. Follow me."

Resitari brought them to a lift which carried them high into the tree, just under the treetops. When they were on the same level as the rest of the resort, Tolina gasped at how concealed it had been from below. It was much brighter since they were closer to the treetops and the bright glow, and she could see most of the guests were Wendi and Vitolas. There were levels of balconies wrapping around hollowed trees with people mingling inside and walking bridges connecting everything together.

Resitari started with the closest tree and pointed to it as they passed. "This is our beverage bar, and this next tree contains the spa." They moved along, and on the other side of the spa was a massive tree trunk with a restaurant inside and as they approached, she pointed to it. "This is our main restaurant. You enter here, but there is a covered deck above the trees where you eat under the starlight." When they came back out from seeing how to access the restaurant, Tolina was so thrilled she held back a squeal as she spotted the rooms. Resitari brought them over another bridge to one of the trunks hollowed out for a room and led them inside.

The room was simple with a large, rounded bed fitted with white sheets against the inside of the hollowed tree, a bathroom with glass walls, and a spiral staircase with a replicator behind it. Resitari led them up the stairs to their treetop covered deck, and Tolina loved that they designed the rooms to be much lower than the restaurant so they could have privacy even on the deck.

"This enclosed deck and your room are both soundproof, and you have a replicator with specialized menus for any of your sexual needs. I hope you two have a wonderful stay."

Resitari disappeared down the stairs and Tolina couldn't help but ask, "Is this a sex resort?"

Kortul acted like she should have known that as he set her container of honey down at his feet. He took her face in his hands, and he watched her as he replied, "This was the original nesting ground for the moths they evolved from. This is one of the most romantic places in the galaxy. We have lost time to make up for, and I knew this would be the perfect place."

Tolina was at a loss for words as he lifted her honey, and they went back downstairs. He set her honey on a table by the bed and scooped her into his arms before he sat down. Kortul spread her legs and softly stroked her pussy. "Are you still sore, or did the salve do its job?"

She didn't feel sore at all, and she smirked at him. "I'm healed." He pressed two fingers inside and she gasped wanting more. He turned her and lay her on the bed before he pulled the top of her dress down, freeing her breasts. Kortul took his time kissing, sucking, and flicking each of her nipples with his tongue while she threaded her fingers through his hair.

He lifted her dress and kissed her in the center of her lower belly before he licked her down to her pussy. Kortul pushed her legs apart and kissed her pussy like he kissed her mouth before he settled on her clit and sucked it between his lips. She moaned and her hips writhed, causing Kortul to growl, and he gripped her thighs to hold her still.

Her muscles tightened as she felt the rush of pleasure pour from her core as the orgasm settled in, and Kortul licked her pleasure up with his tongue. "I could eat your pussy all day, and I think I might."

Chapter 31

She Does What?

After he made her cum twice more, he cleaned her with a wet cloth and fixed her dress. "We need to eat something and discuss our plans."

Tolina agreed, and he grabbed her favorite honey before they started for the restaurant. When they arrived, they were led up a spiral staircase to the treetop deck and they were seated by the edge where they could enjoy the view. The waiter set water on the table, and he tapped the holo-screen in the middle with the menu. "Would you like a bowl for your honey, Mrs. Saltic?"

Tolina smiled at hearing 'Mrs. Saltic.' she loved how it sounded now. "Yes. Thank you."

Kortul moved to the chair next to her and pulled her into his lap before he whispered against her ear, "If you smile like that over 'Mrs. Saltic' again, I will rip this dress off and fuck you on this table in front of all these people." She bit her lip and held back a giggle. *Do I want that?* Kortul stared at her in disbelief. "You are the perfect woman for me. You wouldn't mind that at all would you?"

Tolina was tempted to straddle him, but she didn't want them to be kicked out. "We should eat and talk so we can go back to our room."

Kortul agreed and set her back in her seat before ordering his food. His bird meat and vegetables were gone in minutes as she slurped down her bowl. When they were finished, Kortul smiled and licked his lips. "Are you ready to talk about tonight?"

"Sure." She had no idea why their sex needed to be planned out, but she was more than curious to find out.

"I know you are still furious about what I did to you." Kortul waited for her to confirm, and she gave him a narrowed glare and a brief nod. "You know how I spanked you before I fucked you?" Tolina held back a whimper of delight and nodded as he continued, "I like to switch."

Tolina was confused, and when she started to understand her face fell. "Wait. What is happening exactly?"

Kortul bit his lip and took a breath before he explained, "I want you to punish me for wronging you and then I want you to fuck me with a strap on. Before you ask, a strap on is something you wear with a dildo so *you* can fuck *me*."

Tolina's mouth dropped open, and she felt a rush like she had never felt before as imagery of her spanking his bare ass before fucking him flooded her mind. "I never dreamed that would come from your mouth."

"Well?" Kortul demanded as he stared at her, waiting for her agreement.

Tolina was confused until she realized what he was waiting for. "Oh! Yes, yes. Let's go. Now."

Kortul resisted the urge to throw her over his shoulder and run back to the room with her. That would defeat the entire point. He grabbed her container of honey, and he had a tough time keeping up with her on the way back to the room. He had never trusted anyone enough to be able to admit what he wanted, but now that all changed, and his cock was already out and so hard it ached.

When they reached their room, he set the honey by the sink, and he turned around to her pointing at the bed. "Take your clothes off and wait for me there." Kortul's heart was fluttering as he stripped off his shirt and pants and sat on the bed like she commanded. Tolina taking a serious approach to his needs reinforced his belief that he had been right about her all along. She stripped off her own clothes and tossed them with his and he watched her ass bounce as she half skipped across the room. He tried to see what she was ordering at the replicator, but she was blocking the screen. She selected a few different items, and when the items were ready, she turned around with a bag in her hands and pointed to the stairs.

Something occurred to him as he was climbing the stairs, Tolina had been through spy training. She was experienced in torture. *No fucking wonder she needed no instructions.* He couldn't help but bark a laugh as the realization fell over him, and he felt a sharp swat on his ass.

"What's so funny?"

Kortul almost came on the stairs, and his laugh became a groan as he grabbed his cock and Tolina slapped him again causing his pleading sound to grow steeper in pitch as he tried to take the next step. He peeked at Tolina behind him seeing her eyes were bright and she had a villainous grin spread across her face. "I've never admitted I wanted this to anyone, and I'm laughing because I am about to cum. I didn't need to explain anything to you. You didn't ask why either because you already know." Kortul paused and watched her maniacal smile turn soft as he continued, "I think you needed this, too."

She crawled over him, and she held her face inches from his as she whispered, "I do need this. Now crawl up the remaining stairs and when you reach the deck stay on your knees facing the wall."

Kortul was an equal amount terrified and turned on as he did as she commanded, and his knees barked in pain as they dug into the hardwood. He knew even without touching his cock he might last one strong slap before he came. As he reached the top of the stairs, his anticipation was so thick he was panting and his skin felt like it would burn away. He crawled across the deck and stayed on his knees facing the wall.

He could hear Tolina behind him as she set her bag down. When she approached him, she grabbed him by the hair and forced his head back and leaned over him. "How do I know if I go too far?"

"I won't tell you to stop." Tolina kissed him before she released his hair.

"Hands on the wall."

Kortul did as she commanded and as his hands touched the wall, she struck him on the ass with a leather strap. He leaned closer to the wall as he groaned, trying to avoid spilling cum too early. When she hit him again, this time on the other side by his hip, he couldn't hold it in any longer and cried, "Oh, fuck!" His cock erupted onto the floor by the wall, and he whispered to himself, "I didn't even touch it."

Tolina broke character for a moment and leaned around him with a curious smile. "Did you just cum?"

Kortul's laugh was a hiss under his breath as he tried to

brush it off. "Shhh. Just keep going. We don't need to talk about that."

Tolina was grinning so wide he could see all her teeth. "I assume that's a first?"

"Maybe." Kortul could feel his face beaming with amusement.

He watched as Tolina filled with pride, and she batted her eyelashes at him before she resumed her focus. She smacked the strap down on his ass and it stung, giving him what he needed, and he could feel his cock become rock hard again. With a few more hits with the strap on his ass and back, Kortul felt his pleasure growing again. His groans were deep and guttural as he felt angry welts growing on his skin.

He leaned over so far that his forehead was almost touching the wood while he caught his breath. He could hear Tolina retrieving something from the bag behind him, and he couldn't wait to find out what she would do next. Kortul could hear an odd humming sound, and he felt her kneel behind him. "Lay your hands on the deck and don't move them."

He did as she asked, and he felt her rub lube on his asshole, and he could hear her lubing the strap on next. It was making a crackling sound and his mouth dropped open when he realized what she was preparing to fuck him with. *That fucking dildo has a micro-current. I love her. I fucking love her so much.*

She lined up with his asshole and grabbed his hips to steady herself as she pressed the tip inside. His ass was twitching with the electro-stimulation, and his voice went from husky and deep to singing through a cry as she filled him.

The tingles and zaps were mind-blowing, and his muscles flexed with the pulses, forcing him to fight to stay in place as she thrust into him. She began slow and careful, but once he was pressing back against her thrusts, she pounded into him, and he was too enthralled in the pain and pleasure to notice he was expressing his delight in low-pitched whimpers and cries. He felt himself near his climax, and he went silent as his cock twitched with the impending cum. Tolina reached around him to grasp his cock with her hands, and she thrust as she stroked him. He came so hard it slapped the floor between his hands and splashed the wall.

Tolina slumped onto him and kissed his back before she turned off the current. "Now, lay down on your back so I can sit on your face," She slid from him and patted his flaming hot ass. He had a satiated smirk on his face when he rolled over, and she loved it. Tolina tossed away the strap on and crawled over him to position her pussy over his face. Her thighs were thick, and she was wondering if Kortul would be able to breathe as she looked down and could only see his eyes. "Can you breathe?"

"Shhh, sit down, my love."

She bit her lip at his endearment, and Tolina dropped her weight onto his face. She grabbed the ledge of the windowsill above her for balance. Kortul reached up and held her thighs, pressing her pussy to his face as he devoured her. He stroked his tongue against her clit giving her such sweet friction she could already feel her orgasm approaching. Her wet pleasure was dripping down her legs before she sat on his face, and now her sensual delight was thrumming so deeply she knew when she came it would be explosive.

When it struck her, her inner muscles pulsed, and she

released the ledge, sliding down the wall as she moaned through the thick orgasm. Kortul held her to his face as he licked her through it and her hips jolted when it became too much.

She lifted herself from his face and crawled off him, but he didn't let her move far as he grabbed her hips. He sat up with her wiggling in his grasp. It astonished her how quickly she could become turned on as he sat her down in his lap. "We aren't quite finished with you yet. Your ass is raw and looks like it hurts. We need to put something on it."

His cock moved under her and rubbed against her ass as he replied, "Let's go downstairs." They descended the stairs, and Tolina had the replicator make a salve. Kortul was already lying face down on the bed, and his ass was swollen and blue. She lay next to him and leaned over his back to rub the salve on his ass cheeks, and he flinched a few times at the contact. His back wasn't as bad, but she rubbed salve there as well.

When she was finished, she set the jar down and he threw the covers over them. Kortul wrapped himself around her and kissed her on the top of her head.

A burst of something much stronger than simple caring feelings crashed into her when he accidentally kissed her antenna, and she pressed herself into him. "You kissed my antenna and..." she trailed off as she felt him lift her hair away from her curled up antenna. He brushed it with his lips before kissing the tip. Tolina trembled with the intensity of his loving feelings flowing into her. Her own feelings had grown so quickly and in the safety of his arms, and she allowed him to experience the intentions and desires of her heart in return. She could feel him tense. "Can you feel me?"

She could feel Kortul's heart rage as he buried his face in the back of her hair and squeezed her in response to her revelation. Tolina hadn't just caved. She had fallen for him headfirst, and now he knew it. He whispered in her hair, "You're mine."

Chapter 32

Too Good To Be True

After the most peaceful sleep of her life, Tolina woke long before Kortul and had to pry herself from his arms so she could make herself a bowl of honey. She was halfway through her serving when he woke up and peered at her through a sliver of his eyelids. "I meant to wake up first." His voice was raspy and tired.

Tolina giggled at him and patted his thigh as she sipped the rest of her honey. When she finished, she cleaned her bowl at the sink and put it away before joining him back in bed. He was still laid out and trying to blink away his sleepiness, so Tolina crawled on top of him to lie on his chest. He stroked his fingers along the swirls of her wings, and she melted into him. The rhythm of his heart was soothing as she wiggled with his light touch along her sensitive wings. His cock was already out and stroking her inner thigh, and she swore it had a mind of its own.

She breathed in deep and smiled against Kortul's chest. "We need a bath." Kortul groaned in agreement as he lifted her along with him. He stood from the bed, and he set her on her feet to stretch before starting the shower.

Still nude from the night before, they quickly washed and as Tolina passed the threshold to step out, Kortul grabbed her and lifted her over his shoulder. She was so ready to start their game, her pussy became drenched as heat burst inside. He lay her on the bed and kissed her, but this time when she kissed him back, she felt true passion take hold of her, and their kiss became needy and desperate. She ran her fingers through his hair, and he slipped his hand under her shoulder and lifted her as he kissed and ran his tongue along her jaw and neck before kissing along her collar bone. Tolina was lost in him as he descended on her breasts and twirled his tongue over each of her nipples as she felt the tip of his cock brush her pussy. As he kneaded her breasts, he trapped her lips in another molten kiss, and she felt his cock rub her pussy again, but this time it pressed in deeper. His cock stroked her clit, and she gasped against his lips. The tip of his cock increased until she whimpered and moaned. He held her face in his hands, watching her closely as she broke apart for him. His cock stroked her clit until she clenched her inner walls, and in that moment, he pressed in at her entrance. She wrapped her hands behind his head as he sank into her, stretching her to fit around him.

She swore his cock was not so large last time. "Why does it feel bigger?"

He kissed the side of her lips and whispered, "I can move it or reshape it. You are tight. I constrict it as much as I can to fit." Kortul demonstrated by curling the tip and rippling it along her inner pleasure point.

Her breaths became quick as he continued the little waves down his cock as he pushed all the way inside her. Her eyes flared as the pleasure cascaded through her with his soft thrusts. When she came, it was a bubbly warmth which floated through her, and Kortul nipped at her bottom lip. He groaned as he came inside her, and his pulsing cock felt like it was filling every space it could fit.

Kortul wrapped her in his arms and held her while his cock remained buried in her. When he released her, he pulled himself free and took a wet cloth to clean her before he went to the replicator. She couldn't see what he was ordering, and she guessed that was payback for not allowing him to see what she had picked out. "I don't want any of this shit." He went back over to the bed before he listed the reasons on his fingers. "Your whole body is a vibrator, I have rope webbing *and* sticky webbing at my fingertips, and clit creams taste nasty."

She moved to the end of the bed beside him. "What is a clit cream?"

"It's an over perfumed cream which increases stimulation to the point of making you cum without any other contact. It's popular, but I think it's the grossest tasting shit I have ever had in my mouth." He hugged her to his side, and he admitted, "I'm having a tough time deciding how to position you because I want to touch your wings, but I also want to devour your pussy at the same time. My problem is that I saw your wrecked shoulders on the medical scan, along with everything else, and now I'm afraid I'll hurt you."

Tolina sighed against his chest, "I was furious at how gentle you were when we were fighting about the dates. I was so angry, and I wanted to be right about all the terrible things about you, but you saw right through my sinking thoughts. Then you let me to see myself through your eyes. I've never wanted to be railed harder in my life. You could have torn me in half. You don't need to worry about hurting me." Tolina laughed a bit before she continued, "I don't know how long it will take, but I'm sure I'll eventually be thankful for what you did." He traced his fingers along her wings, and she wrapped her arms around him. "I have an uncomfortable question."

He chuckled a bit under his breath. "You? Never."

She scoffed and flicked his nipple with her tongue. "You seem to know what someone with wings loves."

"Oh, I see. No, I've never been with a Vitolas person. I love yours because they're yours." Tolina thought that was all he wanted to express until he brushed his lips against her antenna, which was peeking just above her hair. His feelings were heartbreakingly sweet this time, and she wanted to tear up.

"What are you thinking about?"

"Us, old."

Overwhelmed, Tolina climbed him and wrapped her arms around his shoulders as she buried her face in his neck. "I'm so sorry I ever doubted your intentions."

"You have no reason to say sorry for anything. You had every reason to doubt me."

As he stroked his fingers along her wings, she had an idea. "You could just flip me upside down."

The world spun, and she was upside down with her arms around Kortul's waist before she could think. He rested her thighs on his shoulders, and he parted her pussy with his nose before he devoured her. He ran his tongue over her clit, and she clamped her thighs around his head. His fingers traced along her wings, and she could feel the consuming shiver developing beside her orgasm.

Kortul sounded like he was eating the best meal of his

life as Tolina gasped with the building pleasure. When her lips parted in a gasp, Kortul's cock pressed in her open lips, and she leaned her head back to take him in. He sucked in a sharp breath, and he clenched his core drawing out more desire and heat from her while she sucked his cock.

She reached down and rubbed her finger around his asshole, making his cock pulse and his mouth turn feral at her pussy. She was close to a shivering orgasm, and as the molten heat began to form a wave of vibrating pleasure, Tolina sucked down on Kortul's cock while she pressed her finger in his asshole. His salty cum burst into her mouth as the deep shaking orgasm he drew from her crested, and he had to wrap his arms around her to keep her from vibrating off his shoulders.

They both moaned and clenched through their orgasms before Kortul rested his face against her thigh. He licked his lips before he kissed her pussy, forcing her to yelp. He flipped her back around and set her on the bed to clean her up. "Did you grab my dick and suck it, or did it stick itself in your mouth?"

Tolina was as confused as she was amused and with a half snarl, half laugh, she answered, "I gasped, and it stuck itself in my open mouth."

"Oh. Sometimes I think my dick makes its own decisions. I'm not really sure how I feel about having a prehensile penis with its own ideas." Kortul's tone was serious, and Tolina had to brace herself so she didn't fall off the bed as giggles overtook her.

He reached over and wiped the cum from her chin before he kissed her. "I want to fuck you in a hot tub. You teased me half to death at the resort hot tub, and I've imagined fucking you in one since."

"Can you do that here? Have a hot tub transported in?" Tolina had never sat in something so wonderful, and sex in it seemed even better.

Kortul nodded and explained, "All of these rooms can be flooded with forcefields holding in the water for the other species who evolved here, the Paddering. They evolved from alligators and occupy the marshes of the planet."

Tolina was obsessed with learning about her new galaxy and the people in it. "Are they bioluminescent too?"

He nodded and smiled at her as he sat down next to her on the bed. "Yes, everything here makes its own light. The Vitolas people evolved first during a period of gigantism on the early planet, then later when the advanced Vitolas discovered a branch of alligators which were developing further, they assisted in a unique way. They played various forms of mentally stimulating music a few times a day for a few thousand years, and it caused an explosion of intelligence in them. The evolution from alligators with evolving minds and bodies into walking, talking, intelligent beings took around fifty thousand years. They have coexisted for hundreds of thousands of years since, and this planet has never seen conflict because of their shared beliefs that this planet is sacred."

Tolina was so lost in his explanation she didn't realize she had grabbed his arm and was holding his hand to the middle of her chest. She giggled when she saw what she was doing and he kissed her head before he revealed, "You've done that a few times, and you didn't notice."

"I have? When?"

"At the city gardens you did it four times."

"Oh." *That means he was stroking my arm as a response*

to me touching him first. Do I really let my guard down that much around him?

"Let's have that hot tub transported to the deck." Kortul waited until she met his eyes and nodded to him before he went to the replicator and did just that. He led her up the stairs to the large hot tub which was already on the deck with steam billowing up. They climbed in, and he pulled her into his lap before he kissed down the side of her neck.

Her heart swelled to bursting as he cradled her in his arms and was more interested in kissing her face than he was anything else. He moved her to straddle him, and he held her face in his hands, "I don't think I could ever live without you. I think I would wither and die. I don't even know who I was before, and now because of you, I feel like I have a life worth living. You are my everything, and I would have done much worse to have you in my arms. I love you more than life."

She knew what he wanted from her, and Tolina wasn't waiting. She kissed him and whispered, "I love you, too. Now, I want you to hang me from the ceiling above this hot tub, eat my pussy, then fuck me. I don't give a fuck about my shoulders. I need this."

Squeezing his eyes shut, he held Tolina to him before Kortul licked the tip of her nose and kissed along her jaw. "I have an idea." He set her beside him and climbed out.

The deck was more than large enough for her to spread her wings, so he hooked his finger at her, and she climbed out and padded over to him. He positioned her in the center of the space. "Spread your wings." She did as he asked, and he ran his finger along one of the unfurling veins on her wings making her gasp and wiggle. When they were spread, he walked around her and reached over her head to gently press her wings together. "Hold them there." Kortul rubbed his sticky webbing along her back and on her skin by either side of her wings and extended it over her shoulder blades. He followed the same placement and layered his rope webbing over the top and spun it over her shoulders.

Kortul extended the rope webbing from his fingertips as he moved toward the wall and climbed it before crawling to the ceiling above Tolina. He tightened the rope in his grip and lifted her while he attached the webbing to the rafter above him. She bounced a few times and giggled to herself, and he couldn't fathom weighing so little. She might have been tall, with head crushing thick thighs, but Tolina weighed half as much as she looked because of her light bones internal body structures.

Tolina knew he had evolved from a spider, but she had never experienced his true nature until this moment. This was Kortul. The *real* Kortul. The raw man before her was who she had been desperate to uncover. She had been mistaken about the man she would find under the surface of the flashy rich asshole she experienced in the beginning. He was kind and attentive. He paid attention to every detail, every quick breath, every glance, and every single smirk. He was everything she could have ever wanted.

Kortul connected his rope webbing to the rafter and slowly descended until he was facing her. With her arms free, Tolina grabbed his face and kissed him as she wrapped her legs around his waist. She let go of him and he continued down to the floor until he was on his feet and disconnected his webbing from his hand. Grabbing her ass first, he pulled her to him and kissed her lower belly as he guided her legs onto his shoulders.

He started with his tongue exploring her pussy as he

stroked her wings, and she allowed the sprouting shiver to consume her. Tolina could feel him smiling at her pussy as his attention moved to her clit, and he pressed his tongue against it. With her internal vibrations, his tongue felt exquisite, but when he began rubbing it against her clit at the same time, she grabbed his hair in a death grip and squealed. The sound came out chopped through her shiver, and she could feel Kortul's amusement as his hot breath at her pussy came out in bursts. He held his tongue to her clit until she was kicking her legs from the overstimulation.

She could feel him shaking his head 'no' as he gripped her ass and forced her pussy back against his mouth. Having lost all control with her shiver and orgasm, Tolina screamed, but Kortul refused to let her go. Her thighs were now shaking on top of her shiver, and she yanked handfuls of his black hair as he assaulted her vibrating clit with his tongue. Another orgasm was closing in, and she threw her head back and released a deep moan as it blasted through her like an eruption of lava, sharp and hot enough to melt stone. Her orgasm ran so deep she couldn't help slamming Kortul with her searing feelings, and he sucked on her clit, causing to her scream as she aimed more of her pleasurable feelings at him.

Kortul was moaning at her pussy. Pausing, he pried her legs apart to peer at her dumbfounded. "You made me cum on the floor!"

"What?" Tolina laughed as she tried to breathe. "You're joking. You made *me* cum so hard I blasted *you* with enough pleasure that *you came too?*"

She and Kortul laughed as he climbed the webbing and faced her, still licking and sucking the results of her pleasure from his lips. "I want to fuck you from behind so I can touch your wings, but I need to cut you down from here."

She nodded and he kissed her, sharing how she tasted with her before he crawled farther up and gathered the webbing she was hanging from and cut it with his teeth. He lowered her to the deck and jumped down in front of her before sweeping her off her feet.

Kortul carried her to the hot tub and climbed in before setting her on her feet. "Grab the edge." Tolina did as he asked, and she felt him grab her hips to line her pussy up with his cock. He pressed his tip inside and pumped a few times before he eased inside of her, stretching and filling her. She angled herself down onto his cock, and he created waves as he thrust and curled his cock downward to rub her where he knew she loved it the most. As he stroked his fingertips along her wings, he stopped at her ass and stroked her asshole with his thumb and began pressing inside, making her squirm and groan.

The combination of the hot water, his thumb in her ass, and his rippling cock overfilling her pussy, had her flowing into the orgasm like it was a river of warm honey. Kortul came along with her and reached around to pinch her clit as he emptied into her, thrusting through her heavy, wet orgasm. She moaned over the release of pressure at her core as he slid from her and her body fell limp in the hot water.

Chapter 33

Perfection

After waking entangled in one another's arms, Kortul and Tolina dressed and were back home before the system stars had risen in the sky, so they grabbed their coats and were on the patio waiting for the light to break over the horizon. Kortul had Tolina wrapped in his jacket, and he leaned in and kissed her under her ear. "I want to announce you as my wife. It's a notice posted publicly, but it means a lot to me. It's something my people do."

"Would this prevent, maybe, other people who you've been with casually from thinking you're still available?"

Kortul kissed her neck before he replied, "Maybe."

Tolina smiled and twisted around to kiss him. "Of course you can announce us. Is there anything else your people do?"

"We have a blood bond marriage ceremony, but we did that when we first met." Tolina stuck her cold hand up Kortul's shirt and pressed it on his stomach. He startled and yanked her hand from his shirt.

"Fuck! Your hand is cold!"

"Do you want to have a real ceremony?" She watched his eyes soften.

He held her hands away from him as he leaned in and kissed her. "I would love that, but let's have it on the island. No cold hands." Kortul was still holding her hands, and she giggled as she tried to pull away, but he used his sticky web, and she wasn't going anywhere.

Mabit appeared beside them intent on watching the stars rise. "When did you two return?"

"This morning. Do you want to join us for dinner tonight?" Kortul released Tolina and peeled away the webbing on her hand before balling it up and sticking it in his pocket. She wrapped herself back in his jacket, and he held her close.

Mabit was overjoyed seeing them together and grinned with pride. "I would love to. Did you two have a nice time?" Tolina's cheeks warmed, and she resisted the urge to bury her face in Kortul's chest.

Kortul answered above her, "It was perfect. I am announcing our marriage today, and we want to plan a do-over ceremony on the island soon."

Tears swelled in Mabit's eyes, and he reached out to set his hand on Kortul's shoulder. "I would love nothing more than to see you two have a ceremony. Kortul, I've waited a long time for you to be at peace. All I've ever wanted was for you to find happiness. I'm going back to my apartment so you two can watch the stars rise together. I'll see you later for dinner."

Mabit transported back to his apartment, and they were alone again on the patio. The stars just peeked over the horizon as Kortul leaned down and kissed one of Tolina's antenna. His love curled through her and wrapped around her heart.

The streams of light were stunning by themselves, but the vibrant rainbow of colors painted across the sky as the starlight shined through the distant crystal islands on the horizon were ethereal. She was happy, even if it felt like she didn't deserve it. Having even a moment of joy was difficult in her former life. Some of her people were positive just because they forced it to be their coping mechanism, but she was never one of those people. The only thing which had ever brought her joy before was an occasional chat with her former bonded and when she killed her targets. She didn't think her love for killing people who deserved it would fade, and she hoped somehow she would be able to continue. Even if she didn't, she knew she would be happy now without it. This new form of happy, this in love happy, felt complete. She marveled at how feeling grounded, supported, and loved could change her entire outlook on life almost overnight.

Kortul's warmth surrounded her as they watched the sky brighten to a periwinkle and then soften to a light blue. He kissed her head and spoke over her hair, "We have a few things on our schedule today. We need to pick up some ingredients at a nearby street market for Brock, and there is a sweet wine I found for you in a galactic market across the city. Also, tonight, we need to have Mabit take our picture to send off for our marriage announcement."

Tolina was giddy over his schedule. It felt wonderful to have simple domestic tasks to do. She seemed thrilled, and he placed his hand over her chest. He could feel her heart racing. "Are you excited about running errands?"

"Maybe. What's wrong with that?" Tolina twisted in his arms to look up at him.

Kortul kissed her on the forehead. "I'm glad it makes you happy because picking up groceries and gifts for Brock is all I really do besides stress out Mabit and Tyce."

Tolina smiled and pressed her face into Kortul's chest. She felt his nipple through his shirt rub against her temple, so she rose up on her toes and bit it. Kortul belted a high pitch scream as he leapt backward into a chair behind him holding his hands over his nipple.

Tolina jumped on him, and the chair fell backward sending them rolling across the patio. Kortul laughed and shouted as he and Tolina wrestled, and in his riotous amusement, he was unable to fight back. She had him in a headlock with her legs locked around his waist as she whispered in his ear, "Don't forget I'm still upset with you. You'll be paying for ruining my dates for a while."

She reached down and pinched his nipple, and he cried out, "Tolina, stop it! Let me go!"

"Never!" She stuck her long tongue in his ear, and he thrashed trying to force her to release him.

He screamed with her wet tongue wriggling in his ear, and in defeat, Kortul broke down laughing and went limp in her grip as he half tried to wave her tongue away. He screeched, "STOP IT!"

It was Tolina's turn to laugh, and she released her grip before laying out on the ground.

Kortul took his opportunity to twist around. He kissed her and nipped at her bottom lip before he grabbed her ass. "Are you ready to go act like normal people in public?"

"You mean I can't tell the random people I see about how I fucked you with a sparking dildo?" Tolina watched

Kortul light up with a grin as he leaned down to kiss her again. This time the kiss was passionate and sweet.

Once they were standing Kortul asked, "Corver, transport us to the sidewalk in front of the building."

On the sidewalk, Tolina was wide eyed and gaping, so Kortul followed her line of sight. There was a sequel to the pornographic comic painted about them on the windows of his building. It depicted three images of Tolina caught in Kortul's web. In one they were facing, the artist had Kortul positioned where he was thrusting his cock in her pussy from behind. Tolina screamed with laughter when she saw Kortul's shocked face, and everyone on the street turned to look at them. They all at once looked at the pornographic comic painted on the windows, which they had been ignoring to that point. Everyone on the street either gasped or giggled when they realized the comic was about them, and all Kortul could do was stare at Tolina and laugh with his hand over his mouth. Kortul avoided looking at her or the painting and stared at the sidewalk to keep from laughing mid-sentence. "Corver, book window cleaning for the building, immediately!"

There was a quick confirmation tone, and Kortul and Tolina slipped away trying to hold in their laughter. "Do you remember those sweets we had in the art district?"

"Yes, I was a little upset you took it and threw it away." That treat had been delicious.

Kortul explained as he wrapped his arm around her, "The sweet had a tiny tracking device which is used to target people for trickery, like painting porn on the individuals place of business or home. The only major crisis we have as a society here is boredom, which for our unruly young has turned into a form of artful street trickery. When people are properly cared for, they don't have many reasons to commit crimes. Our queen hears all cases herself, and she strives to be as fair as possible. She already dropped the hunt for the murderer of the rapist at the resort."

Tolina had not told Kortul the truth about that yet, but maybe one day she would admit to it. She was too used to keeping things in her pocket for a later use from her training, and she couldn't help it. Plus, she didn't want to talk about it at the moment. There were too many people on the sidewalk. "Why are there no depictions of your queen?"

"She's not Wendi, I'm sure you have seen a portrait and didn't know it was her. She comes from a long-lived species of giant tarantula who never developed a body form like us. Queen Batton is the last of her kind at three hundred years old. She will live to be at least two thousand. She hears court cases, and then she hosts constant private parties to keep herself busy. Her kind reproduced by laying a single clone egg at the age of two hundred, but she made the choice in her youth to crush that egg and allow us to govern ourselves when she eventually passes. It takes a lot of resources to sustain her, and she feels she has become a burden on our society rather than a guiding leader. She believes it is time for her kind to end, and this was a collective agreement her people made long ago as Wendi people spread across the planet. Her people chose to stop allowing their eggs to mature in their plan to give us the planet, and she feels she is completing their commitment. Her people helped continue the symbiotic bond the Eckolie and Wendi had together as we evolved. They ruled this world for over a million years. This planet has always had a peaceful history, and my people cherish that."

"It feels like I landed on some kind of afterlife paradise.

Am I dead? Be honest." Tolina scrunched her nose and bit her bottom lip as she stared at Kortul.

"No. You are not dead and in an afterlife paradise. We are a matriarchal society."

"I love it here. I see why your people are so protective of your planet and don't allow outsiders."

They came to an open market with fruit and vegetable stands lining the closed off street. Kortul led her to a stand with a red twirled up gourd and a round, yellow vegetable with peeling flaky skin the size of her head. "What is that?"

"An onion." Kortul tapped his pocket communicator on the payment kiosk before they walked away.

Tolina recalled what an onion was and was positive she had never seen one that large. *No wonder I didn't know what the fuck that thing was. The fruit and vegetables here are gigantic!* "Why is everything humongous?" Tolina was obsessed with an orange like fruit she spotted which was so huge it came with its own hover device.

Kortul looked at her confused as they left the market and stood by the street. "Corver, I need a transport to the Huyl's Galactic Market in Southdown." He twisted his lip to the side before he answered her, "What are you talking about?"

"That onion and gourd are enormous. I have never seen either that size before."

"Oh right. We are bored, remember? It is common for our people to compete to see who can grow the biggest fruit or vegetable. We grow some of the highest quality food in the galaxy. I'll have to take you to our free use agricultural ocean platforms. They're on the other side of the planet right now. It's where most of this is grown."

The transport arrived, and they were swept across town,

and walking into a colossal galactic market in a matter of minutes. Goods from all over the galaxy were stocked to the ceiling, several stories above them. It was organized by planet and system, and she was obsessed with this place and couldn't wait to come back and explore more of it. He led her onto a hover-cart, and he selected the wine he was searching for on the holo-screen. The hover-cart shot them to the top row and then across the store to a wine cooler. Kortul reached in and retrieved a single bottle of wine and tapped his communicator on the payment kiosk to purchase it. The hover-cart quickly brought them back to the front of the store, and within a few minutes they were back in the transport.

Back home, Kortul set the bags and wine on the counter before he pointed to his room. "My cocks been hard since I saw the comic on the window, and we need a shower before our guests arrive."

"I watched you cum in your shower one night," Tolina admitted as she looked up at him.

He shot her a devilish grin. "I know, my love."

In the bathroom, he turned the water on while she stripped her clothes off. Once his clothes were in a pile beside hers, he wrapped his hand around her neck and pressed her against the shower wall. He tilted her face and met her lips with his, diving his tongue in her mouth, and sending heat searing through her.

He stroked her nipples with his thumbs while his cock rippled at her pussy and pressed against her clit. She shifted her hips, and his cock gave her the perfect rhythm and friction to bring her pleasure to the surface. Tolina felt him press lightly on her neck as she crested, and she came so hard it triggered her shiver. Kortul smiled against her lips as she gasped, and he stole her breath with another kiss as pleasure burst through her.

She angled her hips to work his cock inside her pussy, and she pressed herself down until she was fully seated before she wrapped her legs around his hips. With her wrapped around him and his cock filling her, she allowed herself to become lost in him. Water cascaded down their bodies, and she reached out her long tongue to lick his nipple. His nipple tightened in response, and she twirled her tongue around it. He synchronized his thrusts and the ripples along his cock, and she whimpered with stinging pleasure as he swelled within her. Kortul curled his cock inward, and it rubbed her just right, sending her flowing into a deep, orgasm that moved through her like a warm stream.

Kortul moaned in her hair before he kissed her antenna as he came in her, sending her into a different realm of loving orgasmic pleasure layered over the ecstasy already moving within her. She blasted him back with her own loving feelings, and she swore she saw tears in his eyes.

When the pleasurable waves cooled, Kortul remained inside of her and kissed her head before he lifted her off him and set her in the shower stream. He carefully washed her before he washed himself. When they were finished, they dried and dressed in lounge clothes before joining Brock, who was cooking in the kitchen.

Brock shooed them from the kitchen when Kortul tried to help, and they sat at the table right before Mabit and Tyce transported in. The two sat down, and Kortul slid his handheld communicator to Mabit. "Can you take our picture for the announcement?"

Mabit gave them a warm smile as he picked up the communicator. "I would love to." He held up the device, and Kortul wrapped his arm around Tolina. They both smiled for the camera and Mabit took a few pictures before handing the device back. Kortul sent off the form with the photo and put his communicator back in his pocket.

"Our marriage will be announced tomorrow."

Tolina could tell this announcement meant the world to Kortul and Mabit. This family was one she was proud to belong to, and she smiled to herself. She was Mrs. Saltic now, and she loved it. Their dinner was filled with smiles and chatter. Tolina felt at home. It was *perfect*.

Chapter 34

Cut

Their day started with a horror film, and when it was finished, they had put on their swimsuits and transported to the patio. Tolina sipped her drink and set it down before he leaned her back for a kiss.

Kortul picked up his tablet to show her their announcement and her heart squeezed with how thrilled he was. He set the tablet down, and his face fell before he grabbed her and yelled, "Emergency..." but his words were cut short by a tiny dart in his neck.

Tolina felt a dart hit her shoulder at the same time, and her body froze in place. The patio disappeared, and they reappeared behind a force field in a cell aboard a transport ship, and Pollard Gondek Tweed the First stood outside their cell. His big ears curled and his big flat brown tail slapped his legs.

Pollard spun his finger in the air, and the two of them were forced to straighten and face him. "Saltic, I have waited a long time for an excuse to be rid of you. You were the only person to ever stand in my way of ownership of your father's company, and after I sell you and your wife to a Gistones farm on Lochpacs, I will legally be able to take everything. With your wealth added to mine, I'll replace and supersede you as one of the wealthiest people in the galaxy. Did you think because I let my son take over the negotiations for my company, that I would be too feeble to come for you? I can't prove it was you who slaughtered him, but someone must pay for this, and you've always been number one on my list. You should've heard the way your father would speak of his useless son and the Corbatton law, forcing him to leave the company to you. How does it feel to know your father cared for his business associates more than his own son or even his partner? Do you want to know why? It wasn't because you were useless. He could have worked with that, but you were both so much worse. You and Mabit were too soft together, and he hated *you* for it." Pollard smiled at Kortul as he continued, "I offered to sell you to Lochpacs once, and he almost let me. I'm so glad he didn't allow it because now I have the pleasure of torturing your wife in front of you before you're shipped off."

Tolina's heart didn't even stutter a beat with the revelation. The only thing she worried about was Kortul becoming distressed. When Pollard walked off, he released them, and Kortul tried to pry the dart from his neck, but it wouldn't budge. "Tolina, I..."

Lifting her hands to place them on either side of Kortul's face, Tolina cut his broken words short and forced him to focus on her. "When it starts, you need to close your eyes. Do you understand me? They don't know who I am, but you do. You need to trust me." Kortul's eyes were bulging from his head, and she could hear his heart thumping in his chest as if it would burst. She placed her hand over his heart and hooked her thumb in his mouth and forced him down to her eye level. "If we need to play a game to make it through this, then that's what we will do. If you watch me during my bloody playtime I will punish you, do you understand me? Don't make me resort to worse."

Kortul was horrified and turned on all at once, and he lied as he nodded, and she released his jaw. He stared at her and breathed, "I love you. I..."

Honey fuck! That didn't work. She could see his mind slipping into chaos, and she gave him her best smile as she softly explained, "Panic helps no one. Deep breaths, and remember who I am."

Kortul stopped and did as she said, forcing himself to calm with slow deep breaths. He did know who she was, and as much as this would destroy him, he knew she could endure much more than he could. It didn't matter though. He would do anything for her except sit by while she was tortured. *Not happening.* When he was calm enough to think, he tried to apologize, "Toli, I am sorry."

"Stop. Never say that again." Tolina snapped before he could say another word and when he started to say something else, she cut him off as she continued, "Without your wealth or looks, and when your layers are peeled back, you are a great man, and you will not apologize- not to me or anyone else. You will not flinch when the worst begins. You will not give them one sliver of satisfaction, do you understand? We will do this together, no matter what happens. Somehow, someone will slip. When that happens, we will be free. We *will* survive this. I love you, Kortul. They're coming."

Tolina could feel the tremors of the boots coming down the hall on the other side of the door. Kortul kissed her with tears in his eyes and locked her in a bruising embrace as the door to the brig slid open and three Zaerini men, including Pollard, came inside.

Pollard waved his hand, and they both froze. He waved his hand again, and they moved apart, straightening to face him. He reached over and pressed a finger to the keypad, and the force field enclosing them dropped. He waved for Tolina to walk from the cell before he replaced the field.

He waved to release his control over Kortul and left Tolina frozen behind him as he approached the cell. "Not a word to save your lovely wife? What is she anyway, a bright pink Vitolas? I bet you love touching those wings of hers."

Kortul closed his eyes and moved away from the force field. His shoulder hit the hard wall of the cell, and he held back a scream of fury. *Do what she told you. Don't watch. She is a professional. We can escape and fix her wings. Fuck, I can't do it.*

Tolina watched as Kortul did as she asked him not to do. He looked right at her. His eyes were haunted as he stared at her.

Pollard released his hold on her through the dart stuck on her skin and he grabbed her by the neck to lift her even with his face. "If you move or use any empathic manipulation, Saltic will be transported into space." She was not stupid. She knew precisely how this would go. She remained emotionless and he dropped her to her feet before pulling a knife from his belt. He stepped around her and tapped between her shoulders. "Unfold them." Tolina sighed under her breath as she unfurled her wings and spread them behind her. She looked up to find Kortul in front of her staring into her eyes and horrified. She shot him a scathing look, but he shook his head no.

Pollard sliced her wing down the center, and she cringed. The pain was consuming and her throat constricted to hold in a cry. "Fuck you, Pollard! Leave her alone!" Kortul's voice was distant as she regained her composure through the agony. Her body knew pain of this degree too well, so by the time Pollard sliced her other wing, she was already giving Kortul a furious look as he shouted with burning ferocity against the force field.

Tolina knew exactly what Pollard was doing as she felt him misalign the cuts and tapped between her shoulders. She curled her wings back against her skin, knowing they would heal wrong, and she would no longer be able to fly. It would take reconstructive surgery and months to years of rehabilitation to recover from this, and even then, she may never fly again. It was an outlawed practice on her harsh world long ago because of its brutality. She refused to allow heartbreak to sneak in, and she held Kortul at the forefront of her mind.

"We have a few days before I can deliver you to Captain Gowler. You'll have plenty of time to heal before we send you two off to your new home." Tolina was lost in her thoughts as they forced her to walk back into the cell, and Pollard restarted the force field before releasing his hold. Her clear blood trailed behind her with every step. As the three men left them alone in the brig, her blood pooled at her feet, and she crumpled to the floor to lay face down and ease the flow.

Kortul fell face down on the floor next to her and reached for her hand. He knew exactly what Pollard had done to her. His words were sorrowful, and his voice cracked as he tried to reassure her, "I swear you will fly again. Stay as calm as you can so you don't lose too much blood."

"I can make my heart slow. I will appear dead, but I'm fine. I need you to trust me. It will take a few hours for me to clot enough to raise my heart rate to a sleeping state. I will need to sleep for at least a day."

Kortul couldn't hold back his tears as they streamed from his eyes. He had never felt so helpless. He didn't think anything could have made him regret pursuing Tolina, but as he watched her breathing slow to an imperceptible level, his heart ripped itself into shreds of grief. *I should have let her go. She would've been happy enough with someone else, and she would still be able to fly. She wouldn't be here at all. This is all my fault. I wish my father would've just killed me.* Kortul couldn't block out the day his father almost beat him to death. If Mabit had not stopped him, Kortul would never have survived. *Mabit, I wish I could warn you Pollard is coming for you.* Brock and Tyce crossed his mind next, and his heart ached for them both. Kortul sunk himself into a thoughtless state of heartache as he held Tolina's hand, which was cooling to the touch. Her skin became dull and lifeless as she slowed her heart, and it was too haunting for Kortul to handle, so he kept his eyes shut. He didn't sleep, but he wasn't fully awake as he lay on the floor of the cell for what seemed like an eternity before Tolina sucked in a deep breath. It was slow and steady, but over the course of a few hours she was breathing normally, and her color had returned. The blood flow from her wings was dry, and the cuts were clotted and forming scabs as Kortul rubbed the hand he still held. She whimpered softly as she began to rouse, and Kortul brushed the hair from her face.

She opened her swollen eyes and whispered, "Are my wings still bleeding?"

He shook his head 'no,' and she tried to smile at him,

but all it did was make him upset, so she squeezed his hand and reassured him, "I know that was hard, but I'm over the hard part. Now I just need another day, and I'll be healed enough to walk. By the time he sells us, I will be able to fight if I need to. Wings heal faster than anything, especially when they're folded. I'm more worried about you and your stress levels. They will target me again, and you need to be ready. They might keep us together just to keep this up. We both know it's better if it's me they target."

Kortul shook his head at her and snapped, "I love you more than life, and I understand you have been through things I can't fathom, but how do you expect me to just let them keep hurting you and not react?"

"You don't have a choice. I am conditioned for this, and they don't know that." Tolina barely spoke over a whisper, but she knew Kortul heard every word. He refused to agree with her after he was forced to watch them cut her wings, and she could see it all over his face.

She sighed knowing the next time they came for her, she would need to reveal to him how conditioned she was to pain. Kortul had shown her his true heart, and it was time she allowed him to see the last part of her she had been hiding away. It was the part of her which joyfully laughed in the face of any foe she was stacked against. He knew who she was, but it was time for him to truly see it for himself.

Chapter 35

One Hundred Years

After spending most of the time on the floor with Kortul spread out next to her as she healed, they were back on their feet for their last day in the holding cell. They would be shipped off soon, and Tolina stretched slowly to loosen her movement so she could fight when the time came.

When she was finished, Kortul inspected her healing wings, and he seemed relieved. "You were right. They have healed quickly. The cuts I can see are scarring over."

He ran his finger along the edge of one of her wings, and she leaned to rest against his chest. "When they hand us over, you need to know what will happen. They think I'm just some woman, and they will use me to control you because you are the target. We will keep this facade whether you like it or not until I see a window. If you don't, I'll need to show you a side of me you don't want to see. I will not allow them to harm you." Tolina sighed as she wiggled her back to loosen her stiff wings. "They are coming. Don't deviate from the plan, or you could fuck us both. Kortul, I need you to swear to me."

"I love you, and I won't lie to you."

Tolina scowled at him as she reached up and grabbed his face before bringing him eye level. "If anything happens to you, I will fracture in an insidious way, and innocent people will die. You swear right now on our future and innocent lives that you will behave."

Kortul snapped at her, "Fuck! I'll try!" He brought his lips down onto hers in a harsh kiss before they heard the whoosh of the door behind them.

"Saltic, it's time for you and your wife to meet your travel captain and owner for the duration of the trip." Pollard waved his hand and forced them to stand and face him. He turned off the forcefield and waved his hand to force them to march toward the airlock at the end of the hallway. The airlock was open and connected to an old light-speed ship. When Kortul did not think it could become any worse, he was proven wrong to an extreme point. The journey to the planet they would be delivered to would take one hundred lightyears to reach. Everyone on the ship would be cryo-frozen for the journey, and they would wake up years later with everyone they've ever known back home either elderly or dead.

No matter what Tolina said, there would be no escaping this to return home. There would no longer be the same home to return to. They were marched through the airlock, and Pollard forced their arms out in front of them to be cuffed. Captain Gowler, a Gistones man with tough light beige skin and a giant, curved brown horn protruding from the forehead of his square, hard face walked up with two of his Gistones guards by his side. The Gistones people evolved from rhinoceros beetles and were known for their wide frame and harsh looks. They were overall a peaceful people, but they had been overrun by a few evil, greedy men like the one purchasing them.

The guards cuffed Tolina and Kortul while Pollard disconnected the darts neurologically controlling them. They were dragged to barred cells across from one another, and when the guard shut Kortul's cell, his guard went into Tolina's cell with her and her guard.

Tolina stared at Kortul who was gripping the bars of his cell, and the skin on his hands was stretched over his knuckles with his iron hold. His eyes were pleading, and she shook her head right before the first guard slammed his giant fist into her stomach, sending her flying backward several feet. The guards laughed as she groaned softly and grabbed her belly as she breathed through the pain. Next was a strike to her face that slammed her against the cold metal wall of the cell as stars burst in her vision. She slid onto the floor, and when her eyes cleared, Kortul was on his knees across from her screaming at the guards.

One of the guards grabbed her arm and threw her into the opposite wall, dislocating her shoulder, and in the impact, one of her fingers was forced from its socket on the same side. When she crumpled back to the ground, she could hear Kortul screaming, "I'll fucking kill you all!" The guards laughed, and as they vacated her cell and locked it. As they exited the brig, they spit on Kortul, and he sneered at them when they turned their backs.

The moment they were alone, Tolina lifted her head, and Kortul was wiping the spit from his chest and face with his hand. "Toli, please say something."

"I'm fine. Need to. Catch. My breath." Tolina slowly

regained her wits from the last impact, and she looked at her dangling arm with a grimace. She closed her eyes and stood just to slam her injured shoulder into the wall to force it back into place.

Kortul had his forehead leaned against the bars as he closed his tear filled eyes and whispered, "I can't believe I'm about to say this, but you were right. You're the strongest person I've ever met."

Tolina sat across from him and rubbed her sore shoulder with a grin, and scoffed at her middle finger when she looked down to it bent to the side. Kortul opened his eyes just as she popped her finger back in place, and she smiled at him. "See. I got this."

Kortul banged his head on the bars, and he could hear boots approaching.

"Don't worry. I've been through much worse. You really need to stop watching. It's not good for you." Tolina was poking at the swelling in her face.

Kortul snarled at her as the guards opened the door. "Fuck. Tolina, shut up."

She laughed as the guards walked in and didn't stop when they approached the cell. Tolina wanted these men to fixate on her so they would leave Kortul alone. She knew the best way to achieve that goal was to be herself. She had warned Kortul, and now he would see the last bit of truth she had to reveal.

The giant man growled, "What is so funny fly? Are you ready for more?"

Tolina winked at him and blew him a kiss, sending him into a rage and he slammed his fist into the bars before pulling a cylinder device from his belt. He waved the now sparking and elongating device at her as it charged, and

Tolina curled her tongue up as he thrust the baton at her. When it made contact, her entire body convulsed with the electric current. She clenched her teeth and fought the electricity, growling as he continued to send the current through her. Her skin began to steam where he held the electric stick. When he pulled it away, Tolina resumed her devious laugh, and across from her, Kortul looked like he was ripping his hair out.

She felt like she had been cooked as one guard opened the door and the other kicked her across the cell, sending her body crashing against the wall. She fell silent, and the guards waited for her to move. When she didn't, they locked the cell and moved on. After the door shut and they were alone, Tolina rolled over and sat by the bars like nothing happened.

Devastated, Kortul frowned at her, "Tolina, what the fuck?" That wasn't a question.

She laughed under her breath as she leaned her sore face against the bars. "I used to get my ass beat every other day like this in training. We all did. I told you. I've seen my own intestines, remember?"

"You are not helping anything." Kortul felt like he would be sick as bile crept up his throat. He wasn't sure how much of this he could handle. His heart was physically aching. He would give his life for this woman, so how did she expect him to push his love for her aside in her most vulnerable moments?

Tolina noticed him slipping again. She grabbed the bars by her face and stood up. "Kortul?" He met her gaze, and she continued, "You need to learn to turn off your emotions if you want to survive this. I know you're afraid it will turn you into your father, but it won't. You have too much heart for that. I want you to practice right now. Push everything away and force your mind to clear. Make a box in your mind and put me in it. Close the box, lock it, and walk away when they come for me. Practice shoving me in the box and setting me aside. It's something we all learned in training. If you don't learn this, your stress will kill you, and I *need you* to stay alive."

Kortul was half listening as he stared at the bars in front of him, and she could see him continuing to fall deeper into despair. Something hard wiggled in her mouth, so she reached in with two fingers and pulled out one of her top teeth on the left side. Staring at the tooth, she huffed a laugh and threw it at Kortul, nailing him in the forehead. It bounced off his face before it skidded back over to Tolina.

"Did you just throw a rock at me?" Kortul had his hand on his forehead with a look of pure dismay in his eyes.

Through her swollen face, Tolina smiled. "No."

Kortul tilted his head trying to see what the dark spot was in her smile as she threw the tooth at him again. This time he caught it. When he opened his hand, he yelped and threw it back at her, hitting her in the chest. "Was that your fucking tooth?! Listen, I love you, but right now, I hate you so much. I feel like my heart is dying in my chest, and you are throwing your fucking tooth at me! STOP IT!" Tolina was already mid-throw, and her tooth smacked him right between the eyes. Kortul sat stunned with his mouth dropped open as he watched her reach her leg between the bar after the tooth, presumably to throw it at him again. Shooting his webbing from his fingertips, he snatched the tooth and tossed it in the back of his cell before Tolina could reach it.

He glared at her. "You are not stopping, are you?"

"Nope." Tolina wagged her long tongue at him, and he

cringed at her swollen, dark purple face. In a serious tone, Tolina asked, "Does my head look like a big blueberry with hair?"

Kortul bit his lips together to hold back his smile, but he was failing, so he dropped his face in his hands and whispered, "I hate you so much right now." Her head did look like a big blueberry with hair.

Tolina started giggling, and it soon turned into a full-blown fit of laughter for both of them. When Tolina calmed enough, she explained, "My only goal is to keep you safe and alive until I can melt someone's brain so we can escape." Tolina paused a moment before she went on, "I hate to tell you, but this is who I am too. You know what I did to all those men, right?"

Kortul looked up at her and nodded as he frowned. "In detail."

"Those deaths brought me immense joy to the point of dancing. The only thing I love more than killing awful people is you and our family. If this situation requires that I take risks to keep your head up, then that is what I will do. I tried to warn you, but you didn't listen. I thrive in situations like this. Do you remember me telling you about my first kill and my leg?" Kortul didn't respond, he just blinked and waited for her to continue. "He brought the butt of the ax on my leg several times before I could flip over. My leg was shattered, and I remember thinking, die or kill him. I forced the pain away and turned to catch the head of the ax when he brought it down for another hit. I used his strike momentum to slip it from his grip. Once I had it, I spun the blade and slammed it into his thigh. He fell where I could reach, and I hacked at his legs until I chopped them off. I may have had a gut-wrenching journey for a rescue signal, but I fell in love with being the hand of death that day. I am willing to do whatever it takes to find a way to escape. It might just take some time."

Kortul seemed to melt onto the floor, and he spread his hands over his face. "You know this is a lightspeed ship, right?"

Tolina knew what he was aiming at. "Let me guess, cryo-freezing and then a four-hundred-year journey before we wake and work until we die?"

"One hundred," Kortul corrected as he peered between his splayed fingers.

She smiled at him and stuck the end of her tongue through the gap in her teeth, and she wagged it at him.

Kortul couldn't help but laugh as he admitted, "Your head does look like a big fucking blueberry."

Chapter 36

Truth

The lights dimmed, and a smaller Gistones man came in to drop off bowls of food. Tolina was given sugar water, while they gave Kortul a bowl of white goop. Tolina watched him scowl at his bowl as she sucked down her less than appetizing sugar water. "You need to eat."

He frowned at her. "It smells like a dirty foot."

"It's a vitamin and protein mix. Hold your nose and drink it. Just pretend it's my pussy."

Kortul shot her a devilish smile. "My love, your pussy and your ass taste like candy."

"Oh." *I should have known that.* All she consumed was sugar. "Wait, my ass? When did you lick my ass?" He wiggled his thumb at her, and she remembered the hot tub. She released another, "Oh," but this time it was louder and full of understanding.

Kortul downed the slop and cringed a bit before he set the bowl down and wiped his mouth. "Your pussy could've tasted like actual shit, and I would have loved it just as much."

Tolina laughed as she checked the swelling of her face, and it had fully spread to the sides. She knew she looked terrible because she had her face smashed many times before, and her whole head swelled the same way each time. Kortul eyes were hollow and dark from the stress and loss of sleep. He needed a lot of uplifting to stay positive and she didn't mind at all. "I would still kiss you if your face looked like a butthole."

Kortul hissed with laughter, and she could see his shoulders loosen and relax. "I would say I would still love you if you were a worm, but you *were* a worm with legs at one point, so I have already proved that. Honestly, walking worms are so much worse, so that should count for double."

Tolina laughed as tears gathered in her eyes, and she wiped them away to see. "Being a caterpillar was terrible. I was endlessly hungry, and when I went through my metamorphosis, I thought I was dying. With my nervous system intact, the rest of my former body liquified and rebuilt into this body. It was like living through a horror movie."

Kortul was captivated by her story although he already knew how it worked scientifically. Hearing it from her point of view during the process was disturbing. "You were *awake*?"

"I was fully aware the entire process. It didn't hurt, but it was the most unnerving and unsettling sensation because I didn't know what was happening. If I had known and understood, it would've been different. Taking that first breath after I broke through my chrysalis was a glorious moment." Tolina remembered something she had pushed from her mind for most of her life, but now it mattered more than ever. "I just remembered there is something about my people I need to share with you." She waited for him to give her his full attention. When he was sitting up straight across from her, she continued, "There is a likelihood I will develop a mental decline in my seventies. It's something that happens to many of our people, and those of us who have been through the Vo-Pess training have a higher rate of decline. I believe it's a cascade of problems from the way our society is run, but there could still be a genetic link."

Kortul gave her a sweet smile of reassurance. "We will face it together if it happens. I treasure every moment with you, and I would give up everything for the time I've had with you. I almost did."

"What do you mean you almost did?" Tolina sniffled back tears.

Kortul licked his dry, cracked lips and admitted, "When I learned your name, I added it to everything I own. If you had left me for someone else, you could have taken everything from me. The court would have sold the company, and that's really why none of the Saltic men before me ever married. I would have been forced to watch you walk away, but you would have been taken care of, so it was worth it. I didn't have much of a reason to live until I met you. I didn't want my life at all without you."

Tolina could feel her heartbeat in her face as she thought back to the moments when her mind began to shift and she fell for him. "The chair at the resort. When I felt you for the first time, that's when I decided to give you a real chance. My heart knew before that though, but I wasn't listening. I was too stubborn to see how perfect you were."

"I am far from perfect," Kortul scoffed as he lay down by the bars and rested his head on his arm.

Tolina smiled at him and corrected, "You're perfect for me."

They both remained quiet for some time, and Kortul recalled their time at the resort. *The murder.* Kortul's face dropped. He sat up with a start and stared at her with heated intensity. "Did you kill that murderer rapist at the resort?"

Tolina grinned and shined with pride, but, she wasn't telling anyone Nire was a victim, including Kortul.

"You cut his toe off and shoved it up his nose! You are fucking wicked." Kortul was rubbing his face trying to comprehend how his wife was such a prolific serial murderer when he thought he always knew where she was. *She must have used her empathic skills to identify him.*

Tolina knew the news had not covered the entire story, so she told him what she could, "I cut his dick off and made him eat it. He choked on it. It was very satisfying."

Kortul couldn't help but laugh in disbelief. "Is that why you and Nire were friends by the time we left? How did you have time to do all of this?"

"You were asleep. I can stay awake for days if necessary." Tolina watched it all make sense in his head.

He twisted his mouth to the side and scratched his head as he admitted, "The only reason I was able to talk Mabit into giving me my father's chameleon armor was because of *that* murder. He thought I was turning into my father, and that I was planning to stalk you, ruin your dates, and force you to be with me. He was right about most of it, but my motives are different. I told him I needed to follow you to protect you, and that was true, but it was the thought of another man's hands on you that was unimaginable. I couldn't stand the thought."

"You threw rocks and rotten fruit at my date." Tolina

scrunched her face, and Kortul cringed. She knew it looked painful and was glad the lights were dim.

Kortul sighed as he told the truth, "Yes, I threw rocks and rotten fruit at the first one, but I did nothing to the second man. He was an asshole all by himself."

"What about my third date? Did you do something to his food? Was that your fault?" Tolina had to ask. She had just left the nice man vomiting in the restaurant.

Kortul nodded as he shot her a nervous grin. "I poisoned his food."

Tolina bit her lip and shook her head in disbelief. *I should have known.* "I left that man puking by the table. He was genuinely kind. I feel so bad."

Kortul snarled at her, "He's doing a lot better than we are right now."

"Great point," Tolina laughed and lay down on the ground. Her face was pounding, and she needed rest.

Kortul closed his eyes, and she watched his chest as his breathing slowed and evened out. When she was sure he was asleep, she forced herself to doze off. She knew she might not be able to have deep, restful sleep, but she could at least try for a nap. She needed to save her energy in case she saw an opportunity for her to take the ship.

Many hours later, lights above brightened, but no one came into the cell block, and Tolina and Kortul both sat up to stretch. They had both slept, and Tolina felt much better.

"Your face swelling has gone down. That missing tooth will take a little getting used to though," Kortul teased, and she grinned at him, making sure she showed off the gap.

"It really is a good thing we found true love in one another because we will both be uglier than shriveled old leather after a few years of hard labor under a bright star."

Tolina could see the hope returning to Kortul, and he laughed, "You'll still want to fuck me even when I look like a raisin?"

"Don't worry. I'll always want to sit on that face."

Kortul added, "So you would kiss me if my face looked like a butthole, and you'll still sit on my face even when I look like a wrinkly raisin? I think that covers it."

Tolina was content for a moment, thankful she was able to pull Kortul from his gloomy doom descent. "We will be happy no matter what. I didn't really even comprehend happy before you. Now that I have it, I will not let it slip away without a fight. Do you see now?"

Kortul's mouth tipped up in the corner, and he answered, "I do. I see that I have the strongest, bravest, wife in the galaxy and that I need to trust her. We need to stop doubting each other."

Tolina scoffed, "We kind of have a problem with that, don't we?"

Kortul rested his head between the bars of his cell and sighed, "For a shitty location, and awful food, this is a great bonding vacation we're having. I feel like we've really grown as a couple in the last few days."

"I wish I had another tooth to throw at you." The amusement dancing in Kortul's eyes meant everything to Tolina, and she soaked it up.

Kortul paused to think as he wiggled his fingers, and then looked back at Tolina's tooth behind him. "I have an idea."

A few minutes later, Tolina learned Kortul's idea had nothing to do with escape. Kortul took his time and made her a disk of rope webbing with sticky web on one side. He slid it over to her before he shot a few balls of sticky web onto the center of the wall behind her. "Stick the disk on the wall."

She did as he asked, and he stuck the other one he made even with hers. He wrapped her tooth in sticky web first, then in rope webbing. "I can't stand to be bored. We are playing a weird version of night-ball."

"I see that. Are we calling this tooth ball," Tolina joked as Kortul prepared to throw the ball of rope webbing with the tooth inside at the disk in her cell.

It landed off center, and he relaxed his shoulders. Tolina scoffed as she peeled the ball from the disk and prepared to throw it at his disk. She was closer than his throw, but not quite to the center. She felt a little spark of excitement. "This was a good idea."

They played for hours before taking a rest, and then they resumed their game for several more hours. They talked about everything from geology on Corbatton and random facts about the animals on the planet all the way to Tolina admitting how much she loved killing. They bounced around from subject to subject, and the conversation only paused while they rested. Tolina was ahead by a small margin when she asked, "Are you ready for tomorrow?"

Kortul shook his head as he tossed the ball in his hands. "No. Have you ever been frozen?"

"No. I heard it's not like sleep, and it will feel like an instant for us." Tolina didn't want to address the obvious problem, the one they had both been avoiding.

Kortul lowered his head and became quiet. "Are we discussing reality right now?"

Tolina squeezed her eyes shut. "I know the post eighty-year survival statistics for my galaxy, and I assume they're not any better here?" Kortul confirmed what she suspected when he rubbed his eyes, trying to hide his tears. Cryo-freezing was a common practice, and it was perfectly safe, but only temporarily. When it came to long term freezing, the survival rates of occupants declined after eighty years. Over a tenth of those frozen would not make the journey.

"We *will* make it. We will both make it there alive. I will *not* say goodbye to you. We will see each other again," Tolina whispered as the lights dimmed and the little man came in to deliver their food for the night.

After staring at one another for hours until they both fell asleep, Kortul and Tolina were awakened by the lights before two thinner framed Gistones men came for Kortul first. When they walked to his cell, they waved for Kortul to stick his hands through the bars so they could cuff him. Once he was secured, they opened the door and led him out. He held his eyes on Tolina as long as he could before he was too far down the hall to see her.

They brought him to the prep room where they stripped off his swim shorts and hosed him off with a cold chemical wash before scrubbing his skin with brushes on sticks. He felt as though he had lost an entire layer of skin by the time they were finished. Once he was forced through the ultraviolet sterilization room, he was shoved into an upright cryo-chamber with a clear glass door. They slammed the door shut and set the lock on the side before walking off.

He had just enough room to raise his arm straight in front of him if he kept his hand flat. There was a vent at the side, and he inspected it as he waited and tried to force himself to think about anything other than what was happening.

The moment Tolina's eyes met his, she made a silly grimace, probably over the scrubbing she just had, and he tried to smile but he couldn't. They shoved her into the cryo-chamber across from him and locked her inside before they left to prepare and lock away the next person.

Kortul and Tolina didn't look away from one another as each one of the chambers were filled. It took hours before they were finished, and Kortul's heart felt like it might squeeze itself into a knot as the freeze countdown began. He watched Tolina as she mouthed 'I love you' to him.

She didn't know their language. She was mimicking what his lips looked like when he said 'I love you' to her. Kortul said it back a moment before he watched as Tolina froze solid, along with her entire row of chambers. The chill struck Kortul right before the silence.

Chapter 37

The Wraimet

Captain Gowler was written above the old cryo-chamber, but it was hard to read now. His cryo-chamber taunted him. This would be his last haul before he retired. The salty air on his ship from the cryo-system had weathered and rusted his name. He was looking forward to yanking his title off and taking it with him when he sold the ship. With the cryo-chambers running, they would be departing for Lochpacs in a few hours when he finished his last system checks.

Studying the monitor at his captain's chair, Gowler noticed a small blip of radiation on his sensors, and he moved to investigate it, but his monitor flickered. He struck the top of the monitor, and it went out a split second before the ship lost power, and emergency backup started. Red lights glowed and highlighted an emergency route to the escape pods.

There was nothing wrong with his ship, and he stormed across the vacant bridge to see if he could access his private tablet, but the device had no power. His mouth went sour as sweat beads formed on his brow. *Something is wrong.* He ran to the viewing window at the front of the bridge and frowned at the primitive planet below. Everyone who traveled to Lochpacs at the edge of the galaxy through the great stretch of empty space knew the rumors about running into a Wraimet. Wraimet were space creatures who could cut all power to a ship to board and devour anything, and everything, living. He had boarded an abandon ship with a salvage crew after an attack, and there was nothing but blood and bits of flesh left behind from the monster. Fear wrapped its cold fingers around his throat when he saw a shadow move, and he bolted. "A Wraimet!" he screamed into the empty bridge as he fled. *That must be what this is!*

Forcing the door open, he rushed from the bridge and signaled his first and second officers, Barwe and Polut, to follow him. "It's a Wraimet!" Gowler barked as they ran, and he could hear two "Aye's," of understanding behind him. There was nothing else in the galaxy he feared. A Wraimet would be coming in through the engine room, and they needed to seal off the entry.

When they reached the hallway to access the engine room, they heard a blast behind them, and all three landed face down. Blood, guts, and uniform pieces from someone in his crew tripped and fell from Gowler and his officers as they scrambled from the ground. Gowler saw a hulking figure approaching in the shadows and a deep, menacing voice spoke as they fled. "Run. I like it."

Gowler screamed at his shipmates, "The fucking pods! Run for the pods!" The three men burst through the door leading to the cryo-chamber rooms, which led to the escape pods at the back of the ship. The people in the chambers were waking, and he intended to leave them as a meal for the creature to save his own skin.

The floor rumbled, and Tolina shivered a bit as she forced her eyes open. In the dim red lights, she watched Gowler and the two large men who assaulted her rush from the cryo-chamber room she and Kortul were trapped in. Across from her, Kortul was waking. Extending her antennae, Tolina reached for the captain's emotions, and his terror sent a chill down her spine. "Fuck. I need out of this chamber." She looked down at her leg with metal bones and cringed. She could use her knee to break the glass, but it would shred her skin. Tolina braced her arms on the glass and lifted her leg just enough to aim before she reared back as far as she could and slammed her kneecap into the glass. The skin on her knee burst open with her hit, and Kortul slapped a hand over his mouth as he watched her beat the glass with her now exposed metal kneecap.

Inside her chamber, her clear blood sprayed as Tolina kept on until the glass cracked in the center. She prepared for a powerful impact and when she hit the glass, it splintered down the middle and spiderwebbed. With a shove of her hands, she was able to shatter the glass, and the shards fell into the metal grate below.

Nude and trembling from the cold, Tolina sprinted to the end of the chamber room and grabbed a wrench before she ran back to Kortul. She started to bang on the side of the glass to break it, but she heard something approaching from behind the door. She looked through the glass at Kortul and she lay her hand over where his hand was pressed against the glass. Remembering the vent on the side, Tolina slid the wrench into the vent and forced it through until she could see it inside the chamber.

She could now hear Kortul, and he was screaming. He began furiously pounding on the inside of the glass with the wrench, and Tolina refocused on the approaching threat.

She turned to face the door and saw a long prying tool leaned in the corner, so she ran and grabbed it before resuming her position in front of Kortul.

The door slid open, and a dark figure stepped toward the open door. In the low light, Tolina couldn't see, so she crouched and prepared for an attack.

Something white flickered before a bright light filled the space.

A familiar little figure stood in the doorway wearing protective gear, and he was holding a small, high powered sonic weapon designed for blasting a victim to shreds.

Tolina dropped the tool and screamed, "BROCK!" She looked back at Kortul who had dropped the wrench, and he was now fully pressed against the glass gaping.

Brock teetered over and lifted his hand to offer her something. "I found on patio with Mabit." It was her armor tab. She slapped it on her hip and spread her armor over her skin. She could feel her armor reconnecting the skin on her knee with the nano-tech, and Tolina cringed as it sealed the injury. She retrieved her guns from her sides and pointed them at the lock on Kortul's chamber. He shielded his face as she blasted the lock.

Tolina swung the door open, and Kortul crashed into her and wrapped his arms around her. He peppered the top of her head with feather light kisses and sobbed, "I'm so fucking mad at you!" Kortul stopped only to look up at Brock before he screamed, "WHY ARE YOU HERE?"

Brock had Kortul's chameleon armor in his extended

hand, "Explain all later. You need new safe. We broke it to get armor. Tyce is in ship, and Mabit protects home."

Kortul released Tolina and grabbed Brock in a twirling hug before he took the armor from him to dress. They looked around at the waking Zaerini people as Brock pulled a tablet from his pack and handed it to Tolina. Tolina quickly sent power back to the chambers, so Brock could open them and explain what was happening.

With Brock working on the chambers, she and Kortul found the bridge. Tolina sat in the captain's chair and accessed the sensors before pressing her hand on the screen and hacking into the ship's ancient computer system with her nano-tech armor. She knew the old ship would have a lock on the crew bio-signatures. With the ship's sensors connected to her suit, she mapped out where all the pods landed on the nearby planet.

"I found them. Are you coming with me?" Tolina asked Kortul, who was standing beside her watching.

Kortul smiled at her as he tucked a bit of her hair behind her ear, "Always."

Tolina stood, and Kortul took her hand as he initiated an armor link so they could still see one another when their chameleon setting was active. Once they were linked, Tolina ordered, "Corver, transport us to the ship."

When they were aboard their ship, Tyce greeted them with a worried smile. "It's good to see you two."

Kortul threw his arms around Tyce and squeezed is best friend until he wheezed, "Go kill those assholes so we can go home."

Smiling and then giggling at Tyce's shock over her missing tooth, Tolina agreed, "I can't wait to kill them. Let's go."

Tolina initiated the ship's cloak, and she transported the ship to the surface of the planet. They exited the airlock, and she made their armor invisible as they descended the stairs to the desolated landscape of dry trees and tall rocky hills in the low light of dusk. Tolina shared the bio-target tracking she had linked with the ship to Kortul, and he followed close behind as she moved for her first target of the five. The crew she was hunting believed a monster had attacked the ship, so a monster is what she would give them.

They were closing in on the first targets, and when Tolina spotted them in the distance, she recognized them as the men who prepped them for the cryo-chambers. Her skin still stung from the scrubbing she endured, and she itched to see their blood. She ran for the first one, and as she did, she kicked up dirt and rocks to ensure they knew something was coming for them. She retrieved and turned on her separator as she closed in, Tolina spoke to Kortul through the armor. "Are you ready for this?"

"More than you can imagine," Kortul confirmed, and Tolina was close enough to jump onto the huge man's back. When she did, his panic burst from his throat in a blood curdling scream as he crashed to the ground. Tolina jumped away and landed on her feet before pouncing on him where he lay. He was face down, and she dragged the separator from his shoulder blade to his waist on his right side. He let out a gurgling cry as his body convulsed. Blood squirted from his back as Tolina started on his leg, slicing him from his ass to his knee and flaying him open. She continued to slice into him until he stopped moving and went silent under her. Tolina noticed the second man crawling away, and she raised her gun and shot him three times, twice in the center of his gut and once in the groin. He gurgled and cried at the fatal wounds as blue blood poured from his mouth.

"We need to move." Wasting no time, Tolina located the next two targets who were running away together.

She took off in their direction, and Kortul followed close behind her. She tossed him one of her guns, and he whistled at it. "I am starting to believe Mabit really does love you more than me."

Tolina giggled as she recalled all her wonderful gifts and his glowing praises. "I have bad news."

"I knew it. He does love you more."

Tolina spotted her targets, and her mind switched back to her task like the machine it was molded to be. These were the two men who gave her blueberry head, and she wanted them to pay a little more than the cryo-scrubbing assholes. She lifted her antenna and conjured up all the most terrifying feelings she had ever experienced before blasting them at the two men. The way they stumbled and began throwing their arms out for protection gave Tolina immense joy as she closed the distance between them.

Moving her feelings to the pain she had experienced at their hands, she discovered she could make them hurt like she did, and they screamed in agony on the ground as they grabbed their faces. They thrashed against her empathic onslaught of pain and horror. When she was close enough for the kill, she climbed over the first one and dove her separator in his chest before dragging it down and cutting a valley into his ribs. Blood poured from the wound, and she walked around him to the second thrashing man to do the same to him. Once her separator was plunged into his chest and he was split open and bleeding, she looked for her final target on her holo-screen, the captain.

He wasn't far, and she smiled. Now that she understood her empathic ability better, she planned to test the limits with the captain. They passed over two hills before Tolina saw him trying to make it to a cave opening. He was much too far from the opening to make it pumping his overly thick legs, and Tolina caught up to him quickly. She took the years of torturous pain and suffering she experienced and swirled the traumatic memories in her mind into a cyclone of anguish. Tolina watch as the colossal wave of horror struck Captain Gowler, and he grasped his chest as he rolled on the ground fighting to breathe. He tried to crawl to the cave, but with every movement he made, she increased her attack. Trying something new, she recalled the way her skin felt when she had been burned with a torch, and she inflated it to envelop her whole body before she slammed it into the captain. The high pitch wailing he released pierced the air, and Tolina relished in his song of death.

The captain fell silent as his heart gave out, and he slumped onto the ground. Tolina sliced her separator across his neck to be sure he was dead before she turned to face Kortul.

Tolina could sense his radiating fear and love for her. "Let's go home and finish this."

Chapter 38

Wings

When they landed the ship in the building hangar, Kortul waited until Tyce and Brock transported home before he faced Tolina. He grabbed her and leaned her back to kiss her before he admitted, "Watching you kill is nothing like the movies. I can't wait to see you slaughter Pollard. I know Mabit has him upstairs tied up on his floor, so the real question is, where do you want to kill him?"

Tolina bit her lip as she considered different locations, and she smirked as she thought of the perfect place. It was somewhere no one would ever find his body. "Let's torture him on the ship above one of the Blifordat volcanoes and then drop him inside."

Kortul caught her lips in another kiss, and he gently held her as he agreed with her idea. "You are a stunning nightmare. It's perfection. Corver, transport us to Mabit's apartment."

Mabit stood in his living room with Pollard face down at

his feet. Pollard's hands and feet were tied together behind his back. His face was bruised and red blood dripped from his lips as Tolina walked over to him and smiled in his face. "Remember me?"

Pollard sneered at her as Mabit laughed, "When he told me what he did to your wings, I let him know you were the one who slaughtered his son. You two have a good evening with him, and please let me know when you return. I've contacted a Vitolas wing surgeon, and she would like to begin your repair as soon as possible."

Tolina hugged Mabit gently before Kortul crushed him in an embrace. Mabit took a few steps away and knelt to wave at Pollard on the floor. Kortul kicked Pollard in the stomach. "Corver, transport three of us to my ship."

Kortul kicked Pollard over on his side to put his feet up on him as he sat in the captain's chair, causing Pollard to grunt and grumble. He entered the coordinates to the largest Blifordat active volcano, and in a few moments, the ship was in position over the bubbling, molten caldera. She wanted to watch him fall up close, so she had the ship angled where the airlock faced the caldera. Tolina smiled at Kortul as she lifted her separator from her armor, and Kortul dragged Pollard to the end of the hall by the airlock.

Using her empathic ability, Tolina rested her hand against Pollards face, and she watched the horror fill his eyes as she pumped years of torturous pain into him. Pollard began to bleed from his eyes and ears as she locked him in her empathic prison of terror. She smiled as his pupils dilated and shrank, over and over. She could sense his brain and heart begin to fail from the unending torment she was inflicting.

She yanked it all back in the last moment so he would be present and alert for his death. He sniffed and fought for air as Tolina reached down with her separator and cut two of his fingers from his hand. He screamed, and she held open his jaw to shove his fingers down his throat. With his jaw forced open in her iron grip, she pressed the fingers down so far, he was forced to swallow them, and he cried as they went down his throat. When she was satisfied, she shoved him against the wall and started at his sternum as she slowly dragged the separator down the center of his chest to his groin, splitting him down the middle. His intestines spilled on the floor as he convulsed and blood poured from his mouth.

Tolina set the separator back against her armor. "Corver, transport Pollard and his bodily fluids a mile above the volcano and record his descent into the lava. Make sure his face is visible. When his body has burned away, end the recording and send it to Mabit, then take us home."

Pollard cried below her before he disappeared. Kortul and Tolina stood in a sweet embrace at the airlock glass and watched as Pollard dropped from the sky and into the bubbling fiery lava below. Tolina giggled as she noticed something flapping behind him. "Kortul, I think those were his guts flapping in the air as he fell."

He fell over onto the panel next to him and rested his hand over his mouth as he tried to hide a laugh. "Toli, you are so fucked up." Kortul held her hand as he led them back to their seats and didn't let go of her as they sat down. He reached over and kissed the back of her hand before he asked, "Do you want to go straight to Vitolas?"

"Kortul, we are naked under our armor. I want a shower at home, fresh clothes, and then we can go."

Kortul's mouth made an 'o,' and he nodded in agreement. He remembered her standing by his sealed cryo-chamber, nude, bleeding, and willing to sacrifice herself to kill a monster to keep him safe. Even in that moment he had not discovered exactly who she was, and now that he knew how sharp and depraved her murderous tendencies were that moment on the ship and so many others had fresh meaning.

When they were back home, and she was nude and washing her hair in front of him, his mind went over every moment she spent focused on him, helping him manage the stress, teaching him how to cope, and keeping his mind from falling into a pit of despair. She had even asked him to bottle his love for her so she could force all the pain onto herself.

She finished rinsing her hair and she met Kortul's intense gaze as she traced her fingers over his collar bones. "You've had that look since we were on the ship. Talk to me." Kortul wasn't sure words would be enough, and he knelt in front of her before he pressed the side of his face against her chest. He held her to him, and she reached down to comb her fingers through his hair. "Everything is making sense now, isn't it?"

Kortul didn't say anything, instead he kissed her between her breasts and held her, listening to her heartbeat. He knew he held the greatest treasure in the universe, and his mind was convincing him he never deserved her. He knew he wasn't good enough for her.

Tolina crawled into Kortul's lap, and he held her as she reached for him with her antennae and placed them against his cheeks. She could feel his infinite gratitude and love, but he felt unworthy too. She shifted around to straddle him and licked the tip of his nose. "What makes you think you don't deserve this? I wouldn't have done those things for anyone else." She stopped for a moment and tipped her head to the side before she went on, "Well, maybe Mabit and Brock too."

"I don't care what you say. I'll spend my life repaying you for what you did. Are you ready to face the world and have your wings repaired?"

"I am now that I have clean hair and you're not looking at me weird." Tolina watched a chuckle bubble up from him and he closed his eyes as he hissed a laugh.

He helped her to her feet, and they dressed in comfortable lounge clothes before they walked into the living room. Mabit, Tyce, and even Brock stood waiting for them, dressed and ready to accompany them to the surgery.

When she looked around at everyone ready to come with her, Tolina decided she was finished with holding back how she felt, and she burst into tears. Kortul hugged her to his strong chest, and she let herself sob into his shirt.

When she was ready, Kortul asked, "Corver, take all of us to my ship." They found their seats as they lifted from the floor, and Kortul entered their destination to the Vumenko capital hospital into the computer. Mabit had found the most skilled wing surgeon money could buy, to give Tolina the best chance at regaining her ability to fly.

They arrived at the Vumenko hospital in the hangar under the building. Using the airlock exit stairs, they filed from the ship and entered a door leading them to the lifts and the first floor of the hospital. Once they were upstairs and Tolina was checked in at the front desk, a surgeon brought Tolina and Kortul to a room to prepare her for the surgery. As they walked the doctor introduced herself, "I am Dr. Terigy. I will need you to undress when we reach the room. Please knock when you're ready. There is a sheet you can use to cover yourself on the table."

Kortul and Tolina went into the room together and she stripped down before she wrapped the sheet around her and sat on the table. Kortul knocked on the door and it slid open for the surgeon to enter.

Once inside she guided Tolina to lie face down and she pulled away the cover to inspect her wings. Kortul tried his best to keep his emotions neutral in case she was reading him, but judging by the surgeon's face, Tolina may not fly again.

"I will do everything I can. The nurses will be here soon to prepare you. I will step out so you can say your well wishes before we begin. Kortul, we will need you to return to the waiting room when the nurses arrive."

He nodded to her and the door slid shut. Tolina was still positioned faced down, and she twisted around to look at him. "I'll be fine. I love you."

Kortul leaned down and kissed her head before he whispered over her hair, "I love you too. I'll see you in a few hours."

Three nurses appeared in the room for Tolina, and Kortul went to the waiting room to join Mabit, Tyce, and Brock. He sat down by Mabit, and they stared at the door in silence.

Hours passed before an exhausted nurse came through the door. "We have only finished with one of her wings. There was extensive damage. If you had brought her in even a week later, we would have had to amputate her wings entirely. The way they were set and healing incorrectly created a blood flow loop, and her wings were dying. If there had not been any intervention, her wings would have begun to rot, and she would have died within months from infection. We have never seen a mutilation this severe in person.

Dr Terigy is confident she can save her basic functions of furling and unfurling, and she is remaining hopeful about restoring her ability to fly. We will bring Kortul back when she is recovering from surgery."

Their nods were accompanied by solemn stares, and the nurse returned to the back, leaving the waiting room in an apprehensive silence. None of them seemed to be breathing at all as they waited for several more hours.

When the surgeon finally emerged from the back, Tolina had been in surgery for half of the day, and Kortul was an emotional wreck from trying to block out everything they had just endured while also worrying for Tolina. "Her left wing was worse than her right, but I successfully completed all the repairs she needs. She was also missing a tooth, so we replaced it. She is in a healing recovery bath for a few hours as she wakes, and then you can take her home. Kortul, you can come back to see her if you would like. She is on a respirator since she is submerged, but she can sense you."

He followed the surgeon down a long hallway to a dim room with a giant clear tank in the center. Tolina was suspended in the center of the viscous liquid with her wings spread behind her. Kortul could not tell her wings had ever been damaged from where he stood, but he knew under bright light her scars would be visible.

He felt her reach for him as her antennae raised above her head. She sent him her love and allowed him to feel how comfortable she was as she wagged a finger at him. Kortul stood by the glass as she healed enough to come home, and when she was ready a few hours later, he was by her side helping her into her seat on the ship after they transported in.

Once they were back in the ship's hangar under his

building. Mabit and Tyce waited for Tolina and Kortul to go home first, and Kortul asked, "Corver, transport me and Tolina beside my bed."

In his room, Kortul helped her lay on her stomach, and he crawled in next to her with every intention of remaining by her side for every moment of her healing.

Chapter 39

Marry Me? Really, This Time

Three months later...
Standing on the beach, wearing a long sleeveless black traditional Wendi women's marriage gown, Tolina looked up at Kortul with love in her eyes. He had a crown of black spires on his head, and he wore an orange and black swirled cloak on his shoulders. Under his cloak he wore a fitted black marriage suit.

Behind them stood Tyce holding the Saltic marriage dagger, waiting for Kortul and Tolina to present their hands to him. The ceremony was silent, meant to allow the couple to make the moment truly about them, and only them.

They presented their hands to Tyce, and he cut each of their palms before Kortul webbed their hands together. Tyce moved around them to join Mabit, Brock, and Nire who all stood watching.

In a traditional ceremony, the couple would whisper their devotion to one another, but Kortul and Tolina decided to do things a little different. Tolina reached the tips of her antenna to rest them against his face, and they shared how they felt without words. Their love had grown over the months, and sharing their feelings with one another was something they did often.

When the ceremony finished, they turned and greeted their friends and family. Nire rushed to Tolina and threw her arms around her friend, "You look gorgeous!"

Tolina smiled and hugged her back. "Thank you. Nire, have you met Tyce yet?"

Nire gave Tolina a knowing smirk and answered, "No, I would love to though." Tolina grabbed Nire's hand and twirled her around to face Tyce.

"Tyce, this is Nire. She and I became friends when I still hated Kortul," Tolina admitted.

Nire angled her head and stared at Tolina, confused. "Wait. You hated him?"

"Oh. It's a long story. I'll explain it next weekend when we go on our trip." Tolina and Nire had been planning a girl's getaway. Tolina had to lay on her stomach while her wings healed, and Nire had sent her kind messages, which quickly developed into a strong friendship. Tolina couldn't wait to tell Nire everything.

Tyce was enamored. "Nire, it's nice to meet you. Would you like to walk with me before the dinner begins?"

Nire pinched Tolina's hip and grinned at Tyce as she accepted and thrust her hand out for him.

The two walked off together, and Tolina saw Kortul and Mabit chatting as Brock teetered back to the resort. She came up beside Kortul as he was taking off his marriage cloak. He handed it to Mabit, and he folded it over his arm.

Kortul grabbed her and pulled her close as Kortul chuckled above her hair. "Mabit?" Kortul waited until

Mabit was looking at him before he continued, "Tolina was the one who killed the rapist at the resort."

Mabit stood quietly as Kortul's meaning developed into a stark realization, and he looked at Tolina with humor in his eyes. "It was you? The only reason I gave Kortul the chameleon armor was to protect *you* from the murderer, but you were the murderer!" Mabit roared with laughter and shook his head, "I wouldn't have believed any of this if somebody had tried to convince me of this story. I need a drink."

Kortul took Tolina by the hand, and the three of them walked along the path to the resort restaurant, which was empty except for Tyce and Nire, who were chatting at a nearby table.

Mabit, Kortul, and Tolina sat with Tyce and Nire, and after they placed their orders, Mabit caught him up on plans. "I will return to the city in the morning, and Brock wants to return with me because he says there was a storm, and he needs to clean the windows."

"He hates when the windows are foggy. He cleans them constantly. Tolina and I wanted to spend at least a day or two here before we go back home." Kortul gave Tyce a serious look. "As for you, I have an offer. Tolina and I will be taking our time healing, and I have no intentions of returning to my position as head of Saltic. I want you to take over as company lead. You'll get my salary and a new ship."

Tyce's mouth dropped open, and he smiled at Nire before he looked back at Kortul. "Yes, of course. A few off-world meetings a year for your salary is nothing. Thank you."

Kortul faced Nire next. "How are you enjoying your new position?" Tolina had a discussion with Kortul about Nire, and she had asked him to offer her a city job at Saltic in management. He had given her one of the three highest paying, leading position, and she just finished the training.

"I haven't started the actual work yet, but I love my team, and I can't wait to start. It's a dream for me to be working in development."

Tolina finished eating a bowl of her favorite honey and asked, "Mabit, how is your quest coming along?" Mabit finally had admitted to Kortul he was dating, but he had yet to update them.

"You know exactly what dating is like in Corbatton City. It is *not* good," Mabit laughed and Tolina joined him, remembering her second date and cringing.

They finished eating and they said their goodnights before heading off to their rooms. Kortul and Tolina could not keep their hands from one another as Kortul asked, "Corver, transport us to our room."

Brock was in a ball on the couch, and it looked like he was asleep, so they tiptoed into the bedroom and tapped on the door controls to slide it shut.

Kortul pinned Tolina on the other side of the door and kissed her before he whispered, "Every day with you is better than the day before, but I think today was the best day of my life. It might take a while to top it."

"We can try to top it tomorrow when Brock isn't in the next room."

Kortul laughed and scooped her into his arms before setting her on the bed and stripping his clothes off. He pulled her dress over her head and twirled his finger for her to lay on her stomach. She bit her lip in anticipation, and Kortul knew how much she loved this every night. He grabbed the healing salve the surgeon had given him, and he began softly working it into the scarred areas of her wings.

She wiggled and twitched with his fingers brushing against her wings folded and curled over her back and legs. He pressed down in the center of her shoulders before her shiver began. Last time he didn't hold her down, and she almost vibrated from the bed. When the shiver slowed, he resumed applying the salve, this time to her other wing, and he prepared for her second exuberant shiver. When it was over, he kissed her shoulder and went around to crawl into the bed beside her. He tugged her against him, and he moved her hair so he could rest his face against her antennae as he did every night.

Tolina lay awake and watched the stars in the sky through the window as she felt Kortul fade into sleep. He had spent the last few months dedicated to her healing, and he had been perfect every single moment. She had been cleared for sex for over a month, but Kortul hadn't tried once. He was far too concerned with helping her heal and regain her strength. They had spent weeks together in their living room spreading her wings and folding them back, over and over until she could do it without any help. When she graduated from that, he had held her above his head as she flapped her wings and practiced flying. Right before they left for the island, she managed to lift him off his feet for a few seconds. It had been their most positive sign yet that she would regain her ability to fly. Tolina allowed sleep to take her away to a peaceful rest, but it didn't last long when a short shadowy figure appeared between her and the windows in their room.

Brock stood in front of her. "Nightmares back. You both gone. Had to be the monster again. Can I sleep with you and Kortul?"

Tolina stared at the little old man with his large droopy

eyes and felt terrible. He had been frightened out of his wits when she and Kortul had been taken, and their rescue had been his plan. She grinned and agreed with no more thought, "Of course." She moved out of his way, and he crawled behind her and onto Kortul's back to curl up and sleep.

A few moments after Brock made himself comfortable, Kortul sighed. "Hi, Brock. Did you have a nightmare again?"

He sniffled and Tolina could see him blink a few times. "Yes. You and Tolina gone."

"We are safe because of you. We love you," Kortul reassured him, and he closed his eyes before he finally fell asleep.

Kortul shifted around to look at Tolina and reached over to brush her hair from her face and tuck it behind her ear. He reached for her hand and held it as he went back to sleep, and Tolina joined them soon after.

The system stars were bright the next morning, and Tolina enjoyed watching the colors in the sky shift from yellow and pink to a periwinkle. Brock was still curled up on Kortul's back, and it was the most adorable thing she had ever seen in her life.

A butterfly, a spider, and a frog- what a sweet, weird little family we have. Tolina was smitten with them, and she scooted back down in the bed next to Kortul to wake him. She leaned in and licked the tip of his nose. The action sent his eyes flying open, and he focused on her. He smiled, and with Brock still asleep on his back, he shifted around and before she could think, Tolina was smashed in Kortul's chest, and she couldn't imagine a better place to be.

Something about their rescue occurred to Tolina and she gasped. *How the honey fuck did I not think to ask until now?*

"Kortul, we need to wake Brock. I need to ask him something."

Kortul reached over his shoulder and gently patted Brock on the head. "Brock? Can you wake up for me? Tolina has an important question for you." Brock yawned and licked his eyeball as he stretched. He climbed off Kortul's back and walked around the bed, rubbing his eyes.

"How did you and Tyce find us when you came to rescue us?" Tolina was so curious it was all she could think about. *How did I miss this part?*

Brock blinked a few times and pointed at her. "You have tracker inside of you. The security system notified, so reset tracker and erased old programing to link you."

Tolina's mouth dropped open, and she slapped her shoulder where her Vo-Pess tracker was. The device had a wire running to her heart as a remote kill switch, and she had not thought about how it could be accessed by anyone other than the Vo-Pess. The system to access the trackers had been disabled by the Vo-Pess before she left Hyret, and she had forgotten about it. The technology here was far superior, and she was thankful for this little frog and his thoughtful action. "You are our hero, Brock. You truly are the only reason we are here." She looked over her shoulder her at Kortul. "It has a kill switch. I need to remove it."

Kortul jumped up and reached for his tablet, but Tolina walked to the replicator and ordered a single scalpel. She was cutting a hole in her shoulder when Kortul joined her in the bathroom.

"I made an appointment... Oh, Toli! What the fuck?" Kortul glared at her with his mouth hanging open. He was standing in the doorway with his tablet in his hands, "I guess

I'll cancel the appointment. I should have known you would do that."

"We should get new tracking implants."

He waved at Mabit who just arrived as Kortul tapped on his tablet to find the best tracking implants. She was beginning to pull out the tracker when he looked up and froze. The long kill switch wriggled inside as she pulled it, out and she gagged a bit as it slid free. "That was disgusting." Kortul was so grossed out he was frowning, and Tolina giggled as she grabbed a nearby metal vase to crush the tracker. He opened a cabinet for an emergency dermal bonder and handed it to her. She used it to close her skin. In the next room they could hear Mabit speaking to Brock, so Tolina and Kortul joined them to say goodbye.

Chapter 40

Magic

When they were alone again, Kortul kissed her on the tip of her nose. "How are you feeling?"

Tolina looked up at him and although she loved seeing his sweeter side, she missed the playfulness they had before her wings had been cut. She could see his nipple through his thin shirt, so she reached up and gently bit it. Kortul screeched and spun her in silk before thrusting her above his head. Tolina went limp with laughter and Kortul huffed as he brought her eye level. "Are you trying to kill me?"

After setting her down, Kortul tore away his webbing, and she had every intention of jumping on him once she was free. He had to take a few steps back when she landed on him. "What are you doing?"

"Messing with you until you quit acting like I'm fragile!" Tolina leaned in and bit down on Kortul's shoulder, making him yelp. He still didn't react physically though, and Tolina laughed like a villain as she crawled over his shoulder and aimed for his ass. As soon as she could reach it, she pinched his butt cheek, and he slapped her ass.

She giggled, and he yelled as he tried to pry her off him, "Fuck! Toli! Stop it! I didn't mean to do that!"

"I'll bite it." Tolina squeezed his ass with both hands.

"Don't you dare."

Tolina was already wiggling down, and Kortul grabbed her and swung her around before holding her out in front of him. He knew Tolina could do anything she wanted to him and there was nothing he could do about it. He was terrified of hurting her, and now she was mixing things in is head. "You're always a riddle I can't solve. I think that's why I fell for you so hard, so fast, but right now you're stressing me the fuck out!"

Tolina scrunched her nose, and her head flopped over as she laughed, "That means I'm not trying hard enough!" She wrapped her legs around his waist and bent backward to pull away from his grip before she shot back between his arms with her pointer fingers in her mouth. Kortul tried to lean back, but she was moving too quickly, and she stuck her wet fingertips in his ears and wiggled them around.

Kortul sucked in a sharp breath before he clenched his shoulders and gagged as he grabbed her waist and ran for the bed. He landed on top of her and grabbed her wrists before straddling her. "That was fucking disgusting!" He was grimacing while frantically rubbing his ears on his shoulders as she roared with laughter under him.

"Give me what I want!" Tolina cried out as she bucked.

Kortul had no intention of that, so instead he yelled, "Corver, emergency transport us to location five!"

Tolina's lime green eyes went wide as they disappeared and reappeared above the water right off the shore of the beach. "Kortul!" was all she could scream before they hit the water, and she felt Kortul wrap his arm around her to haul her to the surface.

The water wasn't deep, and he stood up with her held out in front of him. "Are you fucking done now?!"

"Never!" Tolina had not felt this good in months. She reached out and tapped his nose, and he released her. She pulled him down to her level for a kiss, and she could taste the salty seawater on their lips. They stood in the water with their lips locked in a passionate kiss as Kortul stroked her wings, drawing out the hint of a shiver. She whispered, "I want to fly."

Kortul nodded, and they walked to the beach where she shivered to dry her wings before she unfurled them. After flapping a few times, she lifted in the air and flew high into the sky like she had never lost the ability. A powerful sob burst from her as she soared through the air, circling above Kortul. Her tears of thanks didn't last long as she spotted the man she loved below on the beach. He was the reason she was in the sky again, and all she wanted was to repay him for every moment he dedicated to her healing. She spotted him watching her fly. *He's always watching me. I love that he's always watching me.* Her heart was full as she aimed for him, angling her wings so she could come in fast and curl them against her skin quicker. Tolina was light weight, but she knew how to use every ounce of it. She was filled with delight watching Kortul try to run when he realized she was diving for him. She lowered nearly to the ground as she closed in, and he looked back and yelped just as she reached him.

Grabbing his shoulders, Tolina furled her tucked wings against her body, and they were back against her skin in a little under a second. Knocking him from his feet, Tolina and Kortul rolled across the sand and came to a stop with Tolina on top of him. She tried to lean down to kiss him, but he grabbed her face to stop her. "No! No sand kissing! Sand in your mouth is almost as bad as in your butt." He paused a moment before he continued, "You know what? Let's pretend like I didn't say that. We need a shower before we do anything else."

Tolina stared at him with her mouth open and her face still pressed between his hands. "You've had sand in your butt? That's terrible."

Kortul huffed, "I thought we were pretending I didn't say that."

"Have you met me?" Tolina swore she saw Kortul roll his solid black eyes, so she leaned back and hooked her fingers in his wet sandy sleep shorts before she started yanking them off. Kortul shot up and tried to grab them, but she was already at his ankles.

There were people down the beach and Kortul sucked in a sharp breath before he yelled, "Corver, emergency transport us to the shower!"

When they arrived in the shower, Tolina fell on his legs laughing, and he reached up to run the hot water which was aimed at him on the ground. Tolina stripped off her shirt before Kortul leaned up and grabbed her to rinse her in the stream. She scrunched her nose as the water hit her and when her face was clean, he crashed his lips against hers in a desperate kiss. He had refused to even think of sex as she healed, but now that he had seen her fly, his desire engulfed him, and all he could think about was watching her cum.

He grabbed the soap, and they washed and rinsed in a flurry. Once they were clean, Kortul couldn't wait any longer, so he lifted Tolina in his arms and ignored drying them as he brought her to their bed. He lay her out and crawled over her, resuming their desperate kiss. As their lips were entwined, he wrapped her wrist in silk, and he only lifted away from her to attach the webbing to the wall behind her. He kissed down the center of her neck before he licked and sucked each of her nipples until she was wiggling and moaning.

Tolina had missed his mouth on her and the way he ran his tongue over her nipples made her pussy cry for him. She angled her hips, and she tried to wrap her legs around him. He pushed her legs apart, and she felt his cock at her pussy pressing in and wetting the tip. Kortul bit her bottom lip as his cock found her clit, and her breath hissed between her teeth as he stroked her. His cock rippled, and she whimpered as the delicate waves added to the slick heat he was creating. Looking into her eyes, Kortul increased his speed, and Tolina gasped as the long-awaited orgasm consumed her. The pleasurable heat seared her core as it spread and enveloped her in its sweet embrace.

Kortul slid inside her as she crested, and she leaned her head back in a silent cry as he filled her. With his hands at her hips, she angled to take him all the way. His cock curled inwards, and when he began thrusting, he reached down between them and pinched her clit. Tolina couldn't hold back the sharp cry from her lips as she came again with a crash and Kortul moaned over her as he neared the edge.

He blasted cum inside her as he thrust one more time, and he had never seen anything more beautiful than his satiated wife spread under him. Their pleasure dripped from them as they panted, and Kortul collapsed to her side. He crawled up and bit the webbing to break it before he wrapped himself around her. After holding her as they calmed, he kissed her head and went to wet a cloth to clean her. While he was between her legs, carefully cleaning away their cum he asked, "Do you want to visit the crystal cave today or tomorrow?"

"Today. I have a surprise for you when we arrive."

Kortul had a strong feeling he knew what she was planning, and his spine tingled with anticipation. They dressed and packed swimsuits before Tolina pointed at Kortul to leave the room so she could pack her surprise. As soon as the door was shut, she ordered what she needed from the replicator and stowed it away in her pack.

She met Kortul in the living room and she sat on the couch for him to slide on her grip shoes while she put on her gloves. When they were ready, she stood by Kortul and he asked, "Corver, transport us to location twenty-five."

The tropical breeze blew through Tolina's hair, and she lifted her antennae to feel the warmth. She followed Kortul as they scaled the cliffside. The scent of the salt in the air exhilarated her as they ascended the steep crystal. When Kortul reached the mouth of the cave, he helped Tolina up, and they set their bags down.

"Take off your clothes and drop to your hands and knees." Tolina held her eyes on him, and he bit his lip as he stripped as quickly as he could, tossing his clothes all over the cavern. Tolina undressed and waited until he was facing away from her to pull a new strap on and dildo from her bag. She stepped into it and strapped it on before lubing the dildo. When she approached Kortul, he was already sweating, and she slapped him on the ass before she lined up with his asshole. After rubbing the lubed tip of the dildo against his tight ass, Tolina grabbed his hips and pressed inside. He groaned as she fully seated herself, and she reached up to grab his hair as she began thrusting. Once she knew he was close, she closed her eyes and forced an excessive shiver to the surface, causing the dildo inside Kortul to become a vibrator.

Kortul released a high-pitched whimper as Tolina released his hair to reach around him and grab his cock. The moment her hand made contact with his pulsing cock, he blasted the ground between his hands with cum and cried out, "Fuck!" before he fell over on his side trying to avoid landing in his own cum. He looked back at Tolina and seeing her standing over him with the strap on made him ache with how empty he was inside. "It feels like the reservoir behind my cock has collapsed in on itself."

Tolina giggled as she unbuckled the strap on to remove it and cleaned it before storing it back in her bag. When she was finished, she came back to Kortul and lay over him to listen to his heartbeat.

When he felt rested, Kortul stroked Tolina's wings before he lifted them both from the ground. He sat on the edge of the mouth of the cave and dangled his feet off the side as he held Tolina. "I have an idea."

He leaned back and twirled her around, so she was upside down and her back was against his chest. Her head dropped down between his legs as he grabbed her hips and leaned up to devour her pussy. The view of the ocean and sky upside down while being pleasured half to death was so overwhelming Tolina couldn't make a sound. There was no sound which could do the moment justice anyway.

Kortul sucked her clit into his mouth, and she clamped her thighs around his head. A cyclone of pleasure struck her, and she shook until her body began to vibrate, sending her into a thrashing, curling, screaming fit of ecstasy.

He licked her through her orgasm and when it faded, he kissed her pussy causing her to tremble before he whirled her around to face him. "An eternity with you wouldn't be enough. I want more than forever."

She kissed him and licked the tip of his nose. "Who knows if forever in the afterlife is even real. What is real is this life we have now, and we can fill every waking moment. We can live each day like we don't have another. We should play night-ball when we go home. You still haven't taken me."

He rolled his eyes and scrunched his nose. "I was hoping you would forget. You'll kick my ass."

"I know. I can't wait!" Tolina grinned and went to lick his nose again, but Kortul threw her from the mouth of the cave and over the ocean. She yelled, "Kortul!" as she fell toward the sea, and he dove in after her. She screamed as she reached the water's surface and not far behind her was Kortul, who grabbed her under the waves before crashing his lips onto hers in a salty kiss.

Epilogue

Tolina twirled and danced to the high energy pop music blasting from her tablet which Kortul was holding nearby as he recorded her. She held up a bloody knife like it was her microphone, and she sang off key to the music. She had a Wendi man convicted of off-world murder and heinous sexual crimes tied to a chair, and she stepped around the blue blood running down his legs and pooling on the floor. He sobbed as Tolina belted out the words of the fun song about love and friendship.

After it ended, she stared at him and pointed her bloody knife in his face where his little toe hung from his nose. "My singing is not *that* bad. You didn't need to cry so loud about it. That was *very* rude."

She danced around him as a new song began to slice his thumb off. He screamed, and she grabbed him by the hair to force his head back. With his mouth wide open, she dropped his thumb inside. He thrashed as she jammed her hand inside his mouth to make him swallow it. It lodged in his throat, and she smiled to herself as he flapped his lips for air.

His lavender face was draining of color with his blood loss, and he began to convulse. She smiled as she stabbed him in the throat for the kill before she whirled around to face Kortul who was admiring her.

Kortul smiled at her, but when he looked over her shoulder, he snarled at her now dead target. "Let's go home. Corver, transport us to the ship."

Tolina sat in the captain's chair, and Kortul handed over her tablet. She sent the recording to the Corbatton Queen, by whom she was protected. Tolina now was a proud Corbatton assassin, and she adored the queen. After some of the most cruel and evil people in the galaxy ended up mutilated and dead at her hands, the queen eventually discovered it was Tolina. Within the first hour of their meeting, Tolina had a new list of targets and full regal protection.

Handing her tablet back to Kortul, he set it in the seat behind him and knelt in front of Tolina with his eyes full of burning need. She pressed her armor tab, and as her armor receded, he ripped her underclothes away. He set her legs on either side of the arms of the captain's chair, and he devoured her pussy. Tolina leaned her head back as Kortul sucked and licked her clit. He added in his fingers and hooked them forward, taking her higher. She breathed deep as her orgasm rolled over her, giving her everything she needed after a brutal kill. It was hot and viscous, soaking into her bones as she dripped with her own cum. Kortul withdrew his fingers and licked them clean.

He tapped his armor tab, and he was nude underneath as usual. His cock burst from his slit, and he wet his tip at her entrance before he slid inside of her pussy and began thrusting deep. He grabbed the top of the chair, and she lifted her antennae to his face to feel him. Kortul's possessive love engulfed her as his cock filled her, and she wrapped her arms around his chest to lift herself so she could lick his nipple. He cradled her neck with his hand, and she sucked his nipple as she felt his pleasure mixing with hers.

Lightly biting down on his nipple as she came, Tolina caused Kortul to cum with a yelp and he trembled as he rode out his orgasm. He reached down and lifted her for a kiss before he asked, "Corver, take us home."

Once home, they bathed and dressed in comfortable lounge clothes. Before they came around the corner, they could already hear children's shrieks of delight from the living room. It was Mabit's birthday, and the entire family was over for dinner.

Mabit, his husband Benet, and their eight children who all looked like Mabit were running and playing a game of tag. Tyce and Nire were just arriving with their three daughters, and Brock and his new girlfriend were cooking together in the kitchen.

Kortul held Tolina close as he admired his beautiful family. This life and the love around him were more than he could have ever dreamed, and he would spend the rest of his life showing them his gratitude.

About the Author

Lauren Logan is a neurodivergent, disabled science fiction romance author from North Texas. After high school and junior college, she attended the University of North Texas and studied Psychology and History. She met her husband in 2008, married in 2010, and they now have two little boys. They all enjoy watching science programs about astronomy as well as staying caught up on the latest Star Trek episodes.

In 2015 Lauren developed a passion for hair and began a journey that would lead her to hair school in her thirties. She specialized in vivid color and within a year and a half she had been nominated as a top 100 pastel colorist in the Behind The Chair global hair awards. Unfortunately, the ultimate hair honor had come too late. A few months before her nomination was announced, Lauren had been forced to quit her dream career as a vivid hair colorist. The loss was devastating and she fell into a dark place.

November of 2020, Lauren was formally diagnosed with an autoimmune disease, Rheumatoid Arthritis. The disease course is aggressive and effects nearly all of her major joints, as well as both hands and feet. She has developed deformities in her fingers, making any chance of regaining her former hair career impossible. On rainy days you can often see her walking with a cane because the changing weather can bring on a flare. Since her diagnosis, she spends much of her time unable to leave her bed due to the constant pain and fatigue. The medication she is prescribed leaves her immunocompromised as well as having many difficult side effects.

Refusing to let her disability steal her ambition and kill her determination, Lauren began writing at the beginning of April, 2022. Over the course of one year, she completed writing two full length Sci-fi novels. Since the completion of the Reticere Series, she is now working on several stand alone novels in the same universe. Writing gives her hope and being an author gives her a future. She pours everything she is into her stories and she hopes you love them as much as she does.

For more information visit:
www.AuthorLaurenLogan.com

facebook.com/authorlaurenlogan
instagram.com/laurenloganart
tiktok.com/@lauren.logan

www.ingramcontent.com/pod-product-compliance
Lightning Source LLC
LaVergne TN
LVHW091658070526
838199LV00050B/2197